SURRENDER

Reese looked at her lips and bent his head down to kiss her. Suddenly, Kit stopped fighting and let his mouth find hers. His lips were soft, almost tender, but the solid flesh of his body seemed to grow harder as she surrendered reluctantly to his embrace. She closed her eyes, letting the pleasure he was giving her drive out all other thoughts.

The heat of the afternoon seemed to intensify the hot, male odor of him, taking her breath away. The brilliant sun seemed to be affecting her. Kit felt dizzy and strangely weightless. Her fingers clutched at his shirt-front, feeling the granite wall of muscle it covered. Something warm and urgent was being unleashed inside her, and Kit fought it, whimpering in her throat, afraid she might give in completely.

At the sound, the locking hold of his arm around her seemed to relax, as if Reese believed he had conquered her. . . .

from LORD OF THE HIGH LONESOME

JANET DAILEY

Happy Holidays

ZEBRA BOOKS
KENSINGTON PUBLISHING CORP.
http://www.kensingtonbooks.com

ZEBRA BOOKS are published by

Kensington Publishing Corp.
850 Third Avenue
New York, NY 10022

All Kensington titles, imprints and distributed lines are
available at special quantity discounts for bulk purchases
for sales promotion, premiums, fund-raising, educational
or institutional use.

Special book excerpts or customized printings can also
be created to fit specific needs. For details, write or phone
the office of the Kensington Special Sales Manager:
Kensington Publishing Corp., 850 Third Avenue, New
York, NY 10022. Attn. Special Sales Department. Phone:
1-800-221-2647.

Zebra and the Z logo Reg. U.S. Pat. & TM Off.

First Printing: October 2004
10 9 8 7 6 5 4 3 2 1

Printed in the United States of America

CONTENTS

LORD OF THE
HIGH LONESOME

CHAPTER I

Winter-gray clouds darkened the afternoon sky. The temperature was falling fast and a cold wind whistled as Kit Bonner waded through a fresh snowdrift the wind had piled on the path to the door. On the front deck, she paused to stomp the snow from her boots, her brown eyes searching the bleak Dakota landscape beyond the living snow fence of trees.

The cold turned her breath into a puffy white vapor and reddened her cheeks and the tip of her nose. Her lips seemed frozen, on the verge of cracking. A creeping numbness was spreading through her body despite the long thermal underwear beneath her jeans and fleece-lined parka.

Yet Kit didn't hurry into the promised warmth of the house perched on the slope of a hill. Her attention was on the threatening clouds, her mind wondering how severe the coming storm would be and how well the cattle on the range would weather it.

A horse whinnied up by the barns, and her gaze moved in its direction. A shaggy-coated bay had its head over the corral fence, its ears pricked toward the outer barn door. Lew Simpson, one of the ranch hands, had just closed the door and was walking away, the brim of his Stetson pulled low, his body leaning into the wind. His destination was the old bunkhouse, where friendly, welcoming smoke curled from the chimney.

Kit's gaze continued its arc until it was stopped by the imposing structure of the main ranch house. For as long as she could remember, it had been referred to as the Big House. From atop the hill it commanded a sweeping view of the ranch buildings and the rugged North Dakota landscape. No smoke came from its chimneys, and there were no lights in its windows. It stood empty, its doors and windows locked and shuttered.

The sight of it set her teeth on edge. With an abrupt turn, Kit reached for the door and yanked it open to stride inside, slamming the door, peeling off her thickly lined leather gloves with jerky movements.

"That you, Kitty?" a voice called from the living room just beyond the front kitchen.

"Yes." She took off the woolen scarf that was wrapped around her neck and over the faded Stetson atop her head.

Heavy footsteps entered the kitchen. "Radio says there's a big storm coming—stockmen's warnings have been issued."

"So I heard." Kit didn't bother to glance at her grandfather as she draped the scarf over a coat hook and began unbuttoning her parka. "I talked to Sam McKenna today. He'll airdrop hay to the stock Lew and Frank can't reach by snowmobile." There was a husky quality to her voice, a sound that could have been pleasant if her words hadn't been so gruff. "I was hoping we'd get a chinook instead of another blizzard."

"If wishes were horses—"

"Yes, Nate, I know." The parka joined the scarf on the hook as Kit impatiently cut in on her grandfather's recitation of the old adage.

There was a second's pause before he asked, "Did you get the mail?" with no reprimand for her curtness.

It was unnecessary since a twinge of conscience took any edge from her reply. "It's in my coat pocket."

With a hand braced against the wall for balance, Kit slipped a snow-covered heel into the bootjack. Out of the corner of her eye, she saw his arm reaching for her parka and the mail tucked into its pocket.

"Anything special in it?"

"Looked like mostly junk mail and a couple of magazines," she answered, taking the boots she had removed and setting them on the newspapers next to the wall. A few forlorn red-and-green garlands still hung there, though Christmas had come and gone this year without anyone making much of a fuss about it. The tree, which she'd cut herself on the wilder part of the ranch, had been fed to the chipper a while ago.

"At least we'll have something to read if we're

snowed in." With the mail in hand, Nate Bonner turned to walk through the kitchen to the living room.

His philosophical attitude was grating. Kit knew there was little that could be done except wait out the storm, but the thought of being cooped up for what might be days made her restless. She tossed an irritated glance at his departing back, shoulders faintly stooped with age, legs permanently bowed, and the thatch of snow-white hair on his head.

When it came to waiting, old people definitely had the advantage. But her impulse to protest his calm acceptance of the situation died away as Kit noticed the lack of spring to his step. She had no right to snap at him and he wasn't to blame for her bad mood.

"Any hot coffee?" she asked instead.

Her faded brown Stetson was the last thing she took off. A cascading tangle of chestnut-gold hair that had been tucked inside its crown tumbled over her shoulders, a gorgeous contrast to the red-and-black plaid of the man's flannel shirt Kit wore.

Like the others in her winter wardrobe, it wasn't exactly flattering, but the thick, serviceable flannel kept her warm—she switched to men's cotton shirts in the summer. Once in a while, one of the ranch hands made some comment about what she wore and her only answer was that men's things were cheaper and lasted longer.

To those few people who knew her well, her choice in clothes just seemed like a protective shell, not very different from her brown eyes that never let anyone see in and the always proud tilt of her chin.

"Coffee's on the stove."

In stocking feet Kit dodged the puddles of melting snow, stepping out of the narrow entryway into the kitchen. She walked to the gas stove, which, like the rest of the house and most of its furniture, was practically an antique. Even the old coffeepot, made of blue-and-white spattered enamel, might be worth something if it wasn't so chipped.

It sat on a back burner and Kit touched its side with her fingers for a fraction of a second to be sure the brew inside was still hot. She opened the cupboard door beside the stove.

"Do you want a cup, Nate?" she called.

There was an instant of silence before he answered with a rather absent, "No, thanks."

Bypassing the china cups and saucers on the shelf, Kit took out an old ironstone mug. A fine film of dust covered the china. It hadn't been used in the four years since her grandmother died, except to be moved and cleaned up some when Kit got around to the housework, which wasn't often.

Her grandfather had gone steadily downhill since then, losing his vigor, his drive. Once, Nate Bonner had seemed ageless to Kit, but not anymore. Though the Flying Eagle Ranch had flourished under his management, now it was Kit who gave the orders and made sure they were carried out.

No one had disputed her right to take over, or complained because she was a woman and young— she had turned twenty-one last fall. Everyone accepted it as just and fair under the circumstances.

In the living room her grandfather sat in one of a pair of old wingback chairs, his head tipped back to peer through the reading glasses perched on his nose. A lamp on the table beside him cast a circle of light onto the letter in his hand, the rest of the day's mail lying on his lap.

The matching chair flanked the other side of the table, its maroon cushions almost threadbare in spots. With her steaming mug of coffee in one hand, Kit walked to it. Her grandmother Martha had always sat there and Kit had taken to using it, rather than have its emptiness be a painful reminder to her grandfather of the loss of his wife.

"Well, how's that coffee?"

She took a sip. "Awful. But it's hot—that's all I need. Thanks, Grandpa."

Resting her stocking feet on the footstool shared with the other chair, Kit leaned back to stare at the tongues of flame licking the logs in the fireplace. It and an oil burner provided heat for the small house. On winter days when the wind was blowing, and there were few days in North Dakota when it didn't, it took both to warm the house. The combination was beginning to thaw Kit now.

She lifted the mug to her lips and drank the strong black coffee, enjoying its reviving heat more than its taste. Her gaze focused on her grandfather's worn cowboy boots, the underslung heels resting near her feet. There were black marks on the leather from the spurs he used to wear, though it was more than two years since he'd been on a horse. Lately he rarely ventured out of the ranch yard except to drive to town.

Sometimes when she looked into his eyes it seemed like she was looking into the eyes of a lost child. Poor Nate, Kit thought. He had always tried so hard all of his life, sacrificing his own wants and needs, and even his pride, to do what he felt was best for his family. There was compassion in the glance she lifted to his face, but he was intent on the letter in his hand.

"Who's that from?" Kit asked, absently curious as she again raised the mug to her lips.

He cleared his throat before answering. "The new baron."

Her fine features seemed to harden, and her knuckles went white in the handle of the coffee mug.

"Do you want to read it, Kit?"

"No!" She set her coffee aside too quickly, sloshing a little of it over the rim and staining the crocheted doily on the tabletop. She pushed herself out of her chair. "We need another log on the fire," she announced and walked to the wood box.

A long silence followed, broken only by the sounds of her movement. When a split log joined the burning coals of others amid a shower of sparks, Kit grudgingly said, "I don't need to read it. You can tell me what it says."

She remained kneeling in front of the fireplace, a poker in her hand, jaw clenched. In spite of her wish not to care, Kit had to know what was in the letter.

"He starts out thanking us for our expression of sympathy at the old baron's death and—"

"Sympathy?" Kit asked, flashing an accusing

glance over her shoulder. "You sent a condolence card?"

Tired eyes gazed back at her from a sun-leathered face, silently asking for her understanding. "I had to. As manager, I sent a card from all of us at the Flying Eagle, for appearances' sake."

Kit turned back to the fire, tears of bitter resentment stinging her eyes. "Well, I hope he rots in hell," she muttered darkly.

"Now, Kitty," Nate Bonner admonished in a low voice filled with pain.

She jabbed at the logs with the poker, sending more sparks up the chimney. "Okay, okay. Go on." She didn't want her grandfather to feel guilty just because he had sent a card. As usual, Nate had meant well.

Sighing, her grandfather hesitated before continuing. "Says he appreciates our loyalty and he hopes that will continue."

"Right. And we should just keep sending the ranch profits to jolly old England, so he can live in style." Her tone was acid. "Damn him anyway."

"Katherine Elizabeth!" Nate never used her full name unless he was really offended by her hot temper. "Your grandmother would turn over in her grave! This fella never did you any harm."

Kit gave him a meek look that didn't match what she was feeling. "Are we allowed to call him 'fella'? Never mind. I don't even care what his name is. I don't want to know anything about him."

With patience born of experience, her grandfather sighed and waited for her moodiness to subside, knowing Kit's curiosity was bound to get the better of her.

"What else does he say?" she asked finally.

Her words brought another sigh and the crackling of paper being folded. "Nothing much. He's thinking of visiting the ranch sometime soon."

For a moment, cold paralysis gripped Kit. "Do you think he really will?"

It was logical for him to assess what he had inherited, get an idea of the size of the property and how the ranch was run. On the other hand, his lordship might be content with the monthly reports and—of course—the income. She hoped so. She prayed so.

"Guess we'll have to wait and see." Nate Bonner slipped the letter back into its envelope and started going through the rest of the mail.

Kit sat back on her heels and stared into the flames. There was not a single part of her body that did not feel the white heat of pride and the burning of injustice.

Absentee ownership of Western ranches wasn't uncommon. Multimillionaires and movie stars sometimes bought them, even way out here, but the Flying Eagle's owners had always been noblemen.

From what Kit remembered of the ranch's history—her grandmother had told her some of it and she'd learned the rest in elementary school—the first Baron Edmonds had come to North Dakota in the 1880s, attracted by the success of the famous Marquis de Mores, who'd brought his rich American wife to the badlands, founded a business empire and even a town.

But the young baron hadn't been a snob, unlike the French marquis. There were no lavish entertainments on the Flying Eagle, no big hunting parties. He'd worked alongside the men he hired, tried almost to become one of them—and then the disastrous winter of 1886 had almost destroyed his dreams.

Which didn't stop him, Kit thought crossly. Unfortunately. He'd even brought his English bride to live on the ranch, but the rigors of frontier life were too much for her. Once there was a baby on the way, they returned to England. Though Baron Edmonds had promised to come back with his son, he never set foot on the Flying Eagle Ranch again.

The first Bonner, James, had arrived just before the turn of the century to help with the fall roundup, liked it, and stayed. Four generations of Bonners had been born on the ranch since then, and Kit was the last of them.

She loved the Flying Eagle fiercely and thought of it as her own, even though she knew it wasn't.

The old nobleman who had just died was Baron Edmonds's great-grandson—and now the ranch was owned by his descendant, someone who had never even seen the place. Kit seethed with the unfairness of it.

"What about something to eat?" Her grandfather's voice broke into her thoughts.

Kit nodded and slowly straightened up. "There's some beef stew in the refrigerator. I'll warm it up."

"You could make some biscuits—got one of those twist-open cans in the icebox. Just put 'em in the oven with the stew, the way Martha used to," Nate suggested.

"All right," she agreed without much enthusiasm.

Although her stomach said she was hungry, Kit wasn't really interested in eating. As she walked to the kitchen, she saw the first flurry of snowflakes whirling outside the windowpane. She crossed her fingers, making a wish that this late-February blizzard would not be as bad as the storms in January.

Kit's wish came true. The winter didn't linger and spring came on time, even if it was blustery. They hadn't lost too many calves and the year was off to a good start.

She sat astride the blaze-faced bay horse, noting the shaggy remnants of winter hair that still clung to its coat. It was a cool May afternoon with a stiff breeze blowing from the north. Her mouth tasted gritty from the fine sand the wind carried, and she knew it powdered her face as well.

Her faded brown Stetson was pulled low on her forehead to keep it from being blown off. As always, her golden-brown hair was tucked up inside the hat where it wouldn't tangle and didn't show. A flannel shirt in green-and-gold plaid provided warmth, as did the quilted black vest zipped to the neck. Leather gloves covered the hands holding the reins. Lithe and slim, she resembled a young boy in her faded and patched jeans and scuffed boots.

Her gaze slowly traveled down the length of

fence row. "What's going on, Reno?" she asked the gelding, who swished his tail by way of an answer. "I don't see a single break in the fence."

But a half-dozen cows and one calf were grazing on the other side of the wire next to the gravel road, proof that there was a gap somewhere. Dismounting, she looped the reins around a post and took a pair of pliers from the saddlebag.

She pulled out a staple holding the top strand of barbed wire to the post. First, she had to get the cows back in before they got hit by a car or a truck. Then she could look for the hole.

Dropping all three strands and stuffing the staples in her pocket, Kit remounted and walked the snorting bay over the lowered wires. The cows raised their heads as she circled them to drive them back to the home range. One black Angus gave her a wild-eyed look and trotted into the ditch, heading the wrong way.

"Get back," Kit said, annoyed. She reined the bay horse to intercept the cow. "Should have known you were leading this bunch. You just can't stay home, can you? Always looking for a loose wire."

With her escape blocked, the Angus rejoined the other cows ambling toward the lowered wires. The cow quickly shouldered her way into the lead and trotted over the lowered wires while the rest followed. They stopped on the other side of the fence, watching as Kit rode the bay over the wires before dismounting to restring them on the post.

Hammering the staple into place again, Kit glared at the ringleader of the escapees.

"I'm not going to keep chasing you back in all

summer," she warned. "One more time and you're going to the sale barn."

The other cows drifted away, but the black one remained until Kit had remounted. There was still the problem of finding where they had gotten out and that meant riding every inch of the fence line. If it wasn't found and repaired, the cow would try the same trick again.

Riding fence was a boring, tedious job, but necessary. Kit walked her horse slowly beside the row of posts and barbed wire, following the dips and rises of the rugged terrain, alert for any looseness in the wire. Still, she almost rode past the spot. If it hadn't been for a tuft of black cow hair caught on a barb, she might never have found it.

But that particular section looked sturdy enough. When Kit pushed at the top wire with a gloved hand, she realized its look was deceiving. The wooden fence post had rotted at the base and could be lifted completely off the ground—wire, post, and all. She fastened it down as best she could and tied a red bandanna to it as a marker. A new steel post was what was needed but it would have to be installed tomorrow.

Her ride had taken her nearly to the lane that led from the gravel county road back to the ranch. Kit decided she might as well check out the rest of the fence before heading back, at least on the stretch of ground that was relatively level. Then a flash of light on metal caught her eye.

A silver Range Rover was parked half a mile beyond the entrance gate and cattle guard. Kit reined in the bay and stared, wondering whose it was. Couldn't be a neighbor's—or at least not a neighbor she knew. She'd never seen it before—it had to belong to a stranger. Or a curious tourist. Either way, not good.

The ranch had always maintained a very low profile to protect the privacy of its owners. That had been true long before Kit was born and it hadn't changed. Whoever this person was had better have a damn good reason for trespassing.

Reining the bay in the direction of the car, she touched a spur to its flank to send the horse cantering forward. A man stood near the front bumper, looking off in the opposite direction. At the sound of Kit's approach, he turned and waited.

She stopped the horse a few feet away and studied the stranger. Tall, with a rangy build, he wore a brown suede jacket cut in a way that accented the width of his shoulders. His hazel eyes returned her cool look with arrogant ease, and that irritated Kit. The bay horse seemed to sense her inner tension and stamped restlessly beneath her.

"Were you looking for something?" Her tone was unfriendly, although her words were polite enough.

"Yes. The Flying Eagle Ranch." His voice was low, with an accent she couldn't quite place. Definitely not from around here.

Kit's gaze flicked in the direction he had been looking in when she had ridden up. "You won't find it out there."

Her reply made his mouth curve in a sexy smile that brought out slashing grooves running from nose to mouth, and the lean hollows of his cheeks. His features were harshly masculine, from the wide, intelligent forehead, down an aquiline nose

to the powerful slant of his jaw. A stiff breeze ruffled the thick, dark brown hair growing crisply
away from his face.

"I was trying to get a glimpse of the brand on
those cattle over there," he explained with a trace
of amusement. "There isn't any sign on the gate by
the road."

"No, there isn't," Kit said. "Are you a salesman?"

"No."

"There isn't any sign on the gate because the
Flying Eagle Ranch isn't open to visitors. In case
you don't know it, you're trespassing on private
property. About a half a mile up the road, there's a
spot where you can turn that thing around. Use
it."

There was a faint narrowing of his gaze, a gleam
entering his eyes that Kit didn't understand. All
she knew was that she didn't like it. It made her
feel defensive, even though she knew perfectly
well that she was in the right.

"Are you ordering me off?"

Just for an instant something in his tone made
Kit question her action. "Are you expected at the
ranch?" she countered.

"No, I—"

"Then, yes—I'm ordering you to leave," she interrupted briskly, reining the bay to the side. "And
I hope you don't force me to call the county sher-
iff. Because if I do, you won't get by with a warning. I'll have you arrested."

Several seconds of charged silence followed before the man turned and walked to the Range
Rover's door. Kit concealed her surprise. For some
reason, she simply hadn't expected this man to

back down. He seemed much too self-assured, or so she had thought.

Now that she was no longer transmitting the tenseness of challenge to the bay, the horse stood quietly along the roadside. Kit relaxed in the saddle as the stranger drove past her.

The heavy layer of accumulated dust and dirt that covered the back and rear bumpers kept her from reading the license plate, but she suspected the man was from out of state.

There was no reason to wait and see if he obeyed her. Precious working time would be wasted if she waited to see whether he used the turnaround a half mile ahead. If he didn't and continued on to the ranch headquarters, Nate or one of the hands would be there to send him on his way.

Turning the horse back to the fence, Kit listened to the pleasant swishing sound it made as it trotted through the tall, thick grasses. She wondered who in town had let something slip about the ranch. Generally, people were aware of the ranch's long-held policy of anonymity and respected it.

After all, they had the Marquis de Mores's twenty-six-room chateau to attract tourists, even though it just looked like a great big house and not particularly fancy. But a marquis—even a dead one—beat out a baron any day.

It didn't matter. The stranger would soon be on his way, if not by her order, then by someone else's. Kit remembered the prickling of antagonism she had felt when she confronted him, but then she had never been easy with strangers.

She was aloof by nature, never worrying about her lack of friends because she never wanted any. Hers was a private, solitary existence. That was the best—and safest.

At the fence line, she turned and followed it past the closed gate. The brisk wind was quickly blowing away the dust the Range Rover had raised, but the vehicle itself was out of sight below the ridge. With a last glance in that direction, Kit dismissed the encounter from her mind and concentrated on the job at hand.

CHAPTER 2

Tired and grimy from the long day's work, Kit rode the bay into the ranch yard. Eager to reach the barn and the night's ration of oats, its step was quick and its ears pricked. But Kit noticed Lew Simpson over by the well and turned the reluctant horse away from the barn.

"What's wrong?" She reined the horse to a stop and leaned forward to see for herself.

Lew Simpson was on the far side of forty, a short, wiry man. His sweat-stained hat concealed the fact that he had only a halo of hair—the top of his head was virtually bald. He'd come to the Flying Eagle before Kit was born, as much a part of her childhood as Nate and Martha. In typical cowboy fashion, he worked hard and played harder.

"The pump was actin' up." He wiped the grease from his hands onto his Levi's and reached for the cover that protected the motor. "I guess it needed a little oil and some cussin'. It's runnin' fine now."

"Good." Kit sat back in the saddle.

"Did ya—"

The clink of metal against metal diverted her attention to the shed. The tractor—the H—was parked in front and Kit could see someone kneeling next to the front wheels.

"Not again," she said resignedly.

"Yeah, I think Kyle's busted it." Lew shrugged.

Kit tried to count to ten but gave up at three. "First the cows and now this—damn it." She snapped a finger in the direction she'd come from. "Lew, there's a fence post rotted at the base about a quarter-mile west of the gate. I tied a red bandanna to it so you can find it—I don't have time to fix it, especially if the tractor's out of commission. Get a new steel post from the shed and replace it—pronto."

Without waiting for a reply, she spurred the bay around and hurried him to the shed. She stopped a few feet from the young guy crouching by the tractor, shooting him an exasperated look. "What now?"

He didn't raise his head, but Kit saw a dull flush creep into his freckled face. Kyle Johanson was no older than Kit, a town boy who wanted to be a rancher. He'd barely known one end of a horse from the other when he'd signed on a year ago, but he tried hard—too hard—and he was ridiculously careless at times. His mechanical skill was about all he had going for him, though he seemed to break things just to repair them.

"Um, it's the steering rod. I think." He shifted uneasily and peered at the wheels in a study of concentration. "Could be broken. Maybe not."

"How did it happen?" Kit demanded.

"I hit a rut. That last rain really tore up the road," he hedged. "I was headed for the yard when—"

"Yeah, right," she lashed out, impatient with his excuses. "Skip it, Kyle. You can't race a tractor!"

"I know," he muttered lamely.

"I want the H fixed by tomorrow," Kit snapped. "And I don't give a damn if you have to drive to Bismarck or Billings to find the parts. Got that?"

"Yes, ma'am," he mumbled, but his light blue eyes flashed her a look of rebellious anger.

Kit knew why. However justified the tongue-lashing might be, his all-important, manly pride was hurt. She checked her temper and nudged the horse away from the tractor, aware that if he objected to her authority, she'd have to fire him— and just now, she couldn't afford to spend the time looking for more help. Discretion insisted that she retreat and not push him any further.

As Kit walked the horse away, she heard Kyle mutter, "What's got into her, anyway? She had no call to chew me out like that. I didn't do it on purpose."

Lew must have been approaching as she left, because she heard him answer in a faintly guarded tone, "Everybody has a bad day now and again."

"She's full of it. No wonder nobody ever asks her out. She's a damn ice queen—"

"That's enough, boy." Lew's voice sliced off the rest of the sentence.

Kit lifted her chin and rode a little straighter in the saddle, but she didn't turn around. Bitterly, she wondered what jerk made up the line about

words were not being sticks and stones—she knew
only too well that they hurt just as much.

Her diagonal route across the ranch yard to the
barn took Kit directly past the front porch of the
Big House with its huge log columns. The rough
planking of the exterior walls suited the sprawling,
one-story structure. Its rustic simplicity and sheer
size was impressive, blending well with the rugged
splendor of the Dakota scenery.

Usually Kit avoided even glancing at the Big
House, but her eyes were drawn to it by some
inner compulsion. The lowering sun cast a long
patch of light into the shadows of the porch and
she could see the heavy wooden front door standing open.

Vaguely she remembered Nate saying something about airing the house this morning and she
figured he had neglected to shut the door. He was
becoming more and more absentminded about
some things.

Kit turned the bay gelding toward the hitching
rail in front of the porch. She dismounted and
wrapped the reins loosely around the rail, walking
up the three steps to the porch, her spurs jingling
faintly.

The sound of her footsteps echoed on the floorboards as she walked across the porch to the
screen door. Reaching to close the front door behind it, Kit hesitated. Nate had probably opened
windows in the house, she decided, and maybe he
had meant to leave it ajar.

She went in and stood for a moment in the wide
entrance hall, fighting a sensation of resentment.
This house always had that effect on her, and there

didn't seem to be a whole hell of a lot she could do about it.

The cool breeze filtering through the rooms had not banished all the staleness from the air and a musty odor filled her nose.

About a half-dozen steps into the hallway, Kit noticed the door to the room that served as library and den was also standing open. Her nerves tensed, their ends suddenly raw and exposed. Unwillingly she let her gaze be pulled to the open door and into the room.

A redbrick fireplace, blackened from decades of use, stood on the opposite wall directly opposite the door. On the floor in front of it was the brown hide of a grizzly bear, its yellow-white fangs bared in a permanent snarl. It was a trophy of the first baron, hunted and killed when it began to attack the ranch's cattle herds. The grizzly had probably been one of the last in the badlands.

But it wasn't the bearskin rug that captured Kit's attention—it was the painting above the fireplace mantel. Despite the dimness of the room, illuminated only by the waning sunlight coming through the dusty windowpanes, Kit could still make out the features of the face in the portrait.

It showed a handsome man in his prime, with wavy, sand-colored hair that fell across his smooth forehead at a rakish angle. His expression was unsmiling, but there was a wickedly engaging glint in the blue eyes staring back at Kit that seemed to draw her into the room with the irresistible pull of metal to a magnet.

Her fingers slowly curled into her palms, turning

her hands into tight, gloved fists. **She** gazed at the image of the first baron's descendant with a loathing that she was unable to control—the force of the emotion made her tremble. Not even knowing that he was dead lessened her reaction to his portrait.

Scalding tears sprang into her eyes, the only emotional release Kit ever allowed herself—but she would not let one slip past her lashes. Not here. Not in this house.

"Was there something you wanted?"

The blandly arrogant voice of a stranger shocked Kit out of her trance. She turned, her eyes wide with alarm, to see someone sitting behind the hardwood desk.

It was the stranger from the road—the one she had ordered off the property. He leaned back slightly in the chair, looking at her with interest. His relaxed air, his attitude of being completely in possession and in command, was the igniting spark to her temper.

"I warned you to get off this ranch!" Kit couldn't believe his nerve. She was hopping mad and she didn't give a damn if he knew it. "What the hell are you doing in here? Who let you in?" She'd have their scalp and his, too, before she was done.

He briefly arched a dark brow, but nothing resembling guilt or any other emotion flickered in the cool hazel eyes regarding her so steadily. The rough angles and planes of his face were immobile.

"No one _let_ me in." He stressed the verb. The line of his lips curved as he spoke, but his cynical smile seemed to mock her anger.

"Well, someone is damn well going to show you out!"

Kit didn't think for a second that she could do it on her own. And she sincerely hoped the stranger would not go peaceably. She would love to see him roughed up a bit and that complacent look literally wiped from his face.

Her angry strides were punctuated by the sharp jingle of her spurs. As she neared the door she could see Lew and Kyle walking by through the fine mesh of the screen. Her outstretched arm pushed the door open, rigidly holding it ajar.

"Lew! Kyle!" Her husky voice was loud in the evening quiet.

Both men turned around to face the Big House, stopping as soon as they heard her. They had a faintly puzzled look, visible even at Kit's distance.

"Come here!" she ordered. "There's a man—"

"We already met the new baron, Kit," Lew said, frowning and cocking his head to the side. "So if it ain't too important, Kyle and me got to make a few calls and see if anybody's got the replacement parts for the H in stock."

The last part of his reply didn't register, only the first—the words "the new baron." She froze. It took Kit a second to realize she could hear the sound of her own heartbeat pounding in her ears.

In slow motion she let the screen door swing shut and saw the two ranch hands hesitate before walking on. With equally deliberate movements Kit turned.

The stranger—she corrected herself—*the new baron* was negligently leaning a shoulder against the jamb of the opened library door, rubbing his chin thoughtfully, his veiled but watchful look studying her reactions.

"Well, well. A real, live baron. Should I curtsy?"

He grinned. "That won't be necessary."

"And how do we address you?" There was an unmistakable edge to her voice.

"The name is Reese Talbot," he offered, without being friendly or hostile. It was a flat statement.

"Why didn't you say who you were?" Kit demanded, incensed that he had deliberately not told her when she'd confronted him by the road. She wondered why he didn't have an English accent—and reminded herself that she didn't want to know anything much about him.

He tipped his head slightly to one side, his gaze hardening. "I'm not in the habit of explaining myself to people who don't know who I am."

This was too much. "Oh. I see. Well, I humbly beg your noble pardon."

"You don't sound humble at all." His eyes narrowed slightly, whether from annoyance or amusement, she couldn't say. Kit felt suddenly self-conscious as he took her in from head to toe.

Her stained hat was still pulled low on her forehead, concealing the glorious hair piled beneath it. A powdering of dust covered her face—she could taste the caked grime on her lips. The man's shirt, the patched jeans, and the bulky quilted vest combined to make her figure shapelessly slender. Spurs were strapped on her boots and leather gloves covered her hands.

A gleam of amused contempt lit his gaze. "Those clothes don't do much for you. I didn't know you were female at first."

"If you think I object to being mistaken for a boy, you're wrong," Kit retorted.

But he didn't indicate one way or another what he thought. "You obviously work here."

Kit hesitated for a fraction of a second. Evidently the new baron, this Reese Talbot, didn't know who she was. In a way it was hardly surprising.

"Yes, I work here," she admitted and added no more.

He continued to look at her in the same unnerving way. "What's your name?"

"Kather—" For some reason, she almost used her full name, as if reasserting her femininity, but she quickly changed her mind. "Kit Bonner."

"Bonner," he repeated the last name. "That's the same as the ranch manager. Are you his granddaughter?"

"Yes." Kit tensed, suddenly defensive, her chin lifting. "How did you know?"

"He mentioned you when I met him this afternoon." Reese Talbot seemed to find her question odd. It showed in the sharpening of his look. "He said you'd ridden off somewhere."

"And you figured that meant a leisurely canter through a meadow, not chasing cows and mending fences," she said. "Am I right?"

"Yes."

Kit had difficulty holding his level gaze and looked away in irritation. "Why are you here?" Her tone was curt and challenging.

"I own the Flying Eagle. I wasn't aware I required a reason to come here." His voice was smooth as steel.

That was a sensitive issue. "You aren't wanted,"

she said bluntly. There would be hell to pay if Nate found out she had said that, but she didn't care. She was struggling to control her temper as it was.

"Obviously not by you." Reese Talbot seemed to find her open hostility very amusing.

"Not by anyone," she corrected him. She was really asking for trouble now. "Any welcome you've received since you've arrived was only out of courtesy."

"And you don't feel bound by any rules of courtesy." He was teasing her as if she were a hissing kitten.

Kit wanted to smack him. As owner, he knew he could get away with saying just about anything, and her only choice would be to put up with it—or leave the Flying Eagle. It was incredibly unfair. "I'm not going to say polite things I don't mean."

"That would be asking too much, wouldn't it?" he said mockingly.

"Look, you descended on us without warning— and you chose not to explain who you were. Don't blame me if I don't roll out the red carpet."

His mouth set in a thin line. Obviously she was trying his patience. Good, she thought. Score one for Kit, and the American team.

"Perhaps I merely wanted to make sure that my arrival would be minus any fanfare," he suggested.

As if. Kit's eyes flashed with fury. "Maybe you just wanted to find out if we were secretly stealing from you or something. As you can see"—her hand slashed through the air to encompass an invisible everything—"we're all living high off the hog. We keep fixing broken-down tractors and chasing crazy cows for the fun of it."

"For your grandfather's sake, I think it would be best if you didn't say any more, Miss Bonner." There was no mistaking the unspoken warning behind his words.

How dare he threaten her—or Nate. Kit paled. She had to swallow an even sharper reply, and turned to leave, wanting to get as far away from him as possible.

"Don't leave yet. I'm not through with you."

His autocratic tone hit her like a lightning bolt. Fighting for every ounce of self-control she possessed, Kit faced him, her brown eyes snapping.

"Do I need your permission to leave?"

He ignored her rebellious stance. "Your grandfather suggested that I speak to you about the house."

Her indignant anger was tempered by caution at the sound of two magic words: "grandfather" and "house." "What house?" Kit demanded guardedly, lowering her head so that the wide brim of her Stetson shadowed most of her expression.

"This house, of course." His reply was smooth enough, but a frown flickered across Reese Talbot's face.

"What about it?"

"It needs more than an airing. It needs a thorough cleaning and the cupboards need to be stocked with food."

"It's your own fault the place isn't ready—you didn't notify us that you were coming," she stated. Not that she would have rushed right over with a feather duster and cans of soup, or whatever it was he expected.

"I am aware of the reason, but that doesn't

change the situation, does it?" Again there was
that flash of white teeth in a cold smile.

"How long are you intending to stay?"

"I have no idea." His tone indicated that it had
no bearing on the matter.

"Well, I'm not a housekeeper and I don't cook."
Her chin tipped up defiantly. That was not exactly
true. She did a fair enough job at both, but only
for people she cared about, like Nate. Not for
barons, who probably didn't eat canned soup anyway. "So you'll have to figure that out for yourself."

"I have all the time in the world to do just that."
His voice had an edge she did *not* like. "And now—
what about the beds?"

"Oh, I imagine the boys could rustle you up
some clean blankets and such from the bunkhouse." Not what he was used to, no doubt, but
that was his tough luck. "And for your evening
meal"—if he thought she was going to invite him
to join her and Nate he was definitely mistaken—
"Frank Jarvis does all the cooking for the boys. I'm
sure he can stretch the meal to include you."

Kit bestowed a cold smile upon Reese that more
than matched his own. She turned abruptly and
walked out, letting the screen door slam shut behind her.

Half expecting to hear him order her back inside, she clumped down the steps to the hitching
post where the bay horse waited patiently. Not a
single sound came from the Big House.

She looped the reins over the horse's neck and
swung into the saddle. The spur she touched to
the horse's flank sent him bounding forward to
the barn. There she dismounted, stripped the sad-

dle and pad from his back, and led him into the corral where she unbuckled the bridle, actions that were accomplished with the swiftness of controlled anger.

She stowed the saddle and bridle in the tack room, and saw Frank, graining the horses they kept at the ranch yard. Kit ignored his greeting. But like Lew, Frank had been around for a while and knew her well. He didn't ask stupid questions if he didn't have to.

With the riding gear put away, Kit left the barn and headed straight for the small house, not even looking at the Big House. The hinges of the door squeaked as she pulled it open and the sound immediately brought an anxious call from her grandfather. "Kitty, is that you?"

"Yes." He was closer, in the kitchen now. "If you're going to tell me that the baron's arrived, I already know it." Unzipping the vest, Kit shrugged out of it and hung it on a coat hook. Then the spurs came off, followed by the hat.

"You talked to him yet?" Nate Bonner asked finally and quietly, already guessing her answer just by the look on her face.

"Yes, I have." She brushed past him into the kitchen.

"Kitty, you can't blame him for what happened." Her grandfather followed, anxious yet gently understanding. "He had nothing to do with it."

"I don't. It was all so long ago it really isn't important anymore." She was lying through her teeth and she knew it. The past had molded her, made her create a hard shell that never let anyone through. Kit stopped beside the counter and glanced at the condensing steam on the glass cover of the CrockPot. "Looks like dinner will hold for half an hour. I'm going to take a shower and change into some clean clothes before we eat."

The subject of the baron's arrival was not mentioned once during the evening meal. Kit rose from the small table in the kitchen to carry the dishes to the sink.

Nate cleared his throat and announced, "The new baron has invited us over to the Big House tonight."

"You go," she replied calmly and without hesitation. "I have a lot of paperwork to do."

"The invitation was for both of us."

"But it was made before he knew who your granddaughter was. Now that he's met me, I don't think he'll be at all sorry if I don't accept." The plates were in the sink and she reached for the milk glasses.

"What happened this afternoon when you met him?" He held a match to his pipe and puffed. It was a habit he indulged in only occasionally and Kit chose not to nag him about it. Nate didn't have a lot of pleasures in his life, and if smoking a pipe was one, then she let it be.

"I thought he was trespassing, a tourist or a newspaper reporter or something, and I ordered him off the ranch. He attempted to put me in my place. Didn't work."

Her clipped answer drew a long sigh from Nate Bonner. "I don't think he knows anything about you or what happened. He seemed surprised that I had a granddaughter. Maybe it would be best if I explained—"

"Don't you dare!" Her calm façade shattered in an instant as she pivoted to face him. The resentment smoldering within her blazed in her eyes. She fought for self-control, not wanting to upset Nate any more than she already had.

"Kit . . ."

She turned back to the sink. "It wouldn't change anything. So if he doesn't know, it won't do any good to enlighten him. Besides, he won't stay for long. Why would a baron want to rough it out here when he's got a castle in England?"

"Well, they don't all live in castles," Nate pointed out. "But you're probably right about the rest of it." He bit the stem of his pipe as he spoke, a faint grimness to his words.

"Of course I'm right." She shrugged. "He'll go and everything will be the way it was before he came."

"Maybe," Nate murmured to himself as he pushed out of the kitchen chair. "Maybe not."

Her heart stopped beating for a second, an icy chill running down her spine. She clamped her teeth together, gritting them in a self-willing determination that it would turn out the way she said. Reese Talbot's presence would cause no more than a mere ripple from a pebble tossed in a large pond, and not the reverberating splash of a boulder.

"Well, I'm heading over to the Big House," Nate announced.

"All right. As soon as I'm done with the dishes, I'm going to get at the paperwork."

"I probably won't be long."

"No, I don't imagine you will." Standing at the sink, her hand poised on the faucet knob, Kit heard herself whisper, "Don't tell him, Grandpa."

His hand rested briefly on her shoulder, a fleeting caress of understanding and reassurance. "I won't, child."

She turned on the water, pride stiffening her back and putting a note of indifference into her voice. "Give the baron my regards."

As the back door closed behind her grandfather, Kit held onto the edge of the sink for a moment, as if she might break somehow if she let go. No matter how much she tried to deny it, she was vulnerable—frighteningly so.

CHAPTER 3

By morning the defensive shell was again in place as she went about her chores, striding across the ranch yard like she owned it, swinging an empty pail.

The ranch's lone milk cow, which Nate had insisted on keeping for the sake of tradition, had been milked, her morning offering strained and in the refrigerator.

Dressed in her usual faded jeans, men's shirt, Stetson, and boots, Kit was returning to the barn. The sight of Lew wearing his going-to-town outfit of a good print shirt and clean denims, heading for the ranch pickup, stopped her short.

"Where are you going, Lew?" she demanded. "Thought I told you to put that new fence post in this morning."

"You did, but the baron asked me to take him in to town." He gestured toward the Big House as if that was enough of an explanation.

A flash of anger sharpened her tone. "I don't give a damn what the baron says!" Kit almost shouted. "You'll do as you're told."

"Don't you go gettin' on your high horse with me, Kitty Bonner." Lew stiffened. "Don't forget I knowed you when you was waddlin' around this place in diapers."

"And don't you forget that I'm the boss," she retorted. "I give the orders around here."

"I was under the impression," a low voice said behind Kit, "that as the owner I had some say, too."

She whirled around to confront Reese Talbot— and met the challenging look in his hooded eyes. Kit hadn't heard him approach and to find him standing so close caught her by surprise.

His height was intimidating, as was the breadth of his shoulders. The man was built—and he radiated an overwhelming maleness that made her take an unwilling step back.

Was he always so alert at this early hour of the morning, as if he was lying in wait and ready for trouble? Disturbingly vital, he seemed to be an immovable male object planted squarely in her path.

"Of course you have a say." Her reluctant admission seemed to please him. "But not when you don't know what's going on. The fence along the road needs repairing and I asked Lew to fix it right away, before the cows get out again. I can't have one of my men wasting time in town with you. "

"One of *your* men?" His voice was tauntingly soft.

Okay—he had her there. Kit sidestepped the question by flicking a sharp glance at the ranch hand. "Get into some work clothes, Lew, and get out on that fence line." She threw Reese a look that just about dared him to countermand her order. "What's the matter with the Range Rover?"

"It has a flat tire and so does the spare. Just my luck." Reese Talbot offered this explanation with a wry smile, his dark head tipped to one side. He gave her an odd look, as if he suspected—what? That she had done something to it on the sly?

As if she wanted him around the ranch, getting in her hair and driving her crazy. Yeah, right. She wouldn't go near his expensive SUV, and she didn't even know where he had left it overnight.

"Anyway, I mentioned it to Lew. He said he was going in to town with the pickup and suggested I ride along."

Kit looked at the ranch hand. "And why were you going in to town?" she demanded.

Lew shifted his stance, looking uneasy. "Sorrell junked one of his tractors and he's been sellin' the parts. Thought I'd check to see if the steering column could be interchanged or modified to fit the H. His place is only a mile or so from town, so I figured there was no sense in making two trips in the same direction."

"You figured," repeated Kit in an angry undertone. "And what about the fence?"

"I was going to do it this afternoon."

"After you blew a whole morning in town."

"I think you'd better go fix the fence, Lew," Reese Talbot suggested dryly. "Miss Bonner can take me to town and check on that tractor part for you."

"Yessir." Lew bobbed his head in agreement and

moved away, obeying this order when he had more or less ignored Kit's.

That irritated her, as did that indefinable air of authority that emanated from the man before her. The fact that he had commandeered her services as chauffeur didn't set well with her, either. Kit was about to inform him that she wasn't his personal driver, but she didn't have the chance.

"Correct me if I'm wrong, but I was under the impression"—there was no amusement in the narrowed look he gave her now—"that your grandfather was the manager of this ranch, and that he gave the orders. Not you."

The ground seemed to rock beneath her feet. It was one thing for her to know that Nate had lost interest in the ranch since his wife's death and had begun neglecting his duties, and another thing for Reese Talbot to know. A sense of loyalty made Kit protect her grandfather as best she could.

"He is," she said calmly. "I, uh, take my orders from him."

"I see," he murmured, but Kit saw that his suspicions hadn't been completely allayed. "Well, is there anything he told you to do this morning or are you free to drive to town?"

Her decision was made in a flash. "I can drive you to town."

"Good." Reese glanced at the gold watch on his tanned wrist.

It was probably a Rolex, she thought with annoyance. Not that she had ever seen one up close or cared to. A baron wouldn't wear anything else. She comforted herself with the thought that it wouldn't last long on a working ranch.

"Is ten minutes enough for you to change?"

"What's wrong with these clothes?" she countered smoothly. They were part of her armor, and she needed it, especially around him. "Why should I change?"

He smiled slightly as he ran an eye over her decidedly masculine clothes and shapeless form. "Why indeed? I suppose that's what cowgirls wear."

"Don't call me a cowgirl."

"I apologize, Miss Bonner."

"And you can stop calling me Miss Bonner. That makes me sound like an old schoolteacher."

"What should I call you?'

She just waved toward the battered old pickup instead of giving him an answer to that prickly question. "If you're ready to leave, I am." Kit walked to the driver's side, aware that he followed.

Her nerves tautened as she realized that she had sentenced herself to spending the better part of the morning in his company. It wasn't wise, not when her emotions ran so high against him. Or at least against the injustice his presence represented.

By the time Reese Talbot had climbed into the other side of the cab, Kit had started the motor and was putting the truck into gear. They bounced out of the rough ranch yard onto the equally jolting ruts of the lane, the old shocks squeaking in protest as they tried to absorb the bumpy ride.

Kit knew if she slowed down it wouldn't be so rough, but just to be contrary, she didn't. "Hang on," she said crisply. "This clutch is a bear." She shifted gears with no finesse whatsoever.

"Why hasn't the road been regraded?" Reese asked, riding out the jolts with apparent ease.

"There's no point in it—not until summer." Kit kept a firm hold on the steering wheel to prevent it being wrenched from her hands. "We don't get much rain in spring, but when we do, it's usually a violent storm." Her tone was matter-of-fact. "So the downpour washes out the roadbed."

The jarring ride continued until they reached the relative smoothness of the gravel county road and left a haze of red dust behind them. Kit's attention was divided between the road, twisting, climbing, and dipping as it snaked its way through the torturous landscape, and the scenic badlands themselves.

Kit never tired of the wild beauty of this terrain, with its stark buttes that jutted into the horizon. The layered rock faces of bluffs displayed striations of color, from the bricklike red of baked clay to yellow and buff, with an occasional seam of black, a low-grade lignite coal.

Below the bluffs grew tall, thick grass, green and rich, the priceless bounty of the so-called badlands. Its dense cover was interspersed with sagebrush and wildflowers. In the twisting ravines formed by runoffs and along the winding streambeds, cottonwoods and willow trees flourished, while stands of junipers clung to the north slopes.

At times it seemed a maze of canyons and gullies and mesas, verdant pastures and impassable rock cliffs. But it always awed anyone who saw it, especially Kit, and she often felt that the wild pulse of this untameable land was her own.

"How old are you?"

The question came out of nowhere, and Kit suddenly became aware of the man sitting next to her in the pickup's cab. That unrevealing gaze of his was watching her and probably had been for some time. His penetrating scrutiny made her nerve ends tingle.

"Twenty-one. How old are you?" She answered calmly enough, she thought, although he had startled her.

"Thirty-five."

"You look older." Kit kept her gaze fixed on the road as they topped a rise.

"Who put the chip on your shoulder?"

"I don't know what you mean," she murmured coolly.

"I think you do," he said. Without looking directly at him, Kit still saw his skeptical smile. "Ever since our first meeting, you've been trying to impress me with how tough you are."

"I don't know what you're talking about." But Kit felt her muscles tensing, although she continued to avoid looking in his direction.

"Well, I am impressed," he offered, but not without some amusement. "You have the hardest shell I've ever seen."

"What makes you think it's only a shell?"

He waited a moment before he answered. "Because, as much you might not like to admit it, you're still made of flesh and blood like the rest of us."

She was startled to hear the click of a lighter. Kit glanced over and saw the first wisp of smoke curling from the tip of the cigarette between his lips.

"Did you ask me if you could smoke?"

"No. Sorry. I thought all cowboys smoked. Actually, I'm trying to quit. I'm down to two a day."

"That's interesting, but I'm not a cowboy and I don't smoke. Well, hardly ever." Growing up with mostly men around, it hadn't been any big deal if she took a few puffs every now and again, once she turned twenty-one.

He exhaled, letting the smoke drift out the open window. "Does your mother let you?"

"I'm a big girl. I make my own decisions." The aromatic scent of the tobacco was pleasant in the dry spring air, and she wanted one. Her grandmother would have said something about coffin nails, she thought with a wry smile. Kit offered a mental apology to Martha, just in case she was looking down from heaven at this particular moment.

"They are . . . tailor-made." His gold-brown eyes appeared to be laughing at her.

"So?" she frowned.

Reese took another cigarette from a gilt-edged box with a name she couldn't read at a glance. "I assumed people around here either chewed tobacco or rolled their own." He lit the second one and handed it to her. "But you don't, of course."

Kit scowled at his tone, knowing he was poking fun at her lack of femininity. She put the cigarette between her lips, the taste of his mouth still warm on the paper. It wasn't a sensation she cared for and she yanked open the ashtray and quickly stubbed it out.

"I'll have to try it sometime, won't I?" was her bland response to his comment.

If anyone had ever grown used to teasing, malicious or otherwise, Kit had. Growing up with cowboys for babysitters on an isolated ranch, being among a handful of students in a rural school where everybody knew everything about you, spending long hours riding the range—all that had taught her to be tough.

It had been years since anyone had been able to tell if a rude remark had hit home. Her aloofness and cool composure had kept her safe and it didn't desert her now. Good thing, too, because Reese Talbot wasn't the kind of man she could just ignore.

"What happened to your parents?" Again, Reese changed the subject without warning. He didn't seem to care that his teasing hadn't aroused a more heated reaction.

"They're dead. Nate and Martha raised me." As an afterthought, she added the explanation. "My grandparents."

"You're doing it again," he observed.

"Doing what?" Kit darted him another frowning glance.

"Trying to prove how tough you are by using your grandparents' first names. Calling them Granddad and Grandma is just too much like family—am I right?" He didn't wait for an answer but went right on talking. "You seem determined not to need anybody." Kit kept her gaze focused on the road rather than take that bait. "What did you call your parents?"

"I don't remember . . . 'Mama' and 'Dada,' I guess."

"Do you remember them?"

"No—not that it's any of your business."

"And do you regret that?"

There was one sure way to get him to shut up—she swerved the truck slightly. He slid hard into the door and slid back when she rotated the steering wheel to where it was before.

"Hey! Keep your eyes on the road!"

"Well, keep your questions to yourself. I didn't ask to be psychoanalyzed, Baron."

"If you don't want to use my first name, I'll settle for Talbot, but no title, please." It was more of an order than a request. "Anyway, the correct form of address is 'Lord Talbot,' not 'Baron.' You wouldn't say 'Hey, Duke,' would you?"

"You know, I probably would."

He had to smile at her irreverent answer. "Just call me Reese."

Reese took one last, long, comforting drag on the cigarette, which he hadn't let go of when she swerved, and ground it out in the dashboard ashtray. "By the way, I'm a U.S. citizen, not a British subject."

"But what do they call you around the castle?" There was more than a little sarcasm in her tone. "Back in England, I mean."

"Sorry to disappoint you, but there is no castle in England, not anymore."

"Oh. Did you sell it?"

"Not me. My predecessor disposed of it."

"What a pity for you," Kit offered. "A title but no castle."

"It was too costly to maintain. If he hadn't sold it, I would have. There's no point in hanging on to property if you don't live there and can't turn a profit on it."

Kit gave him a long look, taking in his chiseled profile. He certainly looked noble. "I understand you inherited a fortune."

Her gaze fell away when he looked back. "You seem to know a lot, Katherine." The way his low voice rolled so mockingly over her given name made her uneasy. But Reese Talbot didn't wait for a response. "Actually, after the death duties—inheritance taxes—there was very little left."

"Except the Flying Eagle, isn't that right, Baron?" She couldn't resist the jab. What he seemed to take for granted was very precious to her—and she had grown up on this land.

"Yes, except for the Flying Eagle, your ladyship."

Her stomach contracted at his flippant response. "Why did you call me that?" Kit demanded, flashing him an angry glance.

"You didn't like it?"

"No, I didn't!"

He nodded as if he'd made his point. "Neither do I. So let's drop the 'Baron.' "

His clipped remark put an end to the conversation for a while. They were driving on a straighter road, past an occasional farmhouse or old homestead that had been abandoned or foreclosed on, with curtainless windows that reflected the brilliant blue sky and empty fields around them. Reese looked thoughtfully at the lonely but beautiful scene.

She answered the question he seemed about to ask. "A lot of people have left in the last ten years. You can't make a go of farming on a small place and there aren't many jobs around here. But I love it. Can't imagine living anywhere else." Her explanation coincided with their arrival in the historic town of Medora, where Kit continued the guided tour.

She pointed out the red roof of the huge house built as a summer residence by the ambitious Marquis de Mores in the early 1880s. It was visible through the budding trees, located on a hill overlooking the town that he had gallantly named for his American wife.

Next, she drew his attention to the flowing waters of the Little Missouri River, which had done most of the work of creating the North Dakota badlands—but Reese didn't seem all that interested in geology.

They drove on to a service station to leave the flat and the spare to be repaired. Kit was well aware of the curious looks she was getting. The few times she was ever seen in the company of a man, it was someone from the ranch—Lew or Frank or her grandfather.

It had to be obvious even to the most casual observer that Reese Talbot was not just a cowboy—not that anyone from around here would mistake him for one. But since he didn't bother to identify himself, Kit didn't, either.

"Where to now?" Kit let the old truck idle in the station's driveway.

"Drop me off at the town center—or the library. Anyplace with a bulletin board. Guess you people don't use the Internet up here."

"Yes, we do," she said indignantly. "Just like anyplace else."

"Well, I want to see if I can get someone local to do the cooking and housecleaning for me—actually, a bulletin board is better."

"I'll leave you in town, then," she said, slipping the truck into gear and easing her foot down on the accelerator.

"Where are you going? To see about the tractor part?"

"Yup." She turned onto the main street, noting that more of its rustic old buildings had been restored. "I wouldn't worry about finding someone, especially these days," Kit pointed out.

"Good," Reese said quietly.

"And people will be impressed when they find out who you are," she added, a little cynically.

"Is there anyone you would care to recommend?"

"No one. You're on your own, Bar—uh, Mr. Talbot." She pulled the truck close to the curb to let him out.

"What time shall I meet you?" Reese stepped out of the car and leaned against the open window frame to look in at her.

"Medora isn't all that big," Kit stated. "When I'm finished, I'll find you."

He seemed to find this funny, judging by the gleam in his eye. Despite his amusement, Kit had a warm sense of satisfaction as she drove away to complete her own errands.

But it was nearly noon before she got back into town. She had encountered one frustration after another, first in finding Sorrell and then in trying to determine whether the part he had could replace the damaged one in the ranch's tractor.

Memorial Day weekend wasn't too far off, which meant there was a scattering of tourists in town. Kit looked at a lot of faces as she drove down the street, without seeing Reese. Finally she parked the pickup in front of the post office and continued the search on foot.

Ignoring the curious looks from the tourists as they wondered if they were seeing a real, live cowboy—or was it a cowgirl?—Kit walked down the street, her head turning and looking, peering into storefronts for a glimpse of the man she sought. The main area of Medora covered no more than a few blocks, and Kit walked it all.

She turned and began to retrace her route to the pickup. As she passed by the Rough Rider Hotel, Kit decided that Reese had given up waiting for her and had caught a ride with someone else back to the ranch.

Then the side entrance door to the small hotel, leading to the restaurant, opened. "Looking for me?" Reese stood in the door frame, seeming to fill it.

Kit stopped abruptly. "Yes." She wasn't about to admit that she'd been about to give up.

"I got tired of cooling my heels waiting for you and decided to have some lunch. Join me?" He stepped backward into the hotel, his outstretched arm holding the door open for her. Kit couldn't exactly say no.

Before she went two steps into the hall, a large hand took her elbow. The sensation of being in his grip momentarily surprised her. Reese Talbot had struck her as being in good physical shape, but his touch revealed a strength that was disconcerting.

Her upturned glance met his lively eyes, and Kit felt a surge of resentment at the way he always seemed to be laughing at her, although there wasn't the ghost of a smile on that hard mouth.

"My table is this way," he explained and directed her to the room on the right.

Their destination was a table for two, against the far wall away from the others. Kit was glad of its location. It made her feel protected, free from curious and prying eyes. Coffee and a water glass were on the table in front of one chair and Kit walked to the opposite side, pulling out the chair and sitting down before Reese could courteously offer assistance.

"Aren't you going to take off your hat?" His hand was on the back of her chair as Kit drew it up to the table.

"No."

"Suit yourself. If I were with any other woman, I would just figure she was having a bad hair day." Reese returned to his own chair, shaking his head. "You're one of a kind, Kit."

"You could be right," was all she would say.

The grooves deepened around his mouth, but it was only a hint of a smile. "I haven't been served yet. Would you like to order?"

"I think I'll have a sandwich," she said. She was hungry and Nate would have fixed his own lunch by now. Eating here would save having to put together a hurry-up meal when they returned to the ranch.

Reese motioned to the waitress, who brought over a menu. Kit glanced briefly at the sandwich section and gave her order to the young girl.

Not wanting to engage in any more small talk with Reese, she began studying the Western paintings on the walls, which complemented the rustic décor of the dining room.

Among the art were sepia-tinted photographs of Teddy Roosevelt, who'd been a friend of the Marquis de Mores as a young man, long before he became president. He had lived in the badlands, Kit knew, at about the same time as the marquis and the first baron.

"Kit?" A questioning female voice broke into her concentration. "Kit Bonner? It is you, isn't it?"

She glanced around to see a blonde woman about her age hesitantly approaching the table. A defensive but proud expression came over Kit's face as she recognized a former classmate.

When the blonde got a full view of Kit's face she broke into a smile. "It *is* you!" She rattled on, "I was sitting over at that table when you came in and I said to my girlfriend, 'That looks like Kit Bonner. I used to go to school with her.' But I wasn't sure."

"Hello, Carolyn." Kit offered the greeting stiffly, not sure of the other woman's motives for seeking her out.

"Wow, it's been ages since I've seen you." The declaration was accompanied by a short, amazed laugh. "Like, not since we graduated, right?"

"I think so," Kit nodded. She remembered her more clearly now. Carolyn Nesbitt had tried to be friendly but Kit hadn't exactly welcomed her well-meaning efforts. Yet Carolyn seemed genuinely glad to see her again after all this time. Kit's lips softened into a wary smile.

"How have you been? You look wonderful, Kit—

so tan. You must spend a lot of time outdoors."
Her blue eyes sparkled as she spoke.

"I'm fine. And you?"

"Great. I'm married, you know." She showed off
the wedding and engagement rings on her left
hand. "It's Carolyn Quinlan now. No kids yet,
though. Bob and I decided to wait a few more
years—you know, have some fun and stuff."

"Sounds like a plan. Well, I wish you both the
best of luck." Kit suddenly became aware that
Reese was standing beside the table. He must have
gotten up when Carolyn came over, assuming that
she was going to sit down or something like that.
All her attention had been focused on her former
classmate, but Reese had seized the chance to
study Kit.

It was disquieting to think that he had been observing her all this time and she felt herself brist-
ling.

When Kit glanced back at Carolyn, she realized
she had drawn the blonde's attention to Reese.
Since he persisted in just standing there, as if he
was trying to win an award for good manners, it
was impossible to ignore him. She would have to
introduce them.

"This is Carolyn . . . Quinlan. We went to school
together," she said to Reese. Okay, he'd figured
that out by now. She felt like a fool.

"So I gathered," he replied. He looked at the
woman facing him and nodded politely.

"Carolyn, this is—" Kit hesitated a fraction of a
second. Her husky voice held a note of challenge
as she continued. "This is the owner of the Flying

Eagle—the new baron." She stressed his title, just to be obnoxious, and got a glare from Reese.

Too bad. He'd told her not to call him by his title but he hadn't said to keep it a secret.

Plainly flustered, Carolyn blushed, then grew pale. She seemed to be trying to make up her mind whether she should merely bob her head or curtsy—if she even knew how. Kit sure as hell didn't. There just weren't a lot of reasons to practice curtsying in North Dakota.

Embarrassed and awed, the blonde girl just stood there. Kit felt sorry for her, but she had no way of knowing that her former classmate would be so overwhelmed.

Reese took charge, extending her a hand and flashing a smile filled with potent male charm. "The name is Reese Talbot, Mrs. Quinlan." He didn't seem to notice how awkwardly Carolyn shook his hand.

"Wow. Um, I mean, how do you do, sir," Carolyn mumbled. "Do we call you Baron, or what?"

"First names are fine with me. Kit knows that I've abandoned the title but she enjoys needling me about it." The persuasive power of his warm voice was already beginning to work on Carolyn. Even Kit could feel its calming and steady effect. He was good at putting people at their ease when he wanted to.

"Well, welcome to North Dakota, anyway," Carolyn said. She almost giggled but seemed to decide against it. "Have you been here before?"

"This is my first visit. I arrived yesterday."

Only yesterday? Kit realized with surprise that

he was right, but it still seemed impossible. The waitress came with their food and the conversation was interrupted until she left.

"Wow—well, okay, I don't want to keep you from your lunch," Carolyn said, looking over her shoulder at her own table and then back. "It was amazing to meet you and everything."

"My pleasure," he said with another flash of that virile grin.

A tentative but friendly smile was on Kit's face when Carolyn turned to her. "It was good seeing you again, Carolyn."

"Same here." Her gaze slid briefly to Reese, then back to Kit, and a glow of happiness radiated from the blonde's face. "Oh, Kit," she breathed, "you must be so happy to have the ba—Mr. Talbot here. I mean, after all this time, you finally get to meet—"

The temperature at the table seemed to drop below zero as Kit withdrew behind a rigidly cold expression that froze the rest of the sentence on Carolyn's tongue.

The blonde seemed to realize that she had said too much. "Kit, I'm really sorry." Her cheeks flushed a deep pink. "I didn't mean anything by—"

"Never mind. It's all right." Kit cut the apology short, feeling Reese's gaze concentrating on her. "See you around, okay?" It was an obvious dismissal.

"Yes, all right, Kit," the blonde murmured uncomfortably. "Well, um, good-bye." She waved her fingers in a childish way at Reese and went back across the room.

Well, hallelujah, Kit thought, watching Reese sit down at last out of the corner of her eye. She avoided looking directly at him, aware of his continued silent study of her. Her pulse was hammering—she could almost hear it.

"I have no use for people like that," Kit announced, her husky voice sounding suddenly tougher. "Look." Her brown eyes flickered disdainfully over the dining room, noticing the heads that had begun to turn in their direction as the whispers about Reese were repeated.

He only shrugged and unfolded his napkin in his lap.

"They'll be fawning all over you just like Carolyn. You may not call yourself a baron, but that won't stop them." Kit turned the salt shaker upside down over her home fries and shook it vigorously. "You might even get in the paper. I can see the headlines: *Blue Blood in the Badlands. Baron Rides the Range.* You won't have any trouble getting a housekeeper."

"Aren't you being kind of hard on her?" His question had a cynically amused ring. "She seems nice enough. I wasn't expecting you to introduce me like that."

"If she had known who you were before she came over, she would have been bowing and scraping like a royal handmaiden," Kit retorted.

"You certainly can't be accused of behaving like that, can you?"

"No, I can't." She met the speculative gleam in his eye and grinned before starting in on her home fries.

"I wonder why she thought you would be over-joyed to meet me," Reese mused.

Kit shrugged dismissively. "Probably because she was. Since I was raised on the Flying Eagle, she expects me to be impressed when the owner—a real, live nobleman—condescends to pay the ranch a visit."

"Your friend obviously doesn't know you very well," he said dryly.

"No, she doesn't. And Carolyn isn't my friend. She's just someone I went to school with."

"I wonder if anyone knows you very well."

"I do," Kit said calmly and picked up her sandwich.

Their conversation came to a standstill as both directed their attention to the meal. They had barely finished when the waitress stopped at their table, a steaming coffeepot in her hand.

"Ready for a refill?" she asked cheerfully.

Reese nodded. "Please."

"How about dessert?"

"Nothing for me, thank you," he said.

"I'll have some French-fried vanilla ice cream," Kit said without a moment's hesitation.

Reese's dark eyebrows shot up. "Some what?"

"French-fried vanilla ice cream," the waitress repeated with a knowing smile.

"I'm going to have to ask the obvious." Again Kit witnessed the potentially irresistible charm of his smile directed at someone else as Reese looked at the waitress. "What is it?"

"It's a large scoop of vanilla ice cream dipped in cinnamon and nutmeg and rolled in Rice Krispies, then dropped in the French fryer for a few seconds. Then it's smothered in hot fudge and topped with whipped cream," she recited by rote. "It's really very good, Baron. You should try it."

Her use of his title revealed how quickly word of his presence had got around. A smile danced at the corners of Kit's mouth as she met his wry glance.

"Sounds delicious, but I'll stick with the coffee," he said.

"Yes, sir." She refilled his cup and deftly cleared the dishes from the table. Before she left, the waitress beamed a bright smile at him. "If you change your mind about dessert, just let me know."

Reese merely nodded and Kit didn't bother to comment on the change in their waitress's behavior. The girl had been conscientious before, but now she was knocking herself out to please. In record time, the gooey dessert was set before Kit. She dipped her spoon into the thick fudge and twirled it around, licking the first bite with the tip of her tongue—until she heard his low chuckle.

She glanced up with a frown and put the spoon down. "What's so funny?"

"You and that dessert." That same gleam of laughter shone in his eyes again. "It's kind of like a ruthless gunfighter banging open the doors of the saloon and ordering—milk."

"What do you mean?" Kit stiffened, sure that somehow or another he had discovered a weakness in her armor.

"Not quite sure how I can explain this without getting your back up," Reese said in a soft, taunting voice. "But your, uh, approach to the hot fudge was pretty sexy. What happened to the tough tomboy routine? If you don't mind my asking, that is."

She turned red. "I do mind," she retorted, even though her toes seemed to curl inside her boots at the way he was looking at her. His intimately suggestive gaze was really annoying. "Do you always analyze other people? I could say something about how your drinking black coffee means—oh, hell. I have no idea what it means." She stuck her spoon in the lump of ice cream and left it there, glaring at him.

Reese didn't care. He silently congratulated himself on picking the perfect place to admire the fire in her eyes and her delicate features. She seemed to do without makeup and it didn't matter. She was gorgeous, even with her hair tucked up under that damn hat and her body pretty much covered up by the man's cotton shirt she wore.

The shapeless cut of the shirt could not conceal the rise and fall of her breasts when she breathed faster, unnerved by his scrutiny.

"Okay, Reese, how about that BLT I just had? What does it mean? Is the mayonnaise symbolic or is it just—dressing?"

He had to laugh. "Sorry. Maybe I got a little carried away. I didn't mean to spoil your dessert and you really seemed to be enjoying it. Go ahead, finish it—I'll shut up."

"Thanks." She picked up the spoon and dug into the gooey treat again but she had lost her taste for it. She ate mechanically anyway, the ice cream sitting heavily on her stomach by the time she was done.

Reese downed the last of his coffee and looked pointedly at her. "Are you ready?"

"Whenever you are," Kit said coolly. If it was possible, she disliked him more at that minute than at any other time in their short acquaintance. He was a much more dangerous adversary than she had first suspected, with a knack for getting under her skin. She could only hope that his stay at the Flying Eagle wouldn't last.

Kit rose from her chair when he did and walked with free-swinging strides to the side entrance door, while he paid for their lunch. They didn't say much on the return trip to the ranch. The Range Rover tires bounced around in the back after they picked them up at the service station and she drove more slowly.

It took forever to get replacement parts out this way—and if he lost his wheels, he would stick around even longer.

CHAPTER 4

Two mornings later, Kit was walking from the barn carrying a pail of warm milk, fresh from the cow. The sky was impossibly blue and the sun was bright; a summery day stretched before her.

The sound of the screen door slamming at the Big House made her stride falter slightly, but she continued on without glancing around. She didn't need to know it was Reese Talbot who had walked out on the outer veranda.

"Kit." His voice commanded her attention.

Since the trip into town, Kit had made certain that encounters with Reese were kept to the minimum—and kept short. It seemed like the easiest way to deal with the situation. This resolve held firm as she altered her course toward the Big House. She stopped at the corner of the house, looking up to the porch where Reese stood.

"What are you doing this morning?" He stood in

the sunlight, his hands on his hips, with an air of quiet authority.

"I'm riding out to the west pasture to check on the herd," Kit answered, glad she had a reason not to volunteer her assistance.

"Good." He nodded crisply. "I'll ride along with you and take a look around myself."

Momentarily taken aback, Kit protested, "But Nate took you on a tour of the ranch yesterday."

"In the truck. I want a closer look," Reese stated.

Her irritation instantly got the better of her. "Whatever you say," she offered in tight-lipped agreement. "I'll take the milk to the house and then get our horses saddled. Be ready in about fifteen minutes."

"Is that an order or a statement?"

"Both." Kit started to turn away, then stopped. "Our horses aren't exactly what you would classify as gentle mounts. Can you ride?"

"Yes." He seemed amused by her question.

"The sun gets pretty hot. Better wear a hat," she added.

"I'm not a complete greenhorn, Miss Bonner," Reese drawled.

"Just thought I should warn you, Baron." She turned away, pail in hand.

He was so damned complacent, she thought angrily, as if he thought he knew everything. She would love to take him down a peg or two. A wicked gleam brightened her dark eyes as she slowed her steps toward the house.

Kit glanced toward the shed a few yards away where Lew, Frank, and Kyle were. All three of them were crouched around the tractor, still trying to complete the repairs and get it in running condition.

"Lew?" she called to the senior hand. When he glanced up, Kit motioned him to her.

He straightened up and walked over to her. "I think we just about got it," he declared with satisfaction.

But Kit's thoughts weren't on the tractor. "Talbot wants to ride out to the herd with me, so would you saddle my bay and catch Dusty for him?"

Lew's mouth dropped open and stayed that way for several seconds. "You don't want Dusty," he protested. "Not for the baron."

"Yes, I do," she insisted with a feline curve to her mouth.

"But Frank"—he motioned to the older cowboy beside the tractor—"just finally caught him the other day. He's been runnin' wild all winter and you know what he's like after that. It takes a week's worth of ridin' just to get the humps out of his back."

"Yes, I know," Kit purred.

"He'll throw the baron sure as hell the first time he steps into the saddle," Lew breathed.

"Talbot assured me that he wasn't a greenhorn and that he could ride."

"And you're goin' to—" He saw the glint in her eye and the look of astounded protest slowly faded into a smile that spread across his whole face. "It's goin' to be a sight to see, isn't it?" Lew chortled softly.

"It certainly is," Kit grinned.

"I'll saddle 'em and bring 'em both up to the Big House," he promised.

"Meet you there in ten minutes," Kit said and started for her own house to put away the milk, a new spring to her step.

Exactly ten minutes later, her boots were clumping hollowly on the wood steps leading to the porch of the Big House. She saw Lew coming from the barn leading two saddled horses. Kit could feel the excitement building within her and fought to contain it.

"Are you ready?" she called to Reese.

"Ready." He pushed the screen door open and walked out onto the porch to join her.

Her gaze ran over him in swift appraisal, faintly surprised at how natural he looked in everyday western clothes. But clothes did not a cowboy make, Kit thought, silently paraphrasing the old saying. She turned away in case those sharp eyes glimpsed something in her expression.

"Lew is bringing the horses," she told Reese.

Standing at the top of the steps, hands on her hips and nerves tingling in anticipation, Kit watched the cowboy approach. One of the two horses Lew was leading was her blaze-faced bay gelding, Reno. But it was the second that drew Kit's attention.

He was a rangy buckskin, buff-colored with a jet-black mane and tail, and black legs. Dusty was so named because any rider who climbed on him invariably ended up dusting the dirt off the seat of his pants. Or at least that was the case whenever he hadn't been ridden for some time, as now. Once he had been ridden regularly he became an honest, hardworking cowhorse.

The buckskin's split personality wasn't visible as Lew led him toward the house. Kit's bay walked alertly, ears pricked, the reins loose, almost crowding Lew. But Dusty was plodding along, ears drooping, seemingly half-asleep.

Over by the shed, Frank looked up from the tractor, took a second look when he recognized the buckskin and straightened, touching Kyle's shoulder to draw his attention. They knew instinctively what was going on and were aware they had a front-row seat to watch the fun.

Lew kept his head down, the hat brim shadowing his face and concealing the mischievous light twinkling in his eyes. Initiating new ranch hands by giving them the roughest horse in the string wasn't uncommon, but hazing a new owner was unheard of. Only Kit would have come up with the idea and had the spirit to carry it out.

"I'll take the bay, Mr. Talbot. You can have the buckskin." She forced an air of indifference into her voice as she skipped down the steps.

Kit had almost reached Lew when she realized she had received no reply and there was no sound of Reese following her from the porch. She stopped and turned. Reese was at the top of the porch steps where she had been.

His attention was on the two men over by the tractor. Then his gaze slid thoughtfully to the buckskin standing so quietly. Reese glanced at Lew, still holding the reins, face averted, before finally meeting Kit's questioning look.

Had he guessed? Did he know what was going

on? How could he? The questions flashed through her mind. Kit's heart was pounding in her throat. He couldn't possibly know, she assured herself grimly.

"Well, are you ready?" she challenged.

"Yes." He descended the steps to Kit. Nothing in his expression revealed that he suspected anything was wrong and she almost sighed with relief. Lew was holding both sets of reins and started to separate those to the buckskin when Reese approached. "I'll ride the bay," Reese stated, taking the reins before Lew could stop him. "The buckskin looks too placid for me."

"No!" The blurted protest leaped from Kit's mouth. He shot her a quizzical look and she attempted to tone down her reaction. "He really isn't placid. You'll see."

"Then you won't mind riding him." Reese shrugged and looped the reins over the bay's neck, moving to its left side.

"But—" Words deserted her.

With a hand on the saddle horn, he paused. "Do you object to switching mounts? Is there some reason why I shouldn't ride the bay?"

"No . . . that is, I always ride him." Frustrated, Kit couldn't seem to come up with an adequate reason not to switch horses.

"Well, this time you can ride the buckskin." Reese swung effortlessly into the saddle, indicating an expertise beyond his simple statement that he could ride. This time there was a competitive glint in his eyes when he looked down at Kit. "Are you ready?"

Her lips pressed into a tight line. Her attempt to

embarrass him had been thwarted. There was nothing to do now but ride the buckskin herself—*if* she could. Stiff-necked, Kit walked to where Lew stood at the horse's head.

"What are you going to do?" Lew muttered through a corner of his mouth.

"Ride him," she hissed. Pulling her hat down tight, she looped the reins over the horse's neck and noticed the way he laid back his ears. "Hold on to the bridle—tight!" Kit ordered under her breath so Reese wouldn't hear.

While Lew tightly gripped the headstall, she crawled slowly and deliberately into the saddle, refusing to even glance in Reese's direction. Kit could feel the horse's muscles bunching beneath her like a spring coiling even tighter. She adjusted the reins to the desired length and made sure she was sitting deep in the saddle. A combination of excitement, fear, and challenge thudded through her veins.

Glancing at Lew, she gave a curt nod and said, "I have him."

The minute he released the bridle and stepped away, the spring uncoiled. The buckskin sprang into a series of stiff-legged jumps across the yard, giving Kit the feeling she was astride a runaway jackhammer. Distantly she could hear the shouts of encouragement from Lew and Frank, but she had no idea what they were saying.

When that didn't unseat her, the buckskin switched its tactics and started sunfishing, jumping and kicking his back legs high in the air, exposing his belly to the sunlight. Kit pulled leather but this wasn't a rodeo contest. The object was to stay on any way she could. She might have, too, but the horse's straightaway line of bucking had brought them to the corral fence. With hardly a miss in his stride, he veered sharply away from the obstacle.

Centrifugal force sent Kit sailing out of the saddle as if she was diving to the ground. Instinct had her rolling almost before she hit the dirt. She ended up sitting on her bruised backside, winded, jarred, and mad. Her hat was cockeyed but still on her head. Kit pulled it straight, aware of the others rushing to her side and Lew walking over to catch the now quiet buckskin.

"Are you all right?" The most unwelcome voice of all that might have asked the question was the one Kit heard. It belonged to Reese.

"No," she snapped and scrambled to her feet without looking at him, brushing the dust from the seat of her pants.

"Looks like I'd better ride the buckskin," Reese said smugly. "You don't seem able to handle him."

Kit jerked her head up to glare at him. She had a fleeting glimpse of the wicked twinkle in his hazel eyes before he turned to walk to the ornery horse. His statement infuriated her, as he had no doubt meant it to—but he might get his comeuppance yet.

Again Lew held the buckskin but this time it was Reese who climbed into the saddle. Fresh from victory, the horse leaped into action while Kit silently and fervently rooted for it. Reese seemed to be glued to its back.

There was a movement beside her. Kit turned to find her grandfather among the onlookers, the bay's reins in his hand. He glanced at her.

"Was this foolishness your idea?" Nate said accusingly.

"Yes," Kit retorted without remorse. "I wanted to prove he isn't as great as he thinks he is."

"Seems to me that he's the one doing the proving," the old man observed.

Kit looked back to see the buckskin cantering in a circle, humping his back. Her plan had backfired royally. Without saying a word, she took the reins from her grandfather and swung into the saddle.

The bay started forward and Kit checked it. She glanced at the faces of the men watching Reese and saw the respect in their eyes. It made her defeat even harder to swallow—and she wasn't exactly proud of her own spitefulness.

More than anything, Kit wanted to leave the ranch yard at a gallop, and alone. Instead, her gaze met that of the buckskin's rider. There was no backing down now.

At a slow, rolling canter, the horses and their riders left the yard, the buckskin following the bay. They rode to the west in silence. The only sounds to break the stillness were the creaking of saddle leather, the rhythmic thud of the horses' hooves swishing through the tall grass, and the trill of a meadowlark.

The terrain finally dictated a slower pace and the two horses settled into a ground-eating walk. Kit shifted in her saddle and winced at the stab of pain in her bruised hip.

"Sore?" Reese asked, with his usual mocking smile.

Kit shot him an angry glance. The expression

on his face—call it lordly arrogance—was hard to take. But it was the knowing look in his gold-flecked brown eyes that really, *really,* got under her hide.

"Yeah, as a matter of fact. Getting thrown off a horse is not my idea of fun." And there were a lot more places that were going to hurt before the day was over, she thought ruefully.

He patted the buckskin. "That was no way to treat a lady, Dusty. Mind your manners next time."

"You guessed right away about him, didn't you?" accused Kit.

"Yes."

She rode in silence for several strides. There was no way any explanation would make her look good but she had to say something.

"It was a stupid prank. Guess I learned my lesson."

"I know."

Kit turned in the saddle to look at him. "Why did you go along with it?"

"Just to see you take that tumble—you had it coming. Besides, you looked pretty damn cute dusting off your britches," Reese said, amusement in his voice.

She stared straight ahead again, seething. "You never would have ridden Dusty if I hadn't topped him off."

"That's something you'll never know for sure."

"You have an answer for everything, don't you?" Kit asked the question through gritted teeth.

He waited a few seconds before replying. "I haven't come up with one for you," he said cryptically.

"Good. I hope you don't. Stay out of my private life. And my thoughts."

She turned again and caught him looking at her with an expression she couldn't really read. He made no reply, and she urged her horse on.

Kit and the bay started down the sloping face of a twisting ravine, Reese following on the buckskin. Their ride to the floor of the canyon meadow was made in silence.

A scattering of cattle grazed on the lush grass, both Hereford and Angus. A pair of white-faced calves were nearby, kicking up their heels in frolicking play. The approach of the riders sent them scurrying back to their mothers, tails high in the air.

Close to the center of the canyon floor, Reese drew his horse to a stop. Kit halted also to see why. He was looking around at the rich grassland, the sage-dotted slopes, and the distant buttes looming on the horizon.

"And they call this the 'badlands' of North Dakota," he mused.

Kit understood what he was getting at, because she, too, found it wildly beautiful. "The Sioux Indians had their own name for it, but French fur trappers called this country the 'bad lands to cross.' Maybe it seemed that way to them after the flat prairies. But it's nothing like the South Dakota badlands—they really deserve the name."

"You've been there?" He sat easily in the saddle, a hand resting on his thigh.

"No, but I've heard other people talk about it," she answered, not in the least bothered that she had been no farther than a hundred miles from the Flying Eagle Ranch in her life. "If you want to see some even more spectacular scenery, you should drive through the Teddy Roosevelt National Park, north of Medora." Kit was warming to a subject she loved best—the land. "We had a cowboy from Texas work for us one year. He said he'd seen some high country before, but this was the wildest, lonesomest land he had ever known."

"He could be right," Reese agreed.

"It hasn't changed that much since the Indians were here. Oh, I didn't get a chance to show you where Teddy Roosevelt had his Maltese Cross ranch on the other side of the Little Missouri River. The railroad brought the ranchers right around then. The only big difference between those times and today is that instead of longhorn cattle coming north on trail drives, we have Herefords and Angus grazing on the land."

"And the buffalo and Indians are gone," he reminded her dryly.

"Yes," Kit admitted. "But I can imagine them here, right where we are. When the Sioux got horses, they became one of the most powerful Plains tribes. Some say they were the finest mounted warriors the world has ever known."

Reese studied her for a long moment. "You love everything about this country, don't you? Its past, its present—" He stopped before he said "its future."

Kit was suddenly reminded that he owned this land. "Yes." Her voice vibrated huskily with the fierceness of her feelings. "And when you love something, it belongs to you in a way."

"Does it?"

It seemed to be a rhetorical question—or at least one that Reese didn't want Kit to answer. With a touch of his heel he urged the buckskin into a canter. He was two lengths away before Kit reacted and followed suit.

The buckskin flushed a cock pheasant from a nearby bush and spooked when it flew up in front of him. The buff-colored horse lunged sideways, skittering away from the game bird. Reese's reflexes were equally swift—he stayed firmly in the saddle despite the sudden change of direction. In full control, he checked his horse's attempt to bolt.

When he had calmed it, Kit had to ask, "Where did you learn to ride?" It was a compliment to his skill in the saddle, though grudgingly given.

"I've been riding since I was small. English-style, western, bareback. You name it and I've tried it." The assertion was made without bragging—it was a statement of experience. "I did some professional showing of hunters for my father when I was younger."

"I imagine you won him quite a few trophies." She heard the bitter tone in her voice but she didn't care.

"A few," Reese admitted, seeming more interested in studying her expression than his answer.

Kit stared at a point between the bay's ears. "I suppose he displayed them in his castle."

His mouth quirked. "To my knowledge, we never had a castle in Maryland."

"Oh, right. You said the castle had been sold— wait a minute. What's Maryland got to do with it? Wasn't the old baron . . . your grandfather?"

"No, he was a distant relative of mine. His grandfather and my great-grandfather were first cousins, I think," he explained. "The baron died without an heir and I turned out to be the closest male relative still living."

"I see," she murmured stiffly. "And are you from Maryland? Don't tell me you drove all the way to North Dakota from there."

"I rented the Range Rover at the airport."

"Not in Fargo. You can't rent a car like that in Fargo."

"No, someplace a little more civilized than that."

Kit wanted to kick him but she couldn't do that too easily astride a horse. "Okay, be cagey."

"I stopped here and there to see some friends, and then took the scenic route."

"I see. You never did answer my question about Maryland."

"Oh—yes, I was born there. My father worked for the British Foreign Service in the diplomatic branch. Actually, I have dual citizenship, but I consider myself an American."

So that explained the lack of an English accent. "I suppose your parents are dead," she said absently, trying to remember what little she knew about the way titles were inherited and realizing too late the insensitivity of her remark.

But he didn't seem to take it the wrong way. "Yes. I'm an orphan like you, only much more recently," Reese said quietly. "My parents were killed in a small-plane crash ten years ago."

"What did you do? Or what do you do for a living?" Again she reminded herself that she hadn't wanted to know anything about the new baron, not even his name. But hearing that Reese had lost his parents, too, made her feel a little sympathy for him, though that wasn't the same as liking him. Kit eyed him thoughtfully.

He shrugged. "My parents were fairly wealthy and I was their only heir. I got an MBA from Yale eventually—when I wasn't trying to figure out the meaning of life in philosophy classes."

"Let me know if you ever do." She had to smile.

"Then I invested the money they left me while the market was booming and I kept the hell out of tech stocks. The collapse didn't hit me as hard as most—in fact, I did pretty well. What else? I dabbled in this and that—and traveled a lot."

He didn't seem proud of his life. In fact, Kit thought he seemed bored.

He studied her for a long moment. "And what about you? You're probably too damn smart when it comes right down to it. Ever wanted to do anything with your life besides chase cows? Did you go to college after high school?"

She shook her head. That had been a bone of contention between her and Nate—the thought of leaving the ranch had not appealed to her and she had put off making a decision about college indefinitely.

"Okay, no answer is an answer, too. I get it. I think."

"Thank you for not playing Twenty Questions with my life. So you live in Maryland?"

"Not exactly. I don't have a home."

"You must have an unusual wife," Kit observed.

Reese cast her a mocking look. "Are you asking if I'm married?"

"Aren't you?" she cantered. She hadn't bothered to look for a wedding ring or noticed that he had that "taken" look of a married man—she simply hadn't been all that interested.

"Have you seen any evidence of a wife?"

"If you mean because you came alone, I'm supposed to assume that you don't have one—well, it didn't cross my mind. Anyway, the wives of the previous owners never seemed to like the ranch much. Some didn't even visit it once," Kit retorted.

"I see. Well, I don't happen to be married. Or engaged. Or committed to anyone or anything in particular—"

His reply caused Kit to jerk at the reins, halting her horse, her eyes widening. "Then what about the ranch? Are you going to sell it?"

He stopped his horse, leveling a look at her slightly anxious expression. "I haven't made up my mind."

Her jaw tightened. "I don't see how you could even consider selling it."

"I haven't said I would." A dark eyebrow lifted at the anger in her words, as if her concern for the fate of the Flying Eagle was somehow amusing. "It might be a good investment. And" —his gaze swept the ruggedly beautiful landscape—"it could make a pleasant retreat for a few months of the year." His gaze returned to dwell lazily on Kit. "What's the matter? Are you afraid that if I sell it the new owner might not keep you on?"

"No," answered Kit with calm certainty. "I'm not worried about that."

Reese seemed skeptical. "You aren't concerned that you might lose your home if I sell out?"

"No matter what you do, I won't leave the ranch," Kit said defiantly. She urged her horse forward to end the conversation.

CHAPTER 5

"He said he might sell." Kit wrapped her wet hair in a towel and turned to her grandfather. "Do you think he will?"

It was more than two weeks since Reese had brought up the possibility that he would dispose of the ranch. Despite her declaration that the sale wouldn't affect her, she knew better. She just hadn't wanted to admit it to him.

"I don't know. He could." Nate didn't glance up from his newspaper.

"Has he said anything about it to you?"

"He doesn't confide such things to me," the old man answered. "Not likely he'll discuss it until he makes up his mind one way or the other. Either way it makes no difference to us."

"I know."

The house they lived in and the two acres around it did not belong to the ranch, so neither Kit nor her grandfather had to worry about having to leave their home after all these years. She had guessed that Reese Talbot wasn't aware that his predecessor had deeded Nate's property away and she hadn't bothered to inform him of it.

The clause was probably buried in a complicated will now making its way through the English version of probate—and if Reese lived in Maryland, maybe he didn't know all the details yet.

Kit sighed, and turned away from her grandfather, who seemed to have become totally absorbed in the paper. Inexplicably restless, she moved toward the back door and the pleasantly cool night air.

The breeze blowing in stirred her long cotton robe against her bare legs. The day had been hot, and despite a shower and shampoo, Kit still felt a bit sticky. Her hair needed to be dried, but the towel would soak up a lot of the wetness and the blow-drying could be done later.

"Nate, I'm going outside for a walk," she called to her grandfather and received an absentminded murmur of acknowledgment.

Pushing open the screen door, Kit walked out into the night. Overhead was a skyful of stars and a smiling moon; and the towering cottonwoods along the Little Missouri formed black cobwebs against the dark landscape. Crickets were singing in the grasses, hopping away in silence when Kit strolled near. The air was heavy with the scent of new hay and she inhaled the pungent fragrance in contentment.

The first cutting was all stacked for next winter's use, a wearying job no matter how it was done.

Reese had surprised Kit by helping with the cutting, proving he wasn't averse to physical labor. If he had suffered from sore, stiff muscles, he hadn't let on. With no small degree of cynicism, Kit thought that he'd probably found the demanding work a change from his normal routine. A steady diet of it would probably wear thin.

Thoughts of him were too disquieting on such a peaceful night. The slight breeze was cooling, the prickling of warmth on her skin already easing under its caress, the cotton robe unbuttoned at the throat. A rustling of the grasses warned her that she was not alone and Kit turned toward the sound.

"Beautiful night, isn't it?" Reese commented.

"Yes, it is," Kit agreed smoothly and resumed her strolling pace with Reese falling in step beside her. "That's one of the nice things about a North Dakota summer. The days may be hot but the nights are usually pleasant."

"Is there anything you don't like about this area?" he said softly.

Your presence here, she could have said, but didn't. "Very little," Kit answered simply. Her wandering path was taking her full circle, leading back to the house.

"Hmm. Are you trying to sell me on the idea of keeping this ranch?"

She couldn't see his face very well in the dim moonlight, but she could feel his eyes watching her. "Would it do any good if I tried?" she asked.

"None at all."

"Okay. But have you decided whether you're

going to keep the ranch or not?" Since he'd introduced the subject, Kit saw nothing wrong with pursuing it.

"No." Reese sounded suddenly impatient with the topic.

"You brought it up. I didn't. No need to get huffy."

He ran his gaze over her, taking in the long cotton robe and the towel wrapping up her hair. "You remind me of a high priestess with that towel on your head," he observed in a lazy drawl.

"You say some really weird things, do you know that?" He had changed the subject and Kit had no interest in any other conversation. She made a slight alteration in her direction to reach the house sooner.

"I was just thinking out loud."

"Spare me." If he started in on one of his explanations, she was going to cut him off.

"Sorry." He didn't look the least bit sorry.

"Well, I have to go in—I have things to do," Kit lied.

"Oh. You didn't look busy when I came out." He gave her a sideways look that really irritated her but he didn't take the hint and go away. "Saturday night and no date, huh? What a sad state of affairs."

Kit lifted her chin and almost lost the towel on her head. "Not at all," she said haughtily. "I prefer it that way."

"Really?" He stood a little distance away, his legs apart and his hands on his hips. His face was in shadow, but his tall body was clearly outlined by the moonlight. He seemed to be waiting, as if the next move was hers.

"So—if you'll excuse me—" Kit quickened her step and began to walk away, but the heel of her slipper caught the hem of her robe and tripped her. She stumbled forward. A muscular arm captured her waist and Reese pulled her to his steadying length. The shock of the near fall and the sudden contact with his very male body momentarily froze her into stillness.

Her hip bone felt the pressure of his muscular thigh. His fingers were spread over the curve of her waist, and his touch seemed to burn through the thin material of her robe, throwing her senses into turmoil.

"I'm all right. Let me go," she ordered him. Her voice was oddly vibrant.

"Of course." Reese acquiesced without hesitation.

The arm around the back of her waist loosened its hold. As his hand fell away, it brushed her hip and the firm roundness of her buttocks. Kit jerked away, her skin tingling where he had touched her and an embarrassed heat flaming her face.

"Stop it!"

"Sorry—I didn't mean—"

"I don't give a damn what you meant. Don't touch me like that!"

He held up both hands. "Whoa. It was not intentional."

Trembling with anger, she wrapped her robe more tightly around herself and stared him down. He looked at her for a long minute before he spoke.

"Tell me something, Kit," he said quietly and curiously. "Who hurt you?"

His question seemed more invasive than his caress. She didn't want to answer.

"Was it a man?"

A bitter, choked laugh came from her throat. "Yeah, you could say that."

Before Reese could say more, Kit hurried up the steps. The light streaming from the back door briefly silhouetted her slender figure, changing the ordinary cotton of her robe to gossamer. Then she was inside, the screen door slamming.

Kit could not forget what had happened in the ten days that followed—the memory of their encounter by moonlight came back to her every time she saw him. All she could do was keep Reese at a distance, even if it meant being cold and rude.

With long, impatient strides, Kit crossed the ranch yard toward her house. It was well past one o'clock, nearly two. The sun was high and hot overhead, and her stomach was rumbling. She had been too busy at lunchtime to eat.

Perspiring from the heat and hungry as well, Kit hurried toward the house, hoping a quick snack would take the edge off.

"Kitty?"

The sound of a female voice brought her up short and she turned toward the Big House and the middle-aged woman standing on the porch, Mrs. Kent, a widowed lady Reese had hired to take care of the house and his meals. Kit still hadn't gotten used to having another woman around the ranch.

"Yes, Mrs. Kent, what is it?" Her demand was abrupt; she was anxious not to be delayed.

The woman smoothed a hand over her plump, aproned figure. She seemed nervous. "Have you seen Mr. Talbot?"

"No, I haven't," she was glad to say.

"Oh." The answer plainly didn't please the pepper-haired woman. "I thought he might be with you."

Frowning, the housekeeper lifted her gaze to the south where the windbreak of trees didn't obstruct the view of the ranch land.

"He isn't. I haven't seen him at all today." Kit stopped hurrying. "Why? What's wrong?"

"He left right after breakfast this morning and said he'd be back for lunch but I haven't seen a sign of him." She looked back to Kit. "I'm getting worried."

Kit let out a long sigh. Lunch would have to wait. "Did he say where he was going when he left this morning?"

"I thought he mentioned something about going for a ride."

Kit made a sweeping inventory of the yard. Reese's Range Rover was there and so was one of the pickups. She had just seen Frank by himself in the other truck, which eliminated that possibility.

"Is he maybe with one of the others?" Mrs. Kent asked hopefully.

"No." Kit had seen all three of the hands within the last hour and a half. Reese had not been with any of them. Her gaze searched over the horses in the corral next to the barn. The buckskin was missing and she knew Reese had taken to riding him. "Damn," she cursed under her breath.

"What do you think we should do?" Mrs. Kent looked really worried now.

Kit didn't answer immediately, looking to the land to the west where it was all too easy to disappear. Reese had said he was going riding and the buckskin was gone. Knowing how ornery Dusty could be, it was possible he had been thrown. Even the best riders could be bucked off by a horse like that. But Kit was convinced that it was more likely he had ridden too far and become lost in the unfamiliar terrain.

"I'll go out and look for him," she said with decision. "Tell Nate what's happened while I saddle a horse. He can take the truck and go look for him. If we aren't back with him by the time Lew and the others show up, you'd better send them out, too."

With a pail of oats as a bribe, she caught the bay gelding and saddled him swiftly. As she rode into the yard, her grandfather was just climbing into the cab of the pickup. Kit paused to speak to him, splitting up the directions they would take to widen the search for Reese. Little more than that was said. Getting lost was serious business in this wild country.

The gnawing hollowness in her stomach was forgotten as Kit rode out. She kept to the ridges, bluffs, and mesas, the places where her view was expanded by the advantage of height. She pushed her mount to cover as much territory as possible.

The bay lathered up quickly in the heat of the afternoon, but he was game.

Kit, too, felt the effects of the summer heat. Perspiration trickled down her spine and formed a rivulet in the hollow between her breasts. The cotton shirt clung to her sweat-damp skin, hugging closely to her curves. There was a salty taste to her lips and the pungent aroma of hot horseflesh assailed her sense of smell.

For well over an hour, she searched fruitlessly, her eyes straining at the sight of each dark shape on the land, only to have it turn out to be a cow or a boulder-size chunk of scorialike rock that had tumbled from a cliff face. The sun was brilliant even beneath the wide, shadowing brim of her hat.

On the point of a bluff, Kit turned the bay to send him down a gentle slope dotted with pillars of sandstone eroded by wind and weather. She caught a glimpse of movement to her left. Kit reined in the bay and stared at the point where she thought she had seen something.

A narrow valley was formed by two ridgebacks. Willows and young cottonwoods followed the winding path of a creek bed through its center, a creek that the summer's heat had probably reduced to a mere trickle. It was in those trees that Kit thought she had detected movement. The horse's side heaved beneath her, glad of the short rest.

A few seconds later, her patience and alertness were rewarded. Reese came riding out of the trees on the buckskin. Relieved satisfaction washed through her at having found him. It didn't last long. The sight of him riding along calmly as if he didn't have a care in the world made her seriously angry.

Kit reined in the bay to the left and urged it down the steeper slope. A patch of loose shale clattered noisily beneath his hooves, attracting Reese's attention. Kit gave the bay his head as he slid and lunged down the hill to the other horse and rider.

Reese glowered at the sight of the lathered neck and flanks of the bay. "What do you think you're doing riding a horse that hard on a day like this?" His harsh voice slashed across her already taut nerves.

"Hey, we've been looking high and low for you!" Exasperated fury quivered in her voice. "Of all the stupid, greenhorn stunts to pull—getting yourself lost!"

"Lost?" He seemed to relax in the saddle, smile lines twitching around his mouth. "I'm not lost."

"What do you call it, then?" Kit challenged him.

"I was just doing some exploring on my own."

"Oh—is that why you didn't turn up at the Big House for lunch, the way you told Mrs. Kent you would?" She didn't spare the sarcasm.

"Is that what this is all about?" Reese looked surprised, in a mocking sort of way. It did little to appease Kit's temper.

"Yes!" she snapped. "The poor woman was worried sick! Nate is out along the river looking for you! And by this time, the boys have joined in the search as well!"

"I did tell Mrs. Kent I'd be back in time for lunch," he admitted unrepentantly. "When the noon hour came around I wasn't hungry so I didn't bother to go back. I didn't think she'd even notice."

His bland indifference made her breath catch in her throat. But not for long.

"Let me set you straight on a few things!" Kit raged, fire blazing in her dark brown eyes. "When someone doesn't show up when he says he's going to, we worry. And when that someone is also unfamiliar with the lay of the land, we take it very seriously. Did you tell anyone where you were going? This isn't friendly country, especially if you don't know its dangers. And it's a hot day—did you bring water?"

"Uh, no. Okay. You're right, Kit. On every point," he conceded.

She was much too angry to notice the leisurely way his gaze was roaming over her, taking note of the way the man's shirt revealed the definitely female curves beneath it and the agitated movements of her breasts in rhythm with her breathing. The flush of anger in her cheeks gave a vibrant glow to her skin.

"Is that all you have to say?" He sure as hell hadn't apologized and he wasn't likely to, Kit fumed.

"No." With an unconscious, masculine grace, Reese swung out of the saddle. "I think we should walk for a while and give you and your horse a chance to cool off."

It was on the tip of her sharp tongue to tell him that she had no desire to cool off, but a glance at the shiny, wet neck of her horse stopped it. The bay did need a breather after the way she had pushed him in her search for Reese.

As he moved to the head of her horse, Kit

placed a hand on the saddle horn and started to swing a leg over the saddle. His hands gripped the sides of her waist and Kit stopped, standing in the air with one foot in the stirrup. Twisting to glare at him, she leaned against the saddle skirt.

"I've been getting on and off horses by myself for years. I don't need your help!"

A steely glint entered his eyes. "That's too bad, because you're going to get it."

His fingers held her tighter. Kit swung at his arm, in too precarious a position to offer more than token resistance. Already he was lifting her clear of the saddle as if her body weighed no more than air. Her feet touched the ground and she tried to wrench away from his hands, hitting at him and kicking.

With consummate ease Reese turned her around, a muscled arm across the middle of her back holding her against his full length. Her arms were pinned against his chest and Kit knew she was no match for his let-me-help-you-little-lady routine. Immediately she stopped struggling and tried to figure out a Plan B.

Plan A, rescuing the ungrateful bastard, wasn't working out. If she could figure out a way to tie him to a tree and leave him for the ranch hands to find, she would do it. But he had her exactly where he wanted her. Damn, damn, damn. She hoped and prayed that no one would see them like this.

If she could get her hands free, she would be able to smack that complacent smile off his face. He seemed to anticipate that she might do just that, though, just as he had anticipated Dusty's wild bucking. He didn't let her go.

"I'm on the ground. You can stop showing off now." Kit spoke through clenched teeth. The heat of his body, so hard and unyielding, was making itself felt and the sensation was unnerving.

There was a mischievous glint in his eyes and a half-smile on his lips. "Do you know," he said slowly, "I've never seen you without that old hat." His voice seemed to come from deep in his throat.

His words registered with a flash of warning. But there was nothing Kit could do to stop him before he tugged the weathered brown Stetson from her head and a cascade of chestnut-gold hair tumbled about her shoulders.

"Well, I'll be damned." There was a chuckle in his surprised statement as he wound his fingers into the silken strands shimmering with highlights of liquid gold in the sunshine.

"Stop it." Kit tried to twist away from his touch, straining against the iron band of his arm across her back, and closing her eyes against the feel of his hand running through her hair.

"Why haven't you chopped it off like a boy?" Reese seemed genuinely curious.

"Because," she breathed out heavily, frustrated by the ridiculous fix she was in, "it's too much trouble getting it cut all the time."

"Is that the real reason?" he asked skeptically.

"Yes!" Kit snapped. "And I didn't ride out in ninety-two-degree heat to talk about my hair!"

He gave her just enough room to get a hand free and she took full advantage of it, slapping him—hard. It was about as effective as slapping a house. He didn't even seem to notice. He looked at her lips and bent his head down to kiss her.

Suddenly, Kit stopped fighting and let his mouth find hers. His lips were soft, almost tender, but the solid flesh of his body seemed to grow harder as she surrendered reluctantly to his embrace. She closed her eyes, letting the pleasure he was giving her drive out all other thoughts.

The heat of the afternoon seemed to intensify the hot, male odor of him, taking her breath away. The brilliant sun seemed to be affecting her. Kit felt dizzy and strangely weightless. Her fingers clutched at his shirtfront, feeling the granite wall of muscle it covered. Something warm and urgent was being unleashed inside her, and Kit fought it, whimpering in her throat, afraid she might give in completely.

At the sound, the locking hold of his arm around her seemed to relax, as if Reese believed he had conquered her. She almost stumbled out of his embrace, then covered her clumsiness by turning away to run a hand through the tousled disarray of her tawny hair. Kit was more shaken by the kiss than she cared to admit.

"You are full of surprises," Reese declared huskily. "Guess there's some truth in that saying about letting your hair down."

Her back was to him and his hands settled caressingly on her shoulders, his warm breath fanning her an instant before Kit stepped away, shrugging free of his touch.

"Don't be too sure about that." Thankfully her voice was fairly steady, even if her heart was still thudding erratically in her chest.

"Admit it, Kit." He made no further move to approach her. "I got to you. Am I the first?"

"Hell, no." She forced that practiced toughness into her voice, hoping he would believe her.

"Hell, yes—I am," Reese insisted with a knowing gleam in his unsettling hazel eyes. "I know I am."

Her level gaze faltered for an instant. "That's what you think."

"That's what I know," he said softly. "I doubt if your experience goes beyond a little teenaged fumbling behind the barn. I'd swear you never made it to the hayloft."

She drew herself up to her full height, summoning all her pride not to be intimidated by the way he towered over her. "Is that something I should be ashamed about?"

"No. On the contrary." Lazily he reached out, his fingers closing around the shirt button nestled in the vee of her breasts. "Every man likes to be the first."

Trembling with fury at the intimate brush of his hand, Kit slapped it away. "You have the time and place mixed up." Her voice was raw. "This is not the eighteenth century or jolly old England. You may be a lord but you can't take your pick of the local virgins."

His eyes narrowed, and a muscle twitched along his tightened jaw. "The women I go to bed with are willing. More than willing. I don't force them."

"Women. In the plural," Kit tossed back contemptuously.

"I'm not a choirboy. And I don't want to be tied down."

"That's more than I wanted to know," she said furiously. "And don't tell me what every man wants!"

"Kit, all I meant **was**—"

"And in case you haven't figured it out already, you're not the man *I* want!"

"That's your choice," Reese snapped. "And believe me, I'm not at all sure I'd want you."

"Good." Her voice was tight. "There's always Carolyn. She couldn't take her eyes off you."

"She's married—and even if she wasn't, she's not my type."

Kit ran a hand through her hair, not used to it being down. "Oh. What is your type?"

"I don't have one. But I like a woman who isn't afraid of being a woman—"

"Meaning I am?" she retorted, before he could finish his sentence.

"Yeah," he said flatly. His gaze suddenly ran over her, piercing and probing. "What did this man do to you? The one who hurt you so badly?"

Everything inside her seemed to freeze up at his question. Kit withdrew behind an impenetrable mask, all emotion—even anger—suppressed. She willed herself to feel nothing.

Her reaction seemed to intensify Reese's curiosity, but he only waited for her to say something first.

"No one asked you to come here." Kit deliberately didn't respond to his questions. "Why couldn't you just be satisfied with absentee ownership? It was good enough for all the others. Why isn't it good enough for you?"

He gave her a long, considering look. "You'd like me to leave, wouldn't you?"

"Yes."

"To leave and never come back," Reese went on.

"You got it," Kit said, the strength of her feelings evident despite the coldness of her tone. "And you will. Someday you will. Then everything will go back to the way it was before you came."

"Will it?" He looked at her quizzically.

"You aren't needed here and you aren't wanted here." She tossed her head back, regal and proud. "So why don't you leave?"

"You've had your say. Now I'll have mine," he said smoothly. "I'll leave when I'm damned good and ready and not a minute before—if I leave at all."

Reese picked up the trailing reins of the buckskin and prepared to mount. Kit stared at him, hating him with all her might and knowing he attracted her physically the way she had prayed no man ever would.

"How can you stay where you aren't wanted?" she demanded.

"You forget" —Reese swung into the saddle and stared down at her— "I own this land. I don't have to be wanted to stay here." His gaze flicked to her shimmering hair. "Don't forget your hat. The sun is strong today."

Turning away, Kit swept her hair atop her head and reached for the hat he'd thrown on the ground. She slapped it against her thigh to knock the dust off, then worked it over the hair piled on her head, tucking the stray locks under the crown. The bay had wandered a few feet away. Kit caught up his reins and mounted.

"How about if I lead the way back to the ranch?" Reese said tauntingly. "I'd like to prove to you that I'm not lost."

"You own this place. You don't have to ask my permission," she responded with a trace of bitterness.

He eyed her for a charged second, his expression hard and grim. Then he turned the buckskin in the direction of the distant ranch yard and took the lead.

CHAPTER 6

Frank Jarvis stood rigidly before Kit, his somewhat paunchy body unmoving, a pinched white-
ness about his sunburned face and a resentful look
in his eyes despite his silence.

"When I tell you to do something, I expect it to
be done!" Kit continued a scolding barrage that
had begun some minutes ago. "I didn't tell you to
do it tomorrow or the day after. I told you I wanted
it done this afternoon. Now why isn't it? What possible excuse could you have?"

"Kyle's horse threw a shoe," Frank began defensively. Among his other talents, which included
cooking, he was also a farrier. "The sorrel already
worn his down to a nub and your bay, Reno, had
one loose. And I figured that since we were done
with the hayin' for a while, we wouldn't be needin'
the mower right away."

"That's not for you to decide," Kit said sharply.

"I told you I wanted it repaired today and that's exactly what I meant!"

She knew she was being unreasonable. Even when the words came out of her mouth she knew she was being unfair. But once she started, Kit couldn't seem to stop. Some inner demon kept driving her on.

And it wasn't easy for Frank to keep taking her abuse. In the first place, like Lew, he was old enough to be her father, and he'd put in his years at the Flying Eagle, enough so the fact that he was conscientious about his work couldn't be questioned. Worst of all, he was being dressed-down by a female. For an old-fashioned type of man, that was hard to swallow.

"Seemed to me the horses were more important," he said defensively.

"You and I have different opinions about what's important," Kit retaliated. "And mine is the one that counts!"

"If you don't like the way I do things—"

"I don't!" Kit could have bitten off her tongue for that.

"Careful there, Kitty." A third voice joined them in the interior shadows of the barn. "If you go to firin' the cook" —it was Lew, standing just inside the door—"you just might find the rest of us walkin' out."

All the fight seemed to go out of her, like the air from a deflating balloon. She turned away from both of them, hiding the sudden wave of vulnerability. "All right. Fix the mower tomorrow, Frank," Kit asked. There was a tired and beaten sound to her voice.

A long moment of hesitation followed and the two men exchanged a glance. "I will," Frank promised finally.

Without moving, she listened to his slow footsteps as he walked through the scattering of hay on the barn floor and his murmured exchange with Lew at the door. It slid open, then closed. Alone, Kit leaned wearily against the rough boards of the barn's inside wall.

What was the matter with her? It had been impossible for anyone to live with her this past week, including herself. She had been like this ever since that devastating encounter with Reese when he had kissed her . . . oh, what a kiss. Then he'd ruined it by implying she was afraid of being a woman—whatever *that* meant.

Was he expecting her to melt in his arms and say yes to everything he asked? Well, she wouldn't. She didn't want him—in fact, she didn't want any man. Passionate yearnings and romantic daydreams were for people who didn't have anything better to do, didn't have a lonely old grandpa to take care of, and a pack of ranch hands expecting her to make all the decisions.

Love was no big whoop—Kit didn't have the time for it and she didn't want the pain.

Dragging her hat from her head, Kit let her hair tumble free, hoping it would ease the pressure pounding in her head. She turned to rest her back and both shoulders against the barn wall, lifting her gaze to the hayloft overhead. A stab of anguish twisted her insides and Kit screwed up her mouth to hold back a sob, succeeding in keeping it to a sniffle.

A sound came from near the door. Someone was in the barn. Immediately Kit straightened, brushing a hand across her face as if donning a mask. When she looked into the shadows, she saw Lew standing there.

"I . . . I thought you had gone." Her voice faltered for only a second before regaining its steadiness.

"You lit into Kyle not more'n twenty minutes ago. Now Frank. I figured it was my turn next," he said pointedly.

She lowered her head. "I don't know what's the matter with me lately." It was the closest Kit could come to an apology.

"I don't know, either, but I sure hope it don't last, 'cause you got all the rest of us snarlin' at each other. This is gettin' to be a downright unfriendly place," he declared in all seriousness.

Kit knew Lew very well. None of this was the reason he had stayed behind when Frank had left. "What do you want, Lew?"

"It's not me that wants anything. It's the boss"— tactfully he corrected that—"the baron. He wants to see you."

The mention of Reese brought every sense to full alertness; Kit was wary as a deer at the first crack of a twig under a hunter's foot. Tension crackled about her.

"Did he say why?" she asked.

"Nope, and I didn't ask. It's been gettin' to where I don't mind nobody's business but my own around here."

Her fingers tightened on her hat, crumpling

the brim. "Tell him I'm busy," Kit snapped, turning away.

"Won't do any good," Lew answered placidly. "He said for you to come as soon as you're free."

There was no way to avoid it. "All right," she agreed fatalistically. "If he asks, tell him I'll be there shortly."

After the barn door had slid shut on Lew, Kit took a few extra minutes to compose herself. There was no thought of disregarding the edict, but Kit would never admit to herself or to Reese just how much he could disturb her.

Nothing in her careless stride betrayed her nervousness. Outwardly she seemed casual, just going about a routine errand. Inwardly Kit was filled with questions that centered on one thing: why did he want to see her?

Since Reese had taken up residence in the Big House, Kit didn't come and go as she pleased through its halls. A fly buzzed angrily as she rapped on the screen door and waited. Almost instantly, Mrs. Kent bustled into view behind the fine wire mesh.

"Oh, hello, Miss Bonner—Kitty." The housekeeper always stumbled over her name, inevitably using both the formal and informal. Kit was accustomed to this nervousness from people who had heard about her, and overlooked it.

"Mr. Talbot wants to see me."

"Yes, he told me." She pushed the screen door open. "Come in. He's in the library."

Oh, no. Not that room. But there was nothing she could do about it. Stiffening her spine, Kit entered. The thick walls made the house slightly cooler and she had to suppress a shiver at the change.

The library door was closed and Kit paused before it as the housekeeper continued on. Her palm felt clammy as she lifted her hand to knock on the door. Immediately, muffled permission to enter was given from the other side.

When Kit opened the door, her gaze was unavoidably drawn to the painting over the mantelpiece. As always, the sight of the handsome, arrogant face in the portrait stirred an antagonism that was almost beyond her control. It was only natural that some of that was transferred to Reese when she turned to find him seated behind the desk, looking very much like the lord of the manor.

"Lew said you wanted to see me." Kit attempted to hide her emotions behind a tone of cool indifference, but the hardness of his expression got to her all the same.

"Have a seat." He nodded toward the straight-backed chair in front of his desk.

"No, thank you." At least this way she could enjoy the rare experience of looking down at him instead of always lifting her gaze.

Kit was aware of the change in his attitude toward her. Where once Reese had looked on her with mocking amusement, he now showed a toughness that reminded her uncomfortably of her own. She could see it in his piercing stare. There was something forbidding in the leanly hollowed cheeks and the austere line of his mouth.

"What did you want to see me about?" She wanted to get it over with and get out.

"Don't worry. It's strictly business." Amused contempt glittered briefly in his eyes.

"I figured." The hat was still in Kit's hand—she wished she had taken the time to put it on and secure her hair under its crown rather than leave it loose to tangle around her shoulders. She hadn't left the hat off to call attention to herself, that was for sure.

"I made a decision about the ranch," he announced, "and I thought I should tell you."

"What is it?" Kit refused to sound overly interested.

"I won't be selling it."

"I'm sure your distinguished ancestors would be glad to know it's staying in the family," was her faintly biting response.

"I knew you would be overjoyed at the news."

Kit shrugged. "Is that all you wanted to say?"

"No, there's more," Reese assured her, leaning back in his chair with every indication that he was going to enjoy telling her. "I won't be leaving for a while—maybe not for a long while."

"That's your decision." Kit shrugged as if it didn't matter to her.

"Yes, it is." He paused for a second. "When I first arrived—"

She interrupted. "If this is going to be a long speech I'd rather not hear it."

Feeling as if the portrait was observing the scene from its place of honor, Kit felt her inner tension mount uncontrollably, her nerves seeming to snap one by one under the emotional strain.

"When I first arrived here"—Reese continued as if she hadn't spoken at all, and Kit tossed her hat on the corner of his desk and jammed her hands into the back pockets of her jeans—"I didn't interfere with the running of the ranch." He paused and gave her a level look. "I sat back and observed what was going on. That first day when I questioned your authority to give orders, you assured me that you received them from your grandfather and acted as a go-between with the men. I had no reason to doubt you."

Kit knew what was coming and braced herself. There was nothing she could do except listen.

"Since then I've had an opportunity to see for myself that your grandfather's management of the ranch is haphazard at best. He's nothing more than a figurehead. You have been the driving force on this ranch."

It wasn't lost on Kit that he had used the past tense, but she kept it from showing. Maintaining her air of indifference, she returned his steady look.

"Why are you telling me this? If you aren't pleased with the way Nate is running things, you should speak to him."

"I chose to speak to you first," Reese said, at his autocratic best, "Because I think you know your grandfather's best years at this ranch are over."

"So he's through, is that it?" Kit challenged. "You're firing him and you expect me to back you up."

"I expect you to admit the truth of what I'm saying."

"You've given no thought at all to the years—the lifetime he's spent taking care of this ranch. You don't appreciate his honesty," Kit said furiously.

"He could have robbed this place blind and been justified. Is this the thanks he gets? You come along and decide he's no longer useful. He's just an old man so you want to boot him out."

His mouth thinned impatiently at her accusations. "I was thinking in terms of retirement—with an adequate pension."

"How thoughtful of you," she scoffed. "Pension off the old family retainer with no thought at all about what he's going to do with his empty days. Just put the old horse out to pasture. You don't care whether or not he misses the harness. Is that the way you repay his loyalty?"

"What about his pride?" Reese flared. "Would Nate want me to keep him on out of pity?"

"No! Never pity! Never from you!" Kit heard herself shouting and turned abruptly away from the desk, straining to control her temper.

"Then that settles it." He, too, made an effort at control.

"Now that you've dispensed with Nate, what about me?" She walked to the fireplace hearth, trying to avoid looking at the eyes of the man in the portrait and intensely aware of those boring into her back.

"Since I'm staying and your grandfather's leaving, I can't believe you'll want to remain," he said finally.

"That's what it all comes down to, doesn't it?" Kit declared. "The reason you're getting rid of Nate is to get rid of me."

"I think we both knew it would come to this," Reese stated. "We knew since the first time we met. The incident last week simply clinched it."

Kit started to smile—fortunately, her back was to him. "How soon are you expecting us to leave?"

"There's no rush. Whenever it's convenient."

"How very kind of you." The smile was spreading, the satisfaction she would soon have warming her soul.

"You won't have to worry. I'll make sure Nate's pension is generous."

Kit turned to face him, a feline purr to her voice when she spoke. "And what if I told you we can be off your property in five minutes, Talbot?"

A guarded look entered his eyes. "What do you mean?"

"All it takes is the time to walk out of this house and to my own." She could see by the brief flicker of surprise on his face that she'd guessed right—he hadn't known. She tipped her head back and gave a throaty laugh. "You obviously can't wait to get rid of me. The truth is that you never can."

His jaw tightened. "Would you mind explaining that remark?"

"It's very simple." The laughter faded from her voice. "You should have checked more closely into exactly what it is that you do own. The house where I live and the two acres it sits on don't belong to you."

Reese was no longer relaxed in his chair. He was leaning forward, his hands on the desk as if he had to keep them there to control his angry surprise.

"It belongs to you and Nate, then," he concluded.

"Yes. You see, the baron, your predecessor"—Kit waved a contemptuous hand toward the portrait—"has already made some provisions for our future."

"How thoughtful of him."

"Yes, wasn't it?" She nearly choked on that, but went on as best she could. "So you really can't get rid of us. You can retire Nate and fire me, but you can't get us out of your sight."

"So that's why you didn't seem to be worried when I said I might sell the ranch." His intense gaze never left her face.

"That's right. No matter what you do, we'll still be here—in the house just down the hill. You'll see us every day," Kit taunted. "So your grand plan to get us out of your life is all for nothing. It can't be done."

Uncoiling himself from his chair, Reese walked slowly around to the front corner of the desk. "How much, Kit?" he asked quietly.

She didn't get the question. "What are you talking about?"

"How much do you want? I'll buy it from you. Just name your price."

That he even *thought* they could be bought off so easily was galling. "Nothing doing," Kit blazed. "Nate brought his bride here. His daughter was born here—and his granddaughter. His wife and his daughter are buried here. Nate will be buried here and *I* will be buried here. We will never sell it!"

"Everybody has a price."

"*We* don't! We belong here. You can't buy us off. We'll be here to wave good-bye when you leave. The land is ours!"

"You can be sure I'll do some checking on that." His look was a forbidding one. "In the meantime, it seems we have a standoff."

His checking would uncover more than a
deeded title. A sense of inevitability consumed her
as she faced the fact that he would know who she
really was at last. Her spine stiffened and she held
her head high. Her posture was proud, for what
pride was worth.

"We were here before you. We'll be here when
you leave," Kit repeated.

His brooding gaze took in her defiant stance.
"Kyle was right. He had a few choice things to say
about you after you chewed him out an hour ago. I
wouldn't even repeat some of the words he used."

Something splintered inside her. "You should
have waited around." Kit wanted him to know it
all, wanted to lash out at him even if it meant reliv-
ing her hated past. "You would have heard what
else he calls me. What everyone has called me.
The baron's bastard daughter."

The white rage of a million hurts trembled
through Kit as she saw his gathering frown, the
sudden intensity of his gaze, and the look he darted
to the portrait above his head.

"He was your father?"

"Yeah. Lucky me." Kit dismissed the subject with
a small but infinitely proud shrug. "On my birth
certificate my father is listed as unknown. And before you point it out, I don't look like him. I take
after my mother."

"But when—" Muscles leaped along his jaw, his
mouth clamping shut as if he regretted the question.

But for Kit the time had come. She wanted him
to know, where once she had dreaded his finding
out.

"The baron paid a visit to this ranch twenty-two years ago, when he inherited it—just like you. But he was in his forties at the time." She glanced up at the painting, feeling the familiar wave of resentment and hurt.

"And your mother?"

"Her name was Sara. She was only seventeen," Kit said. "So she fell in love just like that—why not? He was handsome, rich, and had a title. Who would want anything more? He must have seemed like Prince Charming coming to carry her away to his castle."

"But your grandfather must have—" Reese began.

Her bitter laugh cut him off. "Must have what? The baron was his boss. And Sara was Nate's only child. Nothing was too good for her—he only wanted her to be happy."

Reese nodded but he didn't seem to have anything to say. Kit went on with the rest of the story, telling it plainly.

"Nate didn't say no when he came around to see Sara or gave her nice things and all that. He didn't know what was really going on."

"And when he found out—what did he find out?"

"The usual story." Kit didn't want to look at the portrait a second longer but she didn't want to look at Reese, either. "The baron was married. He couldn't possibly leave his wife for her, blah, blah."

There was a muffled curse behind her, but it seemed merely like an expression of her own violent feelings. What had begun as an attempt to hurt Reese had become an emotional release. The

words, the story that Kit had never uttered to anyone, had to be told.

"So the baron just got out, fast. Obviously, he
didn't want Sara in his life. He deeded the house
to Nate and arranged for my mother and me—she
refused to have an abortion—to receive an income
for the rest of her life.

"I don't understand why your grandfather continued working for him."

"That's Nate," Kit said staunchly. "He's always
done what's best for his family, no matter what. He
felt so guilty, as if he was to blame for not figuring
it out sooner. I don't think his pride would have let
him run away."

"Tell me about it. Men will do anything to pre-
serve their pride."

Kit nodded. "I'm sure he thought people would
find something else to talk about after a while. He
had a home here and work he loved. He was
among friends and could provide for his family."

"What happened to your mother?"

"She died within a year after I was born." A new,
raw edge entered her words. "Car crash. She went
out with a bunch of kids who were drinking and
having a good time—she was still a kid herself. Not
ready to be a mother. Not able to be anything else
because of me."

"You don't know that, Kit," Reese said quietly.
"Sounds like she never had a chance."

"Yeah, well—I usually didn't think about her too
much, except on some holidays. Like Mother's
Day and Christmas. Nothing I can do about it."

"But Nate and Martha must have—" he began.

She cut him off with a wave of her hand. "They

did their best. Hey, they raised me—I thought grandparents were all anybody had when I was really little. They protected me. But the day I got on that school bus, everything changed."

Kit looked up at the portrait again, hate in her eyes. "The older kids knew the baron was my father and told me I was a bastard—I didn't even know what it meant at first, but I got the idea that it made me different from them, and in a way that I couldn't change. And once they got started, they didn't stop."

How it had hurt when they called her names, and added a few for her mother. Kit could still vividly remember the bewildering pain their taunts caused. In the beginning, she had been too young to conceal her sensitivity. Knowing they could get a reaction from her had only added to the children's malicious delight in teasing her to tears.

Two things Kit learned very quickly. Coming home crying upset her beloved grandparents. They had explained, as much as a young child could understand, why she was different from the others. Although they had never used the word "illegitimate," Kit sensed the shame that lay behind their voices.

Raised in much more conservative times, they had strong feelings about what had happened, and their daughter's senseless death gave them no chance to come to terms with it. Kit, motherless and abandoned by her father, knew how to hide her own pain, if only to ease theirs.

Secondly, she learned that if she stayed away from the other children, it didn't give them a chance to hurt her. This aloofness, this holding herself apart from them, kept the story from dying. The children concluded that she did it because she thought she was too good for them, that she acted like royalty. The die was cast for the rest of her school years, and Kit became an outsider—and very good at protecting herself from hurt.

"So that, dear cousin, five or six times removed, is the story." The remark was flung over her shoulder at Reese but Kit's gaze returned to the portrait, riveted on it with a hatred that made her clench her fists. "I'm not even a love child," she said with quiet fury. "Just the product of that man's lust."

"The baron died without issue, Kit. You were his only child, as it turned out. Why didn't you contest my inheritance of his estate?" Reese questioned.

"And resurrect the whole scandal? No, if I had made a claim, it would've been all over the news, and not just locally. I have more compassion for Nate than that," she said, wondering why Reese had thought otherwise. "He's an old man, as you said. He deserves some peace after all this time. Besides, you're welcome to it. I want nothing that belonged to him."

The look she flung at the painting showed a bitter contempt that seemed to be building. There was nothing that Reese could do or say to ease the pain of so much hidden turmoil. "So he's the one who hurt you—I knew someone had," he said at last.

There was a long pause—and her anger exploded.

"I hate him!" The hoarse cry rang in the room. "I hate him!" Every inch of Kit vibrated with the violence of her emotion. "I hate him for what he did to my grandparents! And I hate him for what he did to my mother! And I hate him for what he's done to me! I hate him! I hate him!"

CHAPTER 7

There were three vases of Indian pottery on the mantelpiece below the portrait. The rage inside Kit exploded and she grabbed for one of them, bent on destroying the image of the man she despised so much. Her arm was drawn back to throw the vase when it struck something hard. The vase crashed from her hand into the empty cavity of the fireplace.

"I hate him!" Hoarse and raw, the denunciation came again.

With her first attempt thwarted, Kit tried again, reaching for a second vase. Reese tried to stop her, but she was a woman possessed. With all her strength, she fought to keep him from taking the vase from her. In the resulting scuffle Kit wrenched free, accidentally flinging the painted clay pot away. It broke atop the desk, scattering broken chips onto her hat.

The library door opened and an openmouthed

Mrs. Kent stood in its frame. "What's going on?" she breathed, obviously wishing she hadn't come to investigate the crashing sounds.

Both Kit and Reese were breathing heavily, separated only by a few feet and eyeing each other with the wariness of fighters about to come to blows again. Neither glanced away when the housekeeper spoke. Kit was still in the grip of her volcanic rage.

"It's all right, Mrs. Kent." Reese dismissed her with an abrupt wave. "There's only one vase left."

The click of the closing door distracted him for only a split second, but it was all the time Kit needed to spin around and seize the last vase. This time she didn't even attempt to throw it at the picture. Her target was the personification of it. She held it threateningly over her head, aimed at Reese.

"And I hate you, too!" There were no tears in her eyes, not even of rage. "You're no better than he was! I hate you!"

With vicious force, she hurled the vase at Reese. He dodged it easily, and it shattered against the far wall. Kit turned back to the mantel, but there were no more vases. She spied the fireplace poker and grabbed for it.

Before her fingers could curl around the handle, her wrist was caught in an iron grip and she was yanked away. Kit managed to twist her arm free and started hammering on his chest with both fists, unaware of how much she seemed to him like an angry, frightened child.

"That's enough, Kit! Snap out of it!" A pair of hands gripped her shoulders, shaking her hard.

It didn't work.

Suddenly she felt herself hauled against him, a steel arm binding her close while his fingers gripped the back of her neck. He kissed her hard at first, then more softly, as if her violent emotions could be loved away. Eventually Kit had to submit.

When her resistance began to ebb, the pressure of his mouth on hers changed subtly. Still firm, still commanding, it coaxed a pliancy from her lips. When he got it, his mouth opened tenderly over hers, consuming, demanding, promising comfort for her lonely soul. The hand at the back of her neck began to massage the taut muscles there, sensually rubbing away the tension that remained.

The arm circling her, locking her to him, became less steely. Seeking and caressing, his hand moved over her back and shoulders and hips, pressing her closer to the hard support of him. There didn't seem to be an inch of her body that didn't feel the touch of his hand or his muscled flesh. There was something healing in that, as if he had the power to take away every invisible scar that thoughtless words had made.

Kit shuddered against him, aware that the unbearable pain she had hidden for so long had been finally assuaged—and her utter vulnerability exposed.

With sweeping mastery, Reese parted her lips, deepening the kiss with a passion that enflamed her senses and ignited a fiery reaction. The sheer wantonness of her response terrified Kit and her hands fluttered in protest against his chest.

"It's all right, kitten." His low, husky voice soothed her as he began kissing her eyes, her nose, her cheek, her brow. "God knows you have good reason to be so angry . . . I'm so sorry . . . so sorry." And he retraced his route all over again, his breath and mouth warm and moist and arousing.

Kit was drowning in his kisses, in a sea of physical sensations, each wave that broke over her more devastating than the one before. The frantic pounding of her heart told her she would do whatever he asked—and she was not ready.

"Reese, don't do this, please." She whispered her plea. "Please let me go, Reese, please. Reese, Reese."

Even as she repeated his name, Kit sought his mouth with hers, hungry for his kiss, his touch. The smell, the taste, the feel of him were all she could comprehend. Kit melted against him and felt herself sinking. As long as she was wrapped in his arms, she didn't care.

Her knees buckled and her hand brushed the bearskin rug in front of the fireplace. Then Reese's weight was pressing her backward, onto the thick fur of the old rug.

His mouth was finding all sorts of erotically sensitive areas along her neck and throat, sending delicious shudders of desire over her skin. Her fingers curled into his tousled hair, keeping him there to continue his sensuous exploration.

His hands caressed her intimately as his body covered hers, his pressing weight a sensation to be enjoyed as his rangy, muscled length stretched above her. Expert fingers freed her shirt buttons and pushed the material aside.

"No bra—oh, God. You're beautiful. So beautiful."

The way her breasts seemed to swell into ripeness at his touch stunned Kit, and stimulated her already heightened yearnings for total possession.

When Reese moved to kiss them, her own fingers tugged at the buttons, finally loosening them all and sliding her excited hands over the hard flesh of his stomach and around to the flexing muscles of his back. Kit pulled him down to her, drawing his mouth back to her lips and glorying in the feel of his naked chest against hers.

Then he was pulling her arms from around him and spreading them above her head. He continued to kiss her lips and her face, but he refused to let her hands roam freely over him.

"Do you have any idea what you're doing to me?" Reese muttered against the curve of her mouth.

Kit could only shake her head. This was new and exciting and frightening. She lacked control and the will to acquire it.

"Kit." There was a sudden urgency in his hard kiss. "I want you. For God's sake, don't say no."

Her breath caught in her throat but she didn't say a thing. Reese read his own meaning into the silence, a white-hot desire seeming to sear from every inch of him. He kissed the rapid pulse in her neck with infinite tenderness. Kit wanted only to say yes—but she became suddenly conscious of a pair of eyes watching them.

The arrogant blue eyes in the portrait above the mantel seemed to stare down at the couple intertwined on the bearskin rug. Kit's stomach churned sickeningly.

With a moan that seemed to come from her soul, she pushed Reese away and scrambled weakly to her feet, filled with self-loathing. Stumbling, gasping with pain, Kit ran to the door, ignoring the startled, questioning sound of Reese saying her name. She was through it in a flash and closing it behind her.

Her strength deserted her and she leaned against the hallway wall, clutching her shirtfront closed. She wanted to sob, overcome by emotions that did not make sense, but her eyes were dry. There were no tears to cool the feelings that seared her as hotly as Reese's touch had done.

Her escape was by no means complete. As if to remind her of it, the library door was yanked open. Reese stood there, dark and dangerous, desire still blazing in his eyes, his shirt hanging open to reveal the hard flesh of his tanned, golden skin.

"Kit—" He started toward her.

She didn't cower, but spat at him like a cornered cat. "Don't touch me!"

Reese stopped, seeing her widened eyes and her defiant stance, even though she was flattened against the wall in fear. There were hesitant footsteps and the shadowy, plump figure of the housekeeper peered down the hallway. Kit knew Mrs. Kent could see their disheveled clothes, and quickly, if shakily, she began buttoning her shirt.

Reese flicked an angry and impatient glance at the housekeeper and took another step toward Kit. "Will you—"

"Don't come near me!" she ordered in a hoarse, raw voice. "Don't you ever come near me again!"

There was strength in her legs again and pride

in her eyes. She walked hurriedly to the screen
door and out onto the porch. Kit didn't stop until
she reached her house, and even then continued
straight to the privacy of her room. Her grandfather stared after her, then looked in the direction
of the Big House.

Kit sat astride her horse, letting instinct keep
her in the saddle. Work, the ranch, the land . . .
that was all she needed, she assured herself, but
the aching pain inside of her echoed the call of another need.

In the past week she had slept little, eaten less,
and driven herself harder than ever before. She
avoided the others, stayed to herself, working from
sunup to sundown. She looked thin and hollow-
eyed—and she was bone weary. But it was better
than feeling and remembering.

Kit hadn't spoken to Reese since she had exchanged those few bitter words with him in the
hallway of the Big House. Where he was concerned, she had developed a sixth sense that
warned her when he was near, giving her the time
to elude him.

Three times he had either come to the house or
attempted to approach her in the yard when others were around. Each time she had walked away
from him, aware that it angered him and that the
others had begun speculating about her actions.

There was no chance that Mrs. Kent had kept
silent about what she had seen. Kit could guess
what the housekeeper had assumed. Although her

grandfather had become rather blind to what went on around him after his wife died, Kit suspected that he knew or guessed something had gone on between her and Reese. But he didn't question her, although a couple of times she had caught him looking at her with a deep sadness in his eyes. It made her feel even worse, but there was no way she could explain emotions she only half understood herself.

She approached the ranch yard through the concealing shelter of the cottonwoods along the Little Missouri River. The afternoon sun was casting long shadows from the buildings. Kit reined in her horse, a chestnut this time. She was giving the bay gelding a rest. Nobody was stirring in the yard.

Her timing seemed to be perfect—everyone was out. A glance at the Big House told her that even Reese's Range Rover was gone. Yet Kit was still wary and rode up to the rear of her house so the building would shield her from the view of anyone watching from the Big House.

Dismounting, she dropped the reins and the chestnut willingly began cropping the grass about his feet. Kit dragged herself up the steps to the house, marveling at how much physical abuse the human body could withstand and continue functioning with a semblance of normality.

Entering the house and walking into the kitchen, Kit stopped at the sink. She turned on the cold-water faucet and reached for a glass. It was hot and her throat was dry, her body parched. As she filled the glass she heard the creak of the rocker in the living room.

"Nate?" she called. "I just stopped by to tell you not to bother to fix me any supper. I'm going out again and it'll probably be late when I get back."

"Isn't it always?" a male voice answered dryly.

Kit froze, the water running over the top of the glass. She knew that low voice. It haunted her like a tormenting ghost. She had heard it in the whisper of the wind through the grass or in the rippling rush of water. It came to her in the silence of sleep, warm and caressing and seductive.

Jerkily she set the glass down on the counter without easing her thirst and turned off the faucet. She didn't risk a glance in Reese's direction as she started for the door and escape. But he had already guessed what her reaction would be and was there to block her way.

"Not so fast, Kit," he warned.

Kit could lift her gaze no higher than the buttons of the shirt stretched taut across his chest. But that sight was equally as unnerving as her gaze. Her hands had explored that hard, muscled flesh and the finely curling hairs below his throat. Kit remembered that rapturous exploration well.

"Get out of my way, Reese." She was thankful she had trained herself for so many years not to reveal emotions.

"Not until we've talked."

"I don't have anything more to say to you, so please get out of my way," Kit repeated.

"I have more I want to say to you and you're going to listen. Let's go into the living room, shall we?" Reese took a step toward her and Kit retreated instinctively. He stopped and she saw the hand at his side double into a fist. "My God, Kit," he breathed angrily. "I'm not going to attack you."

She flashed a wary look at him and had to fight to keep from reeling. She was incredibly attracted to the aggressive sensuality etched in the male lines of his face—and fought it. She had to fight it. His hazel eyes blazed over her, noting her thinness and the dark circles beneath her brown eyes.

Kit forced herself to appear calm, not wanting him to perceive the trembling inside her. "I can't be blamed for questioning your reasons for wanting to see me," she retorted at last.

"I came to talk. That's all. I don't want to touch you, Kit."

There was an elemental crackling in the air between them. Kit knew there was cause for his warning. Even now, with this cold war between them, the physical attraction ran high—on both sides, she suspected. Just one touch, one caress, would be dangerous, and that was what Reese was telling her.

"Shall we go into the living room?" He repeated his earlier request.

Kit shrugged and turned in compliance. "Where's Nate?" she demanded, knowing the old man wouldn't be there when she entered the room. And he wasn't.

"He's gone to town on an errand."

She couldn't sit down. For this meeting she would need to be on her feet, mentally as well as physically. Reese didn't avail himself of the chairs either.

"Oh—an errand you arranged?" she said accusingly.

"Yes. I noticed that you've been making a habit of slipping into the ranch in the middle of the afternoon when everyone else is gone or working elsewhere," he admitted.

"So you found an excuse to get Nate out of here and waited for me to come," Kit murmured.

"Do you really think you could continue to avoid me?"

"I tried. Guess I didn't try hard enough." She flashed him a bitter smile.

"Don't be so damn cool, Kit." The muscles in his jaw flexed in an effort to retain control of his temper.

Her legs felt incredibly weak. So much for her hope to stand up to him—she badly needed the support of a chair. Kit walked to the nearest one, sinking into it with a let's-get-it-over-with sigh.

"What did you want to speak to me about?" Kit draped her arms along the length of the armrest and crossed her legs, hoping to appear indifferently interested in his answer.

It had the desired effect—his gaze hardened.

"As if you haven't guessed," he retorted sarcastically.

"Let me see. Last time we spoke, we discussed your plans for Nate's retirement. Is that why you're here? To go over the details with me?" she challenged.

"You know damn well it isn't."

"My dear cousin, the only other thing we talked about was you buying this house and property. Have you come to make an offer? We're not selling—not at any price."

"Cousin," Reese repeated with a sardonic curl to his upper lip. "Is that what you're going to use to keep me at arm's length? Any blood relationship between us is down to a few corpuscles by now."

He came to stand beside the chair. Kit had to force herself not to cringe from him. She stared at her fingers playing nervously with the doily on the armrest. She could feel his eyes studying her as surely as if he touched every feature of her face. In the end she could stand it no longer and pushed out of the chair to put a safer distance between them.

Hugging her arms about her, Kit turned to face him. "There isn't any relationship between us, Reese. And there isn't going to be one."

"Liar." The confidence in his reply shook Kit to the core.

She turned away, hugging her arms even tighter around her. "Get to the point, Reese. Say whatever it is you came here to say and get out!"

"You've gone back inside that shell of yours, haven't you?" he said with a sigh. "You had a taste of what it's like to really feel something and it frightened you."

"And you're analyzing me again," Kit murmured tightly. "If you really want to know, that encounter sickened me. Not that my feelings are any of your business."

"Would you look at me? I don't like talking to your back," Reese snapped.

Kit didn't move. She preferred it this way. She could pretend she was listening to a disembodied voice. It helped her block out his presence.

"I said, look at me!" Her elbow was seized and Kit was spun around to meet the sorely tested patience in his expression.

She jerked away, trembling violently in reaction. "Don't touch me!" she cried, feeling the crack in her very brittle poise.

Swearing under his breath, Reese looked away and raked his fingers through his rumpled hair. Kit felt her heart skip a beat.

"Damn," he muttered. "This isn't going at all the way I planned it." He turned back to her, lifting his hands to hold the air on either side of her, obeying her request not to be touched while instilling the sensation. "When you told me that story about the baron being your father, I—"

"You don't believe me. You think I was lying." Kit stiffened. "I'm sorry I can't offer you any proof, but there's always DNA testing."

"I believe you," Reese corrected firmly.

"And you feel sorry for me—and maybe just a little bit guilty." Her eyes flashed.

"Yes, I felt sorry for you."

"Thanks," Kit lashed out. "But I don't need your pity or sympathy or compassion!"

"I understand you a lot better now. I know why you act so tough and keep people at a distance. That's the only way you can feel safe and protected. If you never let people too close, they can't hurt you."

"Would you just shut up? I don't know where you got the idea I want to hear this!" She knew that she was afraid of how easily he saw through her defenses—and how insecure that made her feel. "If that's all you came to say, you can get out!"

"That isn't all," Reese retorted. "That was quite a revelation—to see the real you. I have to admit that you surprised me. Now, why you ran out of the library the way you did is something else—"

"You mean you had no plans to seduce me? You just sort of went along to see what I'd do?" Kit taunted.

"No, damn it! But yes, I was going to make love to you!"

"Thanks so much. Sorry I ruined it for you. Nice of you to throw me a few crumbs of attention before you walked out, Reese!" There were tears in her eyes as she shouted at him and the memory of her own abandoned behavior in his arms.

"I didn't intend for any of that to happen!" Reese shouted back. "Do you think I want to get mixed up with a little hellcat like you?"

"Ooh, 'hellcat'—I like that. Sounds dangerous. And you sound scared. Have I made it clear that I don't want to get mixed up with you, either?" Kit was trembling. Everything inside her seemed to be caving in.

"That makes two of us, then, doesn't it?" His harsh gaze caught the shimmer of tears in her eyes.

A groan seemed to come from somewhere deep inside his chest. In the next instant, Kit found herself imprisoned in his embrace.

"I wish I didn't want you so damn much," Reese muttered against her hair, a rough desire in his voice. "Told myself over and over to forget about what happened—that it would just burn itself out and be over if I'd given in to it."

A sob of pain came from her throat and Reese began raining ungentle kisses on her upturned face. There was such raw ecstasy in his embrace, such strength in the arms that held her close. His virility thrilled her to the core.

"Now that I know what those men's clothes are hiding," Reese murmured thickly, his hands caressing her breasts, teasing her nipples through her shirt with expert gentleness, "seeing you around the ranch yard drives me crazy. I actually know what it means to want to tear someone's clothes off, Kit. God, I want you."

He kissed her long and hard. Kit had neither the strength nor the will to resist. She submitted to his hunger, feeling his trembling struggle for control as he tore his mouth away. She put her head against his chest—the erratic hammering of his heart sounded as loud as her own.

"I know I rushed you the last time, Kit." His hands roughly stroked her hair. "You were just so hot—but you weren't emotionally ready. It must have seemed so new and frightening to you—I promise I'll take it slow." He smiled patiently but his tone was passionate. "I want to carry you out of here to my bedroom and keep you there for a week—a month." Reese lifted her head, cradling her face in his hands. The sensually dark and dangerous look in his eyes took her breath away. "I need you, Kit. And you need me."

But not forever. He wouldn't need her forever. And Kit knew that wasn't enough for her. She recoiled from the knowledge and from Reese's arms, turning her back on him and on the truth.

"I don't need you." Kit's voice choked up. "I don't need anybody."

"Let me show you what I mean." His hands slid

around her waist, crossing in front to cup her
breasts and draw her back to his masculine length.
"Don't worry, kitten. You've got me—"

A deep, reluctant sigh slipped from her lips.
"For now."

The screen door slammed. It took a few seconds
before they realized the significance of the sound.
Reese was just lifting his head, his hands tighten-
ing on her waist to put her away from him when
her grandfather appeared in the doorway from
the kitchen to the living room. One look seemed
to tell him the whole story.

Kit wanted to die at the look of intense pain that
flashed across his worn features. She swayed
alarmingly and Reese's hands stayed where they
were.

"I was afraid something like this would happen,"
Nate said tiredly, staring at Reese. "When I saw you
the first time I was afraid for my Kitty, especially
when she reacted so violently to you. She usually
doesn't care much one way or the other about
strangers. I tried to pretend it was because of who
you were, but—well, never mind. Are you in love
with my granddaughter?"

The hands around her waist held her a fraction
tighter. Kit's head was swimming. She had no idea
what to do or say.

"Nothing's happened, Nate." By avoiding the
question, Reese had given an unspoken answer.

Before Reese's reply, her grandfather had
looked beaten, used-up, old beyond his years. Now
a vigorous fire seemed to take hold of him.

"Nothing is going to happen, either!" he
barked. "You sent me on a fool's errand so you

could be alone with my granddaughter. Now I'll thank you to take your hands off her and get out of my house—or by God, I'll kill you!"

It was only Reese's hands that kept Kit from collapsing. When they were removed, Kit felt herself slipping over the edge of consciousness and gave a frightened cry, calling out as everything went black.

CHAPTER 8

She seemed to be tumbling in slow motion into an abyss—a black, bottomless pit. Kit struggled to stop the fall, crying out for Reese to save her, Reese who had let her go. For a second she felt his hand catch hers, then it was gone. A sensation of nameless terror engulfed her.

Other hands reached out to her, but they hadn't the strength to help. Kit kept falling, falling. She glimpsed Reese but always out of reach, those strong, tanned hands beyond the grasp of her fingers. She could hear herself crying brokenly like a child. She never cried.

When Kit thought she would be lost forever in the swirling black void, the familiar pressure of his hand gripped hers, holding on and not letting her fall any farther. After that there was just a pleasant floating sensation that slowly and very gradually brought her to the surface.

Kit blinked her eyes and stirred. Sunlight was

streaming through the window, so glorious, so brilliant, so very different from the blackness she thought she'd never escape. A slight breeze blew away the last cobwebs. Suddenly it all seemed so crazy. Had it been a nightmare?

"Have you finally decided to come back to us?"

Kit turned her head, discovering it was resting on a pillow and she was lying in bed—her bed. Reese was sitting in a chair beside it. At the moment it seemed very natural for him to be there. When she looked at him he slipped his hand from the loosened grasp of her fingers and sat up straighter in the chair.

"What happened?" Her voice sounded funny, a little thick. "How did I get here?"

"You collapsed," Reese explained. Kit didn't think she'd ever seen his brooding male features look so gentle. "The doctor said it was probably a combination of exhaustion and not eating. He asked if you'd been under emotional stress. He checked you out pretty thoroughly but he thought you'd be better off at home than in the hospital. Gave us his beeper number just in case and said we could call him at any hour. In a few minutes, I'll let him know that you came to."

Exhaustion, Kit thought. Yes, she had been working very hard and sleeping very little. Emotional stress? A wave of memory swamped her and Kit went white. Her grandfather had walked in and found them together in the living room. His harsh, angry voice came back with piercing clarity. *Get out of this house or I'll kill you.*

"What are you doing here?" she said softly, suddenly alarmed.

"I've been holding your hand for the last twelve hours." His eyes crinkled at the corners when he smiled, something she hadn't seen happen before.

The rest of her mind was registering the length of time he had been sitting there. He didn't seem too uncomfortable, although there was the shadow of a day's growth on his hollowed cheeks and jaw.

"But Nate—" Kit started to protest.

"Didn't have any choice in the matter," Reese interrupted smoothly. He reached for the water pitcher and glass on her bed stand. "How about a drink?"

She bobbed her head numbly, stunned by his previous statement. Her grandfather had been adamant—and furious. She knew him very well and Nate never said anything he didn't mean.

There was a puzzled, doubting look in her brown eyes when Reese moved to sit on the edge of the bed. Supporting her head with one hand, he lifted the water glass to her lips with the other.

"You blacked out, and you weren't making any sense when you regained consciousness. Took forever for an EMS crew to get here, and it was a good thing the doctor was riding with them, or you would've gone to the hospital."

"The nearest one is miles and miles away," she whispered.

"Yeah, so they said. Anyway, the doctor gave you a sedative—"

"A shot?" She looked at her arm, noticing the little cotton ball under a bandage for the first time.

Reese smiled again. "Don't tell me Wonder Woman is afraid of getting a shot."

"Well, no. But what was I saying?"

"You were calling my name. Nate finally gave in and let me sit with you until you quieted down and fell asleep. He stuck around for a long time, though. Guess he realized I wouldn't try to take advantage of you."

Kit flinched at his words and turned her head away, burying her cheek in the pillow. At the caressing touch of his hand on her hair she closed her eyes tightly.

His voice came softly. "That was meant to be a joke, Kit."

"Go away, Reese," she said softly. "I'm all right now. There's no reason for you to sit there anymore."

"Yes, I can tell you're feeling better." He sounded suddenly impatient. "You're beginning to sound like your old self again."

"Leave me alone. I don't need you anymore." Kit only wanted to deny him, deny the emotion pulsing through her.

"All right," Reese agreed curtly. "But before I go, there's one thing I want you to know. I'm not going to let you crawl back inside your shell and hide, even if it means I have to go in there and drag you out. Do you understand me?"

"Go away, Reese. Just go away," she cried angrily, because it would be so easy for him to do what he said. He straightened from the bed and walked to the door. "And don't bother to come back!" Kit hurled at him as he opened it.

His only response was a twisted smile. Kit wasn't sure what that meant.

Reese had barely left when Mrs. Kent appeared, bringing some nourishing hot broth and giving Kit a curious look. The housekeeper repeated the doctor's recommendation of at least two days of complete rest and explained away her presence in the house by saying that Reese had asked her to lend a hand.

Staying in bed for two days seemed impossible. However, with the aid of a sleeping pill left by the doctor, Kit practically slept around the clock the first twenty-four hours. Around noon of the following day, she had been awake for a couple of hours and had eaten a light breakfast. Her grandfather had come in to sit with her, but they had remarkably little to say to each other, both of them feeling the constraint of the situation.

Kit was lying in bed, trying not to think about anything, but it wasn't easy to keep her mind blank. She heard the back screen door open and close, and her grandfather speak to someone.

It was Reese's voice that responded. Kit tensed when she heard footsteps approaching her room, then recognized the placidly even tread as her grandfather's. It didn't occur to her to feign sleep when he opened the door.

There was no expression whatsoever on his age-lined face. "Reese is here to see you again." His choice of words indicated it wasn't the first time in the past twenty-four hours that Reese had stopped in to check on her progress. "Shall I send him in?"

Kit's answer was a sharp, negative shake of her head. When he left and closed the door, she rolled onto her side, curling up into a tight ball of pain.

Nate's stoic attitude hurt worse than his anger could have.

Not once had he questioned her about Reese, never asking how involved she had become with him. Kit was too ashamed of the feelings she couldn't control to talk to Nate about them. She felt she had let him down.

Reese stopped by several times in the next two days and every time Kit refused to see him. With Nate standing guard, there was little objection he could make. And Kit lingered in bed a third day, just to avail herself of her grandfather's protection.

The fourth day she was sick of it. She resumed her duties around the ranch but she was still weak and forced to limit the amount of work she did, depending on how strenuous it was.

It seemed inevitable that she would encounter Reese. He was by the barn talking to Frank when she rode in on her first afternoon out of bed. Kit was too tired to avoid meeting him. She made no objection when he stepped forward to hold her horse's head while she dismounted.

"How are you, Kit?" he asked, leveling those hazel eyes at her.

"Fine," she lied.

"I stopped by to see how you were getting along, but Nate said you didn't want to see me."

"That's right." She hooked the stirrup onto the saddle horn and began loosening the cinch.

"How's life inside the shell?" Reese asked. "Were you afraid you wouldn't be able to get back in if you saw me?"

"Look, Reese," Kit began impatiently. "I'm tired. I'm really not up to your stupid discussions."

"I can see that." His sharp gaze took in the faint pallor beneath her tan and her I've-had-it look. "But I won't take advantage of it. Not this time, anyway." He walked away, leaving Kit trembling with weary anger at his response. She wanted to kick him for talking to her like that, and kick herself for listening in the first place.

During the course of the following week she saw him many times. He always spoke, sometimes only a courteous greeting, other times inquiring about some aspect of the ranch work. But his casualness didn't fool Kit. The look in his eyes told her that he hadn't forgotten their irritable exchange of words and was simply biding his time.

It was a drowsy Sunday afternoon that found Kit prowling restlessly about the house. It was too hot to be doing any work. She could hear Lew and Frank out tinkering in the shed. Kyle had gone home for the day to visit his family and Mrs. Kent had the day off.

Her grandfather was sitting by the window, facing the ranch yard, with a book in his lap. He preferred reading to sitting in front of the old color TV, though Kyle had managed to install a satellite dish over the bunkhouse that brought in too many channels for him to watch. But these days even reading didn't hold Nate's interest for long.

Kit saw him looking out and did the same through the panes of another window. Reese was

riding the buckskin, leaving the yard, heading
west. Some of the tension left Kit when she saw him
disappear from sight.

"I think I'll go for a walk, Nate," she said. "Down
by the river. It should be cooler there."

"Okay."

They both knew the river was in the opposite direction from the one Reese took, but neither mentioned it. Before leaving the house, Kit changed
into a pair of cutoffs and sandals. They would be
more comfortable than heavy jeans and she could
easily slip her sandals off to wade in the shallow
rapids at the bend of the river.

It was cooler in the shade of the towering
cottonwoods. The ground beneath was covered
with the white fluff from their seed pods, with little
wisps of it floating in the air. A slight breeze ruffled the leaves, the sound nearly drowned by the
laughing water of the rapids.

Kit waded for a while, leaving her sandals on the
bank. When she got tired of that, she sat on a
water-smooth boulder near the center of the river
and dangled her feet in the water, letting the gentle rush cool her.

It was with reluctance, a sense of passing time
and supper to be fixed, that she finally left her
perch and waded back to the riverbank where she
had left her sandals. There was no way to dry her
feet, so it took some doing to get them back on.
Eventually succeeding, Kit started back to the
house, her attention on the ground, intent on not
tripping over exposed roots or fallen branches.

A horse snorted and Kit looked up, stopping abruptly at the sight of Reese astride the buckskin at the edge of the trees. He had seen her and was waiting. Somehow she knew that avoiding him would be useless because he would simply follow. Kit could only hope that she could brazen her way past him.

"Wow. It's a crime to cover up legs like yours in jeans." Reese observed her shapely legs with approval as Kit walked closer.

His remark suddenly made her self-conscious about her skimpy—for her, anyway—attire. "How did you know I was down here?" she demanded.

"I was up on the ridge and caught a glimpse of a woman wading in the river." A wicked light danced in his eyes. "I knew it wasn't Mrs. Kent because her hair is pretty gray. And she wouldn't look that good in cutoffs, even from a mile away."

When Kit would have walked past him, Reese nudged the buckskin forward to block her path. "Come on." He extended a hand to her. "It's a long way up the hill to the house. I'll give you a ride."

But Kit didn't trust him to take her to the house and ducked under the horse's head. "No, thank you. I'd rather walk."

"Kit." There was a wealth of exasperation and impatience in the sighing way he said her name and the shake of his head. He reined the horse around to walk beside her. "It's hot and there's no sense wearing yourself out climbing that hill when you can ride."

The house was just out of sight beyond the slight rise. Kit stared fixedly in its direction, ignoring the bobbing head of the buckskin beside her. She walked briskly, feeling the pull on the muscles in the back of her legs at the steadily increasing slope.

"I told you I'd rather walk," she repeated forcefully.

"You're going to ride." Reese leaned out of the saddle to hook an arm around her middle and scoop her off the ground, hauling her across the front of his saddle almost before Kit knew what was happening.

"Put me down!" She struggled and kicked and tried to slide out of his hold.

"What's the matter?" he teased. "Don't you see us riding off into the sunset together?"

"Give me a break!" Kit struck at him but he easily pinned her arms to her sides.

"You know something?" Reese laughed in a really annoying way. "You always hiss and claw before you start to purr, kitten."

"No," she gulped.

"Yes."

He turned her around deftly and captured her lips with a swift kiss. His arms held her even closer and he managed the reins somehow—quite the horseman, Kit thought resentfully, though she secretly enjoyed the kiss.

His fingers slid through the golden-brown silk of her hair, and one hand held the back of her head. He gave her another kiss, a longer one, which just about demolished the rest of her inhibitions.

"You want me," Reese muttered, "just as much as I want you. Admit it, Kit."

He was asking too much of her. She snapped out of the spell, realizing how quickly and easily her feelings could betray her pride.

"No! History isn't going to repeat itself. Don't even try it, Reese!" Kit protested. Her arms strained against his chest, fighting for a single inch of space between them. "Put me down!"

Still holding her, Reese swung out of the saddle, stepping to the ground before setting her feet down. She would have run instantly but his hands stayed on her shoulders, keeping her right where she was.

"Quite a performance. You're not that innocent, Kit," he said cynically.

"Don't tell me who I am or what I should think. All you want is—"

"I have more reasons for wanting you than just physical gratification, but we're getting off the subject," Reese snapped. "You can't always run away, Kit."

"Oh, here we go again. The Traveling Psychologist and Dusty the Wonder Horse. Step right up, folks. All your problems solved for a nickel."

Reese glared at her. "Very funny. You still haven't answered the question. Are you running from me?"

"No, I'm escaping!"

"From a fate worse than death?" he jeered.

"Yes. I'll never give in to you."

"Not because you're afraid of me. You're afraid of yourself." He took his hands from her shoulders and she rubbed them one by one with her hand, easing the tension of his grip.

"That's ridiculous," she said firmly.

"A moment ago you mentioned history repeating itself."

She tossed her head back. "Have you forgotten? My mother was seduced by the last baron. He wanted her just as much as you want me, I guess. And look what happened to her."

Reese was quiet for a moment. "Well—she didn't ever get a chance to explain her side of the story. Or at least you haven't told it to me."

Kit sighed. "It's pretty obvious, isn't it? I mean, she did let herself get taken in by all his fancy talk. And she let him make love to her, didn't she?" It hurt to make those admissions about her mother, but they were the truth as Kit saw it. "She didn't stand up to him or tell him to stop or that she ought not to be doing this."

"Maybe she didn't know how to say any of those things at the age of seventeen. Not everyone is as tough as you, Kit. But—"

"But what?" Her chin tilted up with that familiar defiance.

"I'm beginning to think you're kind of a coward."

She raked him head to foot with a furious look. "How can you say that? How can you accuse *me* of that?"

"Because you are afraid. Your mother risked her heart and she got hurt but she kept right on living. And she cared enough about your life to have you. Young as she was, I have a feeling she did the best she could."

"How the hell would you know?"

"Okay, I'm guessing—based mostly on what you've told me."

"Damn you, Reese! Who asked you, anyway? Why do you care?"

His face darkened. "Because I do—even though you don't. But I don't think you're brave enough to really care about anybody—I shouldn't have been such a goddamned fool."

"That's not true!" Kit covered her ears with her hands to shut out his hammering, hateful words.

Reese pulled them away. "Have you ever said 'I love you' to anyone? I bet you haven't," he answered the question for her. "And I wouldn't lose the bet. Because saying 'I love you' would mean you cared. And if you cared, you might get hurt."

"Shut up!" She took a few, faltering steps in the direction of the house and stopped to have the last word. "Why don't you go away? Just go away and never come back!"

He stood there glaring at her, his hands on his hips. Then he turned away and climbed into the saddle. With a flick of the reins, he spun the buckskin around and rode out toward the range. Kit ran a little farther up the hill, then collapsed in the tall grasses and started crying as if her heart would break.

She was dry-eyed when she walked into the house much later. She didn't say a word to her grandfather about her meeting with Reese.

Two days later, Kit was stepping out of the barn after milking the cow when she saw the Range

Rover parked in front of the Big House. Puzzled, she stared. That wasn't where it belonged. Her frown deepened as Reese walked out, dressed in a suit and carrying two large pieces of luggage.

Slowly, unwillingly, Kit crossed the yard and approached the car. Reese was stowing the luggage in the rear compartment, half-hidden by the swung-out door. He didn't even glance up when she stopped by the front bumper, milk bucket in hand.

The housekeeper came bustling out of the house onto the porch. "You forgot your shaving kit, Mr. Talbot." She started down the steps, holding out a small, brown leather case. She spied Kit standing by the car and stopped on the last step, glancing uncertainly toward Reese.

"Thank you, Mrs. Kent." He came around to take the shaving kit from her, still without so much as a glance to acknowledge Kit's presence. "I appreciate your staying on another couple of days to close things up. Lew or Frank will take you into town whenever you're ready to leave."

Close things up. The phrase struck Kit like a slap across the face. That sounded much more permanent than a simple trip to God-knows-where.

"I don't mind." The woman hesitated, then added, "I enjoyed working for you, Mr. Talbot, truly I did."

"Good-bye, Mrs. Kent." Reese shook her hand and gave her a perfunctory smile.

"Good-bye, sir." There was a slight catch in her voice. She cast one last, dismissing glance at Kit and walked back up the steps into the house.

Still Reese ignored her, carrying the shaving kit

to the rear of the Rover and tossing it in atop the rest of his luggage.

"You're leaving," she finally blurted out the words.

"Yes." Reese slammed the rear door shut.

"For good?"

"Yes." He walked to the passenger door, opened it, and started to slide behind the wheel.

She caught at the door to keep him from closing it. Reese finally looked at her, one foot resting inside the car, his face closed, revealing nothing.

"Without even saying good-bye?"

"I thought we'd said our good-byes," he answered coldly.

"I—" What could she say? He was so aloof, so withdrawn. Kit shuddered and looked away.

"How does it feel, Kit?" he said softly.

"What?" Her voice was small, no more than a thread of a sound. There were tears at the back of her eyes, stinging and smarting.

"You won. I'm leaving and you're staying," Reese elaborated. "How does it feel to get what you want?"

"I—don't know." She stared at him, searching his impenetrable eyes.

"It is what you wanted, right?"

"Yes," Kit breathed an agreement. But the past tense would have been more accurate. It was what she *had* wanted. Only now . . . She had never believed he would actually leave.

His mouth curved in an unfriendly smile. "I hope you enjoy your victory celebration." He started again to climb into the car. "Have a drink for me."

"Why?" Kit forestalled him again.

"Why what?" That piercing gaze was on her again.

"Why are you leaving?"

"Because of you." He gave her a polite smile. "To borrow a cliché from an old Western—this place ain't big enough for both of us."

"And you're leaving," Kit repeated what she had found so difficult to accept.

"It has to be me," Reese informed her. "You couldn't survive anywhere else. There wouldn't be any place you could hide."

Kit flinched at his words, as he had meant her to. "You don't have to go."

"Don't I?" He laughed. "It doesn't matter. I want to go."

"You do?" That hurt more than anything he could have said. If she had felt she had driven him away somehow . . . but to have him want to leave— Kit found that painful.

"How can that be a surprise when you act like you know it all? News flash—you don't. There's a great big world outside this ranch, Kit, and everybody in it doesn't play by your rules."

"Just because you don't want—" *Me.* She almost said it but stopped herself.

His temper was rising—she could see it and hear it in his voice. "I'll tell you what I don't want—your constant anger. Deal with it and get over it. You've had some bad blows, I know that, but you can't keep attacking people who are on your side."

She had to admit, if only to herself, that he had a point, but she didn't reply.

"Take a few chances in life, Kit. Start small. Wear a dress once in a while. Go really crazy—wear perfume or anything that doesn't smell like horse sweat, manure, and hay. You don't have to jam your hair under a dirty hat and dress like an old cowboy so no one will look at you. And do something about that damn chip on your shoulder while you're at it."

Kit seriously considered smacking him—but that would only prove him right.

"You could even get off the ranch and get an education—you're probably smarter than I am. There's nothing inferior about you unless you want to think so."

Each sentence hit its mark. Kit was surprised to discover that she was still standing after that barrage. But Reese wasn't finished.

"You just have too damn much baggage—about everything. Someday you'll figure out that you can't change the past—only yourself. Hell, I can't make that happen, Kit. But I want a woman who's not afraid to be a woman. And not afraid to be human."

Kit let go of the door and stepped away. Her face felt frozen as she looked at him.

"Good-bye, Kit."

He gripped the door for a second, then slipped all the way behind the wheel, and slammed it shut. The motor roared to life and the tires spun before acquiring traction. Kit watched him drive out of the yard until the dust settled.

CHAPTER 9

Dazed by an event she was not prepared for, Kit walked blindly to her house. As if she were a robot programmed for chores, she walked into the kitchen, strained the milk from the pail into a pitcher and set it in the refrigerator. She rinsed out the pail and set it on the porch, somewhat soothed by the timeless ritual.

Like her grandmother, she did it because it made Nate happy, if for no other reason. They could just as easily buy their milk in town, of course, but Martha had always been proudly old-fashioned, just like her husband.

When she went back in, her grandfather was standing in the living room archway.

"Reese has gone," she said.

He nodded. "I know."

"He isn't coming back," Kit added.

"I know."

"How? When?" The emotional numbness was

beginning to wear off and a million doubts assailed her. It wasn't right that Nate had known and not told her.

"He came over this morning and told me," Nate explained.

"He wasn't going to tell me," Kit murmured with a faint sob in her voice. "He was just going to leave. If I hadn't seen him—" The lump in her throat choked off the rest of the sentence.

"It took me by surprise, too, Kitty." He seemed to be attempting to console her.

"Did he"—Kit hardly dared to hope—"did he ask you to tell me anything?" Perhaps he hadn't planned to leave without giving her a message of some sort. Although why she thought so after his parting shots, Kit didn't know.

"He—" Nate hesitated, then shook his head sadly. "He didn't mention you at all."

"Oh." The world was beginning to shatter. If Reese could see her now, he wouldn't find any chip on her shoulder.

"You didn't want him to go, did you, child?" he asked gently.

"No." Huge and round, her brown eyes were brimming with tears, turning into pools of misery. "He was right about me, Nate. He said I was afraid to care. He said I kept running from people, shutting them out because I was afraid they might hurt me. And it's true, Nate." She sobbed and tried to smile. "I am afraid of—having feelings. Getting my stupid heart broken. Stuff like that."

"Oh, Kit, Kit." His sad voice seemed to take on some of her pain. He moved toward her and she crossed the space to wrap her arms around him and bury her face in his shirt, the tears spilling over her lashes.

"Do you know," Kit said wistfully, "I don't think I've ever told you that I love you, Grandpa."

"You didn't have to," he assured her. "I've always known it."

"I should have said it."

"There, there, child." He patted her head and rocked her gently in his arms..

"I love him, too." She told him what in her heart she had longed to tell Reese, all her troubled thoughts pouring out.

"I kinda figured that out for myself," Nate murmured. "You know, Reese and I talked now and then. I think he wanted me to know more about him, understand where he was coming from—and he hinted at his feelings for you. Got the idea that he was waiting to see what you would do next, Kit."

"I never was sure of what I wanted, Grandpa." Unconsciously she wasn't even using his given name any longer. "But nothing happened. He kissed me but he never made love to me."

"I believe you."

"He wanted to, but I kept running away. I wish I hadn't now." She tipped her tear-drenched face to look up at his lined features. "Isn't that awful? I wish he had made love to me. I wish I was going to have his baby. How crazy is that? Then I would have something of him to love now that he's gone. I want it so much it hurts."

A sharp pain flashed across his face and his hands shook a little. "You sound just like your mother, Kitty. That's almost exactly what Sara said to me."

"She . . . she wanted to have me?" Kit wiped the dampness from her cheek with the back of her hand, sniffling a bit as she tried to find control.

"Oh, gracious, yes," Nate smiled. This time there was a shimmer of tears in his eyes. "Whatever made you think that she didn't?"

"I . . . don't know. I thought she might have resented me because I was—a reminder of what happened," Kit explained hesitantly. "She certainly couldn't forget it and move on with me around. And having a baby when she was so young must have changed her life so much."

"Sara loved you. She loved you even before you were born. And afterwards"—his smile broadened—"she wouldn't let you out of her sight. Always holding you and talking to you and watching you sleep. She spent practically every minute with you just as if"—his voice faded slightly—"just as if she knew she didn't have much time."

"What happened? You and Grandma said she died in a car crash, but I always wondered . . . was there more to it?" she asked, then saw how sad he looked and added, "Do you mind talking about it?"

"No." He stroked her hair, brushing it away where it tried to cling to her damp cheek. "We probably should have done it before. But Martha and me, we told you when you were a child what we felt you should know then. We thought when you grew up, if you had any more questions, you would ask. When you didn't, we thought it best to leave it alone."

"I'd like to know more—about Momma."

"She did die in a car crash. That was true," he

began. "Because some folks around here thought she was wild, having a baby out of wedlock and all, there was talk that she had been drinking. But she hadn't. And she wasn't even behind the wheel. Took them five hours just to pull apart the wreckage and they found her in the back." He paused, struggling with the agonizing memory. "Her best friend had three beers before they left the party. Doesn't take much to put a teenage girl over the limit. Less than five minutes later, that car was wrapped around a telephone pole. Your momma was younger than you are now, Kit."

"I did hear some talk," she said, wrenched by the knowledge. "When the kids who teased me got done, they started in on her—on Momma. And it made me think that she didn't want to live, because she'd done that—maybe because she didn't want me."

Her grandfather held her close again. "No, no— she wanted to see you grow up. She always used to talk about what you would be like when you were a teenager—you were a stubborn little thing, even as a baby, Kit. But your momma hoped you would have it all—do well in school, get all dolled up for the senior prom, graduate and go off to college—"

"She didn't get to," Kit said softly.

"She wanted to do a lot of things but it just wasn't to be. I know she didn't want to leave you."

"If she saw me now, I have the feeling she would be disappointed." Kit sighed.

"I don't think so. You didn't have it so easy, Kit. She'd understand if you took the wrong path for a while. She wasn't perfect, either."

"My father—the baron—did she hate him after

the way he treated her? Or did she still love him?" she questioned.

"Sara loved him. She fell in love with him from the first minute she laid eyes on him. She found out almost at the beginning that he was married, but she never told Martha and me. That didn't stop her. She knew she could never marry him. The baron's wife was an invalid, from what I understood, and he wasn't going to divorce her. Guess he had a little bit of decency to him, for what it was worth." He paused.

"Later Sara told us that she decided if she couldn't have the baron, she'd have his child. She wanted something of him she could love when he was gone." Nate pressed a kiss to Kit's forehead. "Do you see what I meant earlier? You said almost exactly the same thing."

But Kit was thinking how instinctively right Reese had been about her mother. She'd risked her heart, had it broken in two, yet remained a loving person.

"And the baron? Did he love my mother?" She had learned so much that she couldn't help wondering if there was more.

"Well, he told her he did, but I can't say whether he actually meant it or whether he said it just to get what he wanted. Although sometimes I've wondered whether your mother would have cared or not if he did."

Kit rested her head against his shoulder. "Maybe he did. I hope he cared a little." For the first time in her life she was willing to give the baron the benefit of the doubt.

"Maybe."

Her own troubles were still very much on her mind, and she gave a deep sigh. "What am I going to do, Grandpa? Reese said he wasn't coming back."

"I know, child, I know," Nate comforted.

"Did he mean it? Won't I ever see him again?" Kit whispered, terrified by the thought and all its implications.

"I don't know." She felt the shake of his head, then heard his sigh. "I'm sorry, Kitty, but he doesn't strike me as the type to say something he doesn't mean."

And Reese had said he was leaving for good. Kit began crying for her blindness, her stupidity, her cowardice, for the loss of something she hadn't known she'd found until it was gone. Her years of holding everything back had damned up a river of tears—but she couldn't hold them back now.

Her grandfather held her closely in his arms with loving unconcern for the drenching of his shirt. Eventually there were no tears left and Kit's sobs were reduced to dry, hiccupping sounds.

Nate pressed his handkerchief into her hand. "There—that's over." He loosened his hold and let an arm curve around her shoulders. "Come over here and sit down. I'll pour you a cup of my famous awful coffee. How does that sound?"

"Sounds good, Grandpa." She wiped her eyes and blew her nose while he guided her to the kitchen, but she didn't really care about the coffee. She didn't care about anything.

Nate Bonner, in his wisdom, sensed that. He set the coffee before her and took another chair from the table, drawing it alongside of Kit. "You think life isn't worth much without him, don't you?"

"Yes," she sniffed, winding her shaking hands around the warm mug.

"You'll find a reason," he promised. "At first, you might only get up in the morning to milk the cow because that old gal will sure let you know if you don't. Later, the fall roundup will start and you'll want to be a part of it. By the time Christmas comes—" He hesitated.

"Well, I can't lie to you, Kit. Getting through Christmas when you're missing someone is about the hardest thing you'll ever do. You and I never celebrated it much after your grandmother died, but maybe this year we'll do something special. We can think about that when you're ready to. In the meantime, just take it day by day.

"When Martha passed, all my reasons for getting on with life went with her," Nate admitted. "At least that's what I thought. But I was wrong. You still needed me. Nothing happens without a purpose, Kitty."

But where was hers? "I hope you're right, Grandpa," she murmured, staring into the black liquid in the mug and wishing she could drown in it.

"Drink up, child," he urged, and Kit obediently lifted the mug to her mouth.

In the beginning it was as her grandfather had predicted. Life didn't seem worth living without Reese. Kit had no one to spar with, no one to please, no one to tease—damn, damn, damn. She didn't want to miss the man, but she did. She didn't even want to get up most mornings, but she would hear the milk cow bellowing up by the barn and drag herself out of bed.

There was no bitterness, only a deep emotional pain that never left her. Minute by minute Kit got through each day. Half the time she didn't know what she was doing. She went through the motions of living, initially for her grandfather's sake and later because it had simply become habit.

The worst times were when the monthly reports and accounts were due. She did them on the computer and sent hard copies to the office of the attorney whose address Reese had provided after he'd come into his inheritance, before she had ever met him. Any checks came from the ranch account with some stranger's signature affixed to them.

July rolled into August, August became September, and Kit's spirit began to heal. She made some changes that were long overdue, if only to boost her own morale. Reese's parting words had an effect—and he seemed to have taken her hardness, her toughness with him when he left.

The men's shirts were abandoned. Those that were still in good condition she packed up in a big box for the church clothing drive. The rest were thrown in the ragbag. She bought new tops, even some sweaters in pretty colors that showed her shape. Her worn and patched jeans got the same treatment. A streak of practicality kept Kit from throwing all of them out, but she supplemented her work clothes with snug-fitting ones that clung to her curves and didn't bag at the seat.

Her stained brown Stetson fell into a camp-fire—and she didn't pull it out. Good a reason as any to buy a new hat. She looked over a catalog of Western wear and chose a cream-white straw cowboy hat with a shallower crown, figuring there'd be no room inside it to pile her long hair. When it arrived a few days later, she was happy to see that she'd got it right. When she rode now, her chestnut gold hair either swung about her shoulders or was caught by a barrette at the nape of her neck.

There were even two new dresses hanging in her closet, thanks to a different catalog—Medora, North Dakota, not being the fashion capital of the world. There was even a bottle of perfume on her dresser, and eye shadow, mascara, and lipstick that she experimented with in private. A little of all of these went a long way, she found, having no one to ask for makeup advice besides two grizzled old cowboys and her grandpa.

Always, there was a silent strength flowing from Nate that kept Kit going on lonely days. To show her appreciation for his unwavering support and understanding, Kit began to take more interest in housework.

Her grandmother had been proud of her home, always wanting it to look its best. At best Kit had managed no more than a lick and a promise, but she thought her grandfather might be missing the care his wife had taken to do it right. Kit discovered that cooking and cleaning weren't quite the drudgery she'd thought, once she got it down to a system. But she still enjoyed ranch work and being outside much more—that would never change.

Along with everything else, Kit began going into town more often. Without her cold, hardened air of reserve, more people greeted her on the street. Kit even began to speak to her distant neighbors and acquaintances.

In true small-town fashion, they remarked among themselves about her new friendliness, commented on how attractive she seemed, and speculated about the haunting sadness that some saw in her eyes. Those who knew about Reese and his sudden departure—and had heard the rumors about the possible affair between them—drew their own conclusions.

Kit no longer bristled when she received sympathetic looks. She was amazed that others might care how she felt. She accepted the fact that they knew something of what had happened between her and Reese, but kept her loss to herself.

She never stopped missing Reese, or regretting their fights, or wanting him. Every hour of every day, Kit longed for him. At times it was just a dull ache, but once in a while it stabbed at her heart like a hot knife. She didn't think it would change for a very long time, if ever, but Kit accepted that. As much as anyone could be, Kit was reconciled to her life.

Bacon sizzled in the skillet, brown and crisp. Kit scooped it out and spread it to drain across a plate covered with a paper towel. She turned as her grandfather entered the kitchen, and smiled.

"Good morning."

"Morning." He looked tired and his thatch of white hair was still tousled from sleep. "It's a bit nippy out this morning."

"Downright chilly." Kit melted a bit of butter in a different, nonstick skillet and broke two eggs into it.

Outside there was a honking sound and Nate Bonner peered out a slightly steamed-over window to see the V-formation of a flock of geese winging their way south.

"Winter's coming for sure," he sighed. "Guess I'd better get the Big House shuttered and ready while the decent weather holds."

She felt a flash of heartache but she kept her feelings to herself. "Yes, you'd probably better," Kit said. She flipped the eggs over with a spatula.

"You going out with the boys this morning?" Nate inquired, tactfully changing the subject.

"Yeah. We should get the last of the cows up to the winter pasture today." Kit slid his fried eggs onto a plate, setting it and the platter of bacon on the table in front of him. She turned back to the stove to crack an egg in the skillet for herself.

"Be cold riding today," he observed as he reached for the bread just popping out of the toaster.

"I'm wearing my thermal underwear just in case you're right." Kit smiled.

"It shows," Nate said dryly.

Kit glanced down at her tapered blouse and snug jeans. With the heavy long underwear beneath, the jeans were almost skintight.

"It does bulge a bit," she admitted with a faint laugh. "But I'll keep warm."

"Figure you'll finish up today?" Nate reverted back to the subject of the day's ranch work.

Kit continued to give most of the orders, but she no longer dictated and didn't want to. In the first numbed weeks after Reese had left, all three of the hands had been quite gentle with her. Since then, a pleasant camaraderie had developed among them. Kit wouldn't have gone back to her old ways for anything.

"Yes, we should," she answered. "It'll probably be late, though. I didn't think Frank would feel much like cooking when we got back so I'm going to invite them over for supper. There's a big pot of chili at the back of the stove, roast beef sandwiches and a couple of salads in the refrigerator. That should satisfy them, don't you think?"

"Should," he agreed. There was a twinkle in his eye when Kit dished up her egg and sat down beside him. "Especially with the chocolate cake you've got hiding in the cupboard for dessert."

"You found it," she said accusingly.

"Tasted pretty good, too."

"Is there any left?"

"Enough for dessert tonight and a snack for me this afternoon," her grandfather said with a wink.

"You and that sweet tooth of yours are hopeless," Kit declared.

"You'd better eat. Your egg's getting cold," he warned. "Want some toast?"

"Please."

"And don't be riding me about my sweet tooth," Nate added. "Yours is just as bad."

Her knife was held at the ready to butter the piece of bread he put into the toaster. She set it down quietly. Her grandfather had unwittingly reminded her of the time when Reese had teased her about the French-fried vanilla ice cream. Kit waited for the pang to subside, glad to be distracted by the toast popping up.

CHAPTER 10

Frost had already turned the tall, thick grass into a swaying carpet of tawny gold. The rugged grandeur of the land did not provide a spectacular display of fall foliage, but there were rusty oranges and yellows of the trees along the watercourses to contrast with the dark green of the juniper-covered slopes. As a rule, fall days were mild and the nights chilly, giving the animals, ranch stock and wildlife alike, a chance to grow winter coats.

Today it had been decidedly brisk with a bite to the wind. A startling blue sky stretched endlessly overhead. The sun was on its swift downward path, shortening the hours of daylight. Winter came early to the badlands, the first snow flurries coming sometimes as soon as late September. They were approaching that time and the air held a warning of winter's cold breath not far away.

A quartet of horses and riders plodded along the dirt track toward the ranch yard. They crested a hill and Kit glimpsed the roof of the Big House through the windbreak of trees. There was a constriction in her chest as she again found it hard knowing that Reese would never enter it again.

"Whew! I ain't never been so tired and sore in all my life," Kyle moaned, wincing as he tried to shift in the saddle. "My butt's really goin' to be draggin' tonight."

Kit mentally shook away her thoughts of Reese. "Right, Kyle," she chided. "You've been sitting on it all day." There was a time when she would have snapped at Kyle for complaining instead of teasing him.

"That's the point," he groaned, and the others laughed sympathetically, aware of their own stiffened muscles from a long day in the saddle.

"What you need is some hard riding to loosen you up. Come on, I'll race you to the barn," Kit challenged, suddenly wanting to hear the wind singing in her ears. Maybe that would get Reese out of her mind.

Before Kyle could accept or reject her challenge, Kit was putting the spurs to the bay. She had a two-stride head start before Kyle gave chase. Both horses flattened out, glad to race as long as they were headed for the barn and oats. Kyle was never able to close the gap. When they reined in at the barn, Kit was the victor.

"You won," he conceded, "but only because you had a head start."

His hand was at her waist to help her down. She couldn't help but recall when Reese had done the same thing, though much more eagerly—it had been the occasion of their first kiss.

She swallowed the lump in her throat and managed a light retort. "Your horse has always been faster than Reno. I won because I was the better rider." She hopped to the ground with his friendly assistance.

"I admit you have the prettiest seat in a saddle that I've ever seen," Kyle said, letting his hand fall away now that she was standing.

His comment astonished Kit. He was actually flirting with her—not in any serious way, but in the easygoing manner of a guy who finds a woman attractive and wants her to know it.

"I'll take care of your horse," he offered.

She no longer thought of such courtesies as attempts to point out that she was incapable of doing things for herself. Instead of strongly objecting, Kit handed him the reins.

"Thanks," she said, and Kyle left, leading both horses into the corral.

As she turned to leave the barn area, she discovered Lew and Frank had ridden up behind her. Lew had dismounted and Frank was leading both horses away. Kit could tell by the bright glitter in Lew's eyes that he had overheard Kyle's comment.

"He was actually flirting with me. Can you believe that?" She laughed out loud.

"I can believe it," he nodded. "You have changed, Kitty. I can remember when a comment like that would have earned a fella twenty lashes or the equivalent from your sharp tongue. It's dulled considerably."

"I guess it has." Looking into his weather-tanned face, Kit knew she had never been properly appreciative of this man's unwavering loyalty and affection. He was like an uncle—something she had never had. "Thanks for being so patient and tolerant, Lew." Impulsively, Kit leaned up and kissed his scratchy cheek.

"For cryin' out loud!" He flushed a deep red. "What ya goin' and gettin' all mushy for?" Despite his embarrassment, he seemed deeply touched and Kit knew she would have done it again, given the chance.

Instead she laughed. "That's what you get for having a woman boss." She walked past him, giving him a pat on the rump, a male gesture that she copied in fun, and Lew sidestepped quickly, even more embarrassed.

"Behave yourself!" he admonished.

Kit laughed and kept on walking. She caught sight of the Big House and the front door standing open. Momentarily her heart gave a leap, but she told herself silently not to be so silly. "Looks like Gramps is still up at the Big House, getting it ready for winter. I'm going to see how he's coming along," she informed Lew unnecessarily. "Don't forget—supper will be ready in forty-five minutes, give or take."

"Don't burn it," he warned.

"I won't." Kit changed directions and started for the Big House. The happiness of the last few minutes lightened her steps as she crossed the yard. Kit concentrated her thoughts on that, putting the pain of remembering Reese to the back of her mind. There was only silence when she set foot inside the house.

"Grandpa? Nate?" she called and received no answer.

But she thought she heard a sound of someone moving about in the rear of the house. After a second's hesitation, Kit went to investigate. The library door was closed and she walked past it, deliberately not looking at it.

It was still the only room in the house that Kit couldn't face.

Dustcovers were draped over the furniture in the living room, and the windows to the west were unshuttered, letting the sunlight stream in to chase away the gloom. Kit glimpsed a movement out of the corner of her eye when she entered the room and stopped. It was only her own reflection in the big oval mirror on the wall, encircled by a polished and ornately carved hardwood frame.

The sight of herself in the mirror caused her to pause. Her hair curled easily about her shoulders, a little tousled by the wind, the gleam of golden sunlight in its brown depths. Her clothes did right by her figure. The proud, defensive look was gone from her features, her lips softened into curves instead of pressed thin.

Kit wondered if Reese would notice the changes if he saw her now. Would things have turned out differently if she had looked like this when they met, been less hot-tempered, less judgmental, less immature? But she would never know the answer to those questions.

His image joined her reflection in the mirror. She blinked and stared at the hard-cut features with their brooding, aristocratic air, that glint of mockery in the piercing hazel eyes, the sensuous mouth and thick, dark hair.

For a fraction of a second she looked at it, then

willed the haunting image to go away. It remained—and moved toward her. Kit went white and pivoted to face it. Reese was standing there—in the flesh.

"Hello, Kit," he said in the low, quiet voice she remembered so well.

"I thought you were a ghost," she breathed.

His mouth quirked in a half-smiling line. "I was surprised by what I saw, too."

"You're back," Kit said. Though why she had to say it when it was so obvious, she didn't know.

"Yes, I'm back."

A warm glow seemed to flood through her body, a treacherous joy leaping in her heart. Once she would have demanded to know why, but the change in Kit had produced a willingness to wait—sometimes—and let life take its own course.

"When . . . did you get here?"

"This afternoon. About an hour ago," Reese answered.

There was not that much distance separating them. One step and Kit could be in his arms, but she didn't attempt to cross it. Not yet. It was too soon. Kit couldn't bear it if he rejected her again. His expression was guarded and she didn't know what he thought of her now.

"You've changed, Kit," he said, his gaze raking her figure.

So he did notice, she thought breathlessly. But did he know why?

"Yes," Kit agreed, "although"—she lifted her arm to sniff the back of her hand, then smiled—"I still smell of horse sweat and manure."

When she lowered her hand, Reese caught it

and brought it to his nose, his breath warm against her skin. His gaze continued to hold Kit's over her hand. "Hmm. There's a trace of perfume, too," he added, letting go a little reluctantly. There was something questioning in the way he studied her face. "You're more beautiful than I remembered."

"I—I'm glad you think so." The words sounded so inadequate when she felt so happy inside. "How long will you be staying, Reese?"

"That depends." But he didn't say on what. "I had some stuff in storage that I wanted to leave here. And I'm afraid I came unannounced again," he said wryly. "Do you suppose Frank can stretch the evening meal to include me?"

"I'm sure he can. No . . ." Quickly Kit retracted her answer. In the surprise of seeing Reese again, she had forgotten. "I invited the boys over to the house to eat with Grandpa and me. So Frank isn't cooking."

"I can drive into town. Maybe I'll eat at the Rough Rider Hotel again. Treat myself to French-fried vanilla ice cream."

"No, please join us," she said hurriedly. "There's plenty of food, honestly."

"I'd like that," he said simply. His gaze brightened as he noticed the way Kit glowed with pleasure. "I saw you when you rode into the yard this afternoon, laughing and joking with the others," Reese mused. "I could hardly believe you were the same Kit."

"Well, I didn't see you. Where's the Range Rover?"

"Around the back. I had the rental agency reserve it—I figured if you saw a different car you'd throw me off the property again. But you got me off the subject. What happened to you?"

She waved a hand airily. "I suppose you could say I've mellowed with age."

"Yeah—you're coming along nicely." He tipped his head to the side at an inquiring angle. "Did a man have anything to do with it?"

Was he testing her? "Oh, yes, definitely," Kit answered.

He lifted one eyebrow. "Anyone I know?"

She smiled. "You know him very well. It's—" The "you" part of the sentence never got out of her mouth.

"Kit!" a voice called from the hallway, and both of them turned at the interruption. "Hey, Kit? Are you in here?" A second later Kyle appeared. Reese was standing slightly to one side, so it was Kit he saw first. "You left your jacket tied on the back of your saddle. Lew told me you were in here so I thought I'd better bring it to you before you started wondering where it was."

"Thanks, Kyle." She reached out for the leather-fringed jacket he was carrying.

But Kyle had stopped short at the sight of Reese. A look of stunned surprise was replaced by a wide grin of welcome. "Mr. Talbot! Wow! I didn't expect to see ya here." Vigorously he shook Reese's hand. "Good to see ya. When did you get back?"

"A while ago."

Kit heard the sudden note of reserve in Reese's voice and stared at him. He did seem withdrawn, with a chilling hardness about his expression. It troubled her, especially the way he avoided looking at her.

Maybe he had guessed what she was going to say before Kyle had entered and was glad she hadn't gotten the chance. What made her think he might have come back because of her? Because that was what she wanted to believe, Kit realized.

It was more than likely he had returned on ranch business. Perhaps he had decided to sell after all and be done with any connection to her for good. It was a sobering thought, one that put the brakes on her runaway imagination.

"This is great!" Kyle declared with an amazed grin. "Wait until I tell the other guys. Welcome back, sir."

"Thanks." Reese's mouth curved but it wasn't a smile.

Kyle remembered he was still holding Kit's jacket. He turned to give it to her, his gaze lighting on her serious expression. He glanced warily back to Reese.

"Uh, was I—interrupting something?" he asked. The question held a note of challenge, as if he wasn't sure Kit needed or wanted his protection.

"No," Reese answered, giving Kit the impression that he had no further desire to be alone with her. "Kit was just inviting me to join you all for dinner." Finally he looked at her, his gaze cold and his tone polite. "I have a few things to unpack. What time would you like me to come over?"

"We'll probably eat in half an hour or so. Anytime between now and then will be fine," Kit answered, telling herself not to be so disappointed.

Depending on how long he was staying, she might still have a chance. Was the magic still there? He had just said that she was more beautiful than he remembered—hey, whatever it took. She'd rope and tie him if she had to.

"Good. See you soon." Reese nodded crisply.

With Kyle beside her, Kit left the house. She felt him eyeing her curiously, probably wondering what had gone on between her and Reese before he arrived, but he didn't ask. Which was good, because she sure as hell didn't feel like answering any questions.

Once outside, he walked with her a little ways before parting to go to the bunkhouse and wash up before the meal.

Although Reese's return had thrown Kit for a loop, the fact that he had come back at all was enough to ease the pain in her heart for the time being. She was smiling as she swept into the kitchen of her own home.

Her grandfather was standing at the stove. He glanced up when she entered. "You saw him, did you?" Nate said, certain of her positive answer.

"Yes." She rushed over to the stove and gave him a quick hug. "He's coming to dinner."

He smiled at the happiness sparkling in her brown eyes. "I put the chili on to heat when I saw you ride into the yard. The table is all set. I figured you'd invite him to dinner and I thought you might want a chance to maybe shower and put on a bit of lipstick."

"Grandpa, you are a sweetie!" Kit declared with a laugh and dashed off to do just that.

She didn't take too much time because she didn't

have long before Reese and the others came. Out of the shower, she toyed with the idea of wearing one of her new dresses, but decided that was too obvious. Dressed in dark blue denims and a flowered blouse, she went into the kitchen. The chili was just beginning to simmer in the pot and Kit took the spoon away from her grandfather to stir it.

"Did Reese say anything to you about why he came back?" she asked.

"Nope. How about you?"

Kit shook her head but didn't have the chance to say anything. Several pairs of boots clomped onto the porch and the back door opened. She glanced up to see Frank walk in, followed by Lew, and Kyle behind him.

"I'll have the food on the table in a few minutes," she promised, turning back to the chili. "Why don't you boys have a chair in the living room until everything's ready."

As they started to file through the living room, Lew teased, "Did you burn it?"

"No, I didn't," she retorted. When Kit looked up, she saw that Reese had arrived. He met her glance briefly and followed the others into the living room, her grandfather joining them and leaving the kitchen to Kit.

A little nervous, Kit took the salads from the refrigerator and started taking them out of the plastic bag to arrange them on the platter. She tensed at the sound of footsteps in the kitchen. When she glanced over her shoulder, Kit saw it was Lew, and relaxed.

Zebra Contemporary

Whatever your taste in contemporary romance – Romantic Suspense … Character-Driven … Light and Whimsical … Heartwarming … Humorous – we have it at Zebra!

And now Zebra has created a Book Club for readers like yourself who enjoy fine Contemporary Romance written by today's best-selling authors.

Authors like Lori Foster… Janet Dailey… Fern Michaels… Janelle Taylor… Kasey Michaels… Lisa Jackson… Shannon Drake… Kat Martin… to name but a few!

These are the finest contemporary romances available anywhere today!

But don't take our word for it! Accept our gift of 3 FREE Zebra Contemporary Romances – and see for yourself. You only pay $1.99 for shipping and handling.

Once you've read them, we're sure you'll want to continue receiving the newest Zebra Contemporaries as soon as they're published each month! And you can by becoming a member of the Zebra Contemporary Romance Book Club!

As a member of Zebra Contemporary Romance Book Club,

- You'll receive three books every month. Each book will be by one of Zebra's best-selling authors.

- You'll have variety – you'll never receive two of the same kind of story in one month.

- You'll get your books hot off the press, usually before they appear in bookstores.

- You'll ALWAYS save up to 20% off the cover price.

SEND FOR YOUR FREE BOOKS TODAY!

To start your membership, simply complete and return the Free Book Certificate. You'll receive your Introductory Shipment of 3 FREE Zebra Contemporary Romances, you only pay $1.99 for shipping and handling. Then, each month you will receive the 3 newest Zebra Contemporary Romances. Each shipment will be yours to examine FREE for 10 days. If you decide to keep the books, you'll pay the preferred subscriber price (a savings of up to 20% off the cover price), plus shipping and handling. If you want us to stop sending books, just say the word… it's that simple.

FREE BOOK CERTIFICATE

Yes! Please send me 3 FREE Zebra Contemporary romance novels. I only pay $1.99 for shipping and handling. I understand that each month thereafter I will be able to preview 3 brand-new Contemporary Romances FREE for 10 days. Then, if I should decide to keep them, I will pay the money-saving preferred subscriber's price (that's a savings of up to 20% off the retail price), plus shipping and handling. I understand I am under no obligation to purchase any books, as explained on this card.

Name _____

Address _____ Apt._____

City _____ State _____ Zip _____

Telephone (____) _____

Signature _____

(If under 18, parent or guardian must sign)

Thank You!

Offer limited to one per household and not to current subscribers. Terms, offer and prices subject to change. Orders subject to acceptance by Zebra Contemporary Book Club. Offer Valid in the U.S. only.

CNHL4A

THE BENEFITS OF BOOK CLUB MEMBERSHIP

- You'll get your books hot off the press, usually before they appear in bookstores.
- You'll ALWAYS save up to 20% off the cover price.
- You'll get our FREE monthly newsletter filled with author interviews, book previews, special offers and MORE!
- There's no obligation — you can cancel at any time and you have no minimum number of books to buy.
- And—if you decide you don't like the books you receive, you can return them. (You always have ten days to decide.)

Zebra Contemporary Romance Book Club
Zebra Home Subscription Service, Inc.
P.O. Box 5214
Clifton , NJ 07015-5214

"How's it goin'?" He leaned against the counter beside her, his astute gaze studying her downcast face.

"Fine. Be ready in a few minutes."

Lew watched her setting out the sandwiches for a few seconds, then asked, "Did he say why he's come back?"

"No." Kit shook her head briefly.

"Do you want me to have a little talk with him?" Lew frowned instantly. "I don't want to see you gettin' hurt by him again."

"No, there's no need," Kit answered, touched by his gallant gesture.

"Do ya still love him?" He lowered his head to peer more closely at her face, revealing his shiny, bald top.

"Yes, I do." She smiled wryly and set the last sandwich on the platter, waving Lew away to the dining room. "Go ask if anyone wants beer, okay? I'm almost done with these." He complied.

Kit picked up the platter and turned to carry it to the table. There stood Reese—who had been behind them, obviously listening. She almost dropped the platter, but his hand was there to save it and set it on the table.

Reese turned back to her and demanded, "Who was that man you were referring to?"

There wasn't any point in holding back now, but Kit was shaking inside. "You, you idiot. Not Kyle, if that's what you thought—*mmf!*"

In the next second his arms were around her and she was crushed to his chest. His mouth came down on her lips, kissing her with an ardor that took Kit's breath away. She strained to be closer to him, arching against his body, happily abandoning herself.

Finally Reese cupped his hands on either side of her face and reluctantly took his mouth from hers. Desire smoldered in his eyes.

"So why did you come back?" Kit asked in a husky voice, now that she was sure of his answer. "Everybody's dying to know. Not just me."

"Because of you. I couldn't get you out of my head. Hell," he chuckled. "I couldn't get you out of my heart. You're beautiful, you're brave—and there's only one of you. I didn't want to fight half the cowboys in North Dakota just because I waited too long."

"I love you, Reese." Kit spoke the words at last. "Only you."

"Glad to hear it, girl. You sure about that?"

She nodded and he kissed her again and would have gone on kissing her, until Lew coughed discreetly.

"About those beers—"

Kit blushed as she looked at Reese through the sweep of her lashes. His adoring and possessive smile made her heart swell with pride. He loved her and nothing could be more perfect than that. He curved an arm around her shoulder, nestling Kit against his side as he turned her toward the living room.

"Come with me," he ordered.

The others stopped talking the minute they entered the living room. Kit's color was still high, but she thought she would burst with her love. She couldn't have hidden it if her life depended on it. The whole world could know, for all she cared.

Reese stopped in front of Nate. "With your permission, I'd like to marry your granddaughter."

Tears shimmered in her eyes as she looked up at the man she loved, hardly daring to believe she had heard correctly. It was a dream, a blissful dream come true.

"I don't need to ask Kitty if it's what she wants," Nate replied, "because right now she looks like the happiest woman on earth. And you and I got to know each other some while you were here. But she is awful young to be taking that step, if you don't mind my saying so."

Reese nodded. "She's promised me that she'll go to college, and see something of the world, and think it over for as long as she needs to—by then she'll understand how great I am."

"I never promised any of that," Kit said indignantly, laughing and holding on to his arm. She stretched up on tiptoe to give him a kiss.

"Well, we can fight about it when we're married. Just in case we ever get bored."

"I don't expect that'll be a problem," Nate said with a twinkle in his eye. "You have my permission. And God bless you both."

"I'm not going to take her away for good, Nate. I just want to thank you for understanding so much and saying so little—and I want to thank you for Kit."

"I wish her momma was here. And my Martha," Nate said softly. "This is a happy day, son."

His voice was roughened by emotion. Kit could hear how deeply he was moved.

"The holidays are coming," Nate said at last. "Thanksgiving's just around the corner. And Christmas. We'd be proud to have you as part of the family, Reese."

It seemed to take several seconds for what was happening to sink in with the others. When it did, there was an explosion of jubilation, backslapping, and congratulations all around. It was several minutes before Lew, who had joined them in the living room, thought to rescue the chili from the stove.

Their thoughts turned to food and the hunger they had temporarily forgotten. As they moved en masse into the kitchen, Reese caught at Kit's hand and dragged her away from the table toward the back door.

"If you'll excuse us for a few minutes?" he asked with a broad smile. "We'll join you later."

"It's cold outside. Better wear a coat," Nate cautioned.

As she and Reese started out the door, Kit saw Lew poke Frank in the ribs and mutter, "It could be freezing and they'd never know the difference."

Outside Kit found out how right Lew was. In Reese's arms she was more than warm enough. It was a long while before either found the time or the necessity for words.

"I thought you wouldn't come back," Kit breathed finally as he cradled her head against his shoulder.

"I couldn't stay away any longer. My home was with you—but I had to leave you to realize that all I wanted was for us to be together . . . right here. No matter what."

"Here?" She raised her head to see if he was

teasing her. "Do you mean we're going to live here? On the ranch?"

"Yes." Reese smiled at her amazement. "Don't you want to?"

"Oh yes, I want to," she said in a rush, then hesitated. "But are you sure you do?"

"Yes," he said, and looked out at the western sun crimsoning the rugged bluffs. "This will always be your home—*our* home," he corrected himself. "And like Nate said, the holidays are coming. Make a list, Kit. We need a turkey, cranberries, tree, Christmas ornaments—"

"Aren't you jumping the gun a little?" she laughed.

"I like to be prepared. And speaking of that—"

He took her by the hand again and led her to the silver Range Rover, opening the back. There was the same luggage he'd left with, and a box on top decorated with red and green. He opened it carefully to reveal glass balls in jewel colors inside a segmented divider. "These are nothing special. But these"—he lifted out the top tray—"are the real treasures."

Kit saw a collection of mismatched ornaments that someone had cherished and packed away with care. Reese reached into the box and pulled out a pipe-cleaner bird with beady eyes.

"I made it when I was six. And this is the rubber Snoopy that always fell off the branch." It was missing an ear. "The dog liked that one." He pulled out paper chains made of faded construction paper that had torn in several places. "Festive, huh? Can't believe I never threw any of it away."

"Don't you dare," she said sternly. "These are your memories."

Reese looked inside the box again and took out a very small box made of rounded black velvet. "Aha—here it is." He set the bigger box aside and opened the black velvet one, revealing an engagement ring. The diamond caught the last red rays of the setting sun and flashed a fire bright as love. "I asked Nate, but I didn't ask you—and I know you'll never let me forget it if I don't." He dropped to one knee. "Marry me, Kit?"

She let out a little shriek. "Oh! It's beautiful! Yes!"

"That's the magic word." He rose and slipped the ring on her finger, and rocked her in his strong embrace. "I got my wish. And it's not even Christmas yet."

She looked up at him as best she could, laughing with joy. "What do you mean?"

He looked inside the box of ornaments, and took out an old glass Santa. "I used to talk to this guy every night after the tree was decorated—I whispered my wish list in his little glass ear. Somehow I usually got most of it. My mother told me years later that was how she knew what I wanted."

"That's a wonderful story. We'll put him on the tree first."

"When we get a tree."

"I know a good place to cut one. About a mile west—"

"You're in charge, Kit."

She nodded, very pleased. It was going to be an absolutely amazing Christmas—and her first truly happy one. Then a thought occurred to her. "What are you going to ask for?"

"That's between me and my man here." He held up the glass Santa and gave her a wicked wink.

"Reese, help me out. What do you want?"

"You. Just you." He folded her in his arms again, and showed her exactly what he meant.

HEART OF
STONE

CHAPTER I

There was a sudden flurry of activity outside Stephanie's office. Located where it was, at the heart of the luxurious New Hanpshire inn, it gave her easy access to all phases of the operation, and she kept her door open. Stephanie enjoyed her partial view of the front desk, and the endless activity there. Guest were always coming and going, not to mention the inn's busy staff.

Across the hall was the housekeeping department—not glamorous but definitely one of the most important facets of a well-run inn. The office next to hers belonged to her brother, Perry Hall, the manager of the inn—and her boss.

When Amanda Adamson, the dining room hostess, went hurrying past Stephanie's door, her curiosity was thoroughly aroused. Something unusual was going on. Even though she had worked for barely three months at the White Boar Inn,

Stephanie felt the accelerated tempo of the inn's pulse, a tense quickening of interest.

The spreadsheet on her computer screen was forgotten as she speared a pencil though the chestnut hair above her ear and rose from her chair. Accounting was invariably the last department to know anything if she followed routine and didn't investigate. Since Perry was her brother, she didn't choose to sit back and wait to be informed.

Once in the hallway, she glanced toward the front desk. Her blue eyes noted the expressions of harried excitement in the faces of the usually unflappable pair in charge of registration.

Stephanie wondered whose imminent arrival was causing such a stir. Famous for its exclusivity—and its very New England sense of discretion—the inn catered to the wealthy and to famous people who preferred to go unrecognized once in a while. Besides, every room was already taken, occupied by guests eager to enjoy the autumn splendor of the White Mountains, and there were reservations all the way through the winter season to spring.

Puzzled by the unknown cause of all this subdued commotion, Stephanie absently fingered the scarab pendant on a gold chain around her neck. She walked over to her brother's office and stood in the open doorway, not wanting to interrupt his conversation with Amanda Adamson.

"Get a bottle on ice, right away," he was instructing her, as Amanda made hasty notes on a pad. Then Perry consulted the business papers stacked high on his desk, looking for something that he didn't find but not glancing up to see Stephanie standing there.

His brown hair was spiky, as if he had run his fingers through it many times. "Fix a tray with a selection of cheeses, pâtés, and fresh fruits to go with it. Better recheck the wine cellar and make sure his favorite wines are in stock, too. Alert the staff. If he decides to dine in the restaurant this evening, I want everything to be perfect. But don't—flowers!" Perry interrupted himself to exclaim. "I nearly forgot the damn flowers." He punched the buzzer to summon his assistant.

For once the young girl appeared within seconds. She looked pale and anxious, more timid than usual. Despite her age, Connie York was highly skilled and competent. Her only real flaw was her marked lack of self-confidence—definitely a drawback in the hotel business, Stephanie thought.

"Yes?" Connie made a question of her response to his summons, her small face pinched into a tense, uneasy expression.

Perry's upward glance finally lighted upon Stephanie, still standing in the doorway, when Connie edged past her, whispering an excuse-me.

"Call the florist. Order something dramatic and expensive—roses, but not just boring ones stuck in a vase. If they can't deliver them in an hour and a half, I want you to pick them up."

"Yes, sir." Connie's dark-haired head bobbed in quick agreement but Stephanie thought she detected a slight note of sarcasm in that *sir*. The girl waited a fraction of a second too long, perhaps to see if there would be anything else.

Perry, who was usually extraordinarily patient with his self-effacing assistant, sent her an irritated look. "It's not going to get done if you stand there, Connie. Go!"

"I know, but . . ." She wavered uncertainly.

"What is it?" he demanded.

Stephanie's gaze wandered over her brother's face. Six years older than she, Perry rarely allowed stressful situations to get to him. He had been more than just her big brother, he had been her idol for as long as she could remember. Life hadn't been easy for him . . . or for her, either. Their mother had died when Stephanie was only four. Perry had taken on a parent's job when he was still a kid himself, fixing meals and more or less keeping house while their father worked long hours as a ski instructor and bartender to make ends meet.

Five years ago, when Stephanie was seventeen, things seemed to be looking up. Perry had won a scholarship to attend a prestigious law school and Stephanie had been accepted by a well-known women's college in New England.

Then everything changed on one terrible day . . . a freak skiing accident left their father a paraplegic, with only limited use of his hands. Perry immediately gave up the scholarship to take the position of assistant manager at the White Boar Inn, and Stephanie stayed home to take care of their father.

Jim Hall's spine had been broken in two—but his heartbreak over seeing his children's chances in life limited by his accident triggered a profound depression that was worse. As the years wore on and complications from his injury weakened his body and his spirit, he had no longer wanted to live . . . and a lethal viral pneumonia had claimed him four months ago. In some ways, his death had been a blessing—for him and for them.

Stephanie hadn't completely adjusted to the absence of a responsibility that had made both her and Perry grow up fast. She couldn't say that she had ever felt free—or even young. Her accounting degree had enabled her to supplement their income by doing bookkeeping at home for local businesses. And when the position at the inn opened up, she was ready to take it, despite a few whispers about nepotism.

She liked working at the inn, liked being around people and being part of things. Most of all, she liked working with her brother. She had the utmost respect for the way he handled a complicated, sometimes difficult job that called for the combined ability of a diplomat and a drill sergeant.

Perry always seemed to be totally in control, whether dealing with a crisis in the restaurant kitchen—usually caused by the temperamental chef—or keeping the housekeeping staff on their toes. Which was why she was surprised by his harried attitude at the moment. It was definitely out of character.

"It's just that . . . I was wondering . . ." Connie was stumbling over the reason for her hesitation.

"I don't have all day. Please get to the point," Perry ordered.

"It's your appointment," his assistant began, intimidated by his abruptness.

"I told you to cancel them." His mouth thinned with impatience.

"Yes, but—" Connie bit her lower lip.

Perry seemed to be mentally counting to ten. "But *what*, Connie?" he asked with forced evenness.

"You have a lunch meeting. With the board of directors. You have to go. You told me a thousand times not to forget about it, and I prepared your presentation."

Perry groaned. "Oh, geez. It totally slipped my mind. It's today, right?"

Connie nodded. "What should I do?"

"Do? There's nothing you can do," he sighed. "I'll have to go, but cancel everything else. Sorry I barked at you—but be sure to get those flowers, okay?"

"Okay." With a nod of her head, the girl disappeared inside her adjoining office.

Returning his attention to Amanda Adamson, who still stood by his desk, Perry raked a hand through his dark hair again. "You know the routine, Amanda. Do what needs doing. I trust you." He glanced at his watch, effectively dismissing the hostess.

Stephanie stepped to one side so the woman could exit. From what she had overheard thus far, she had a general idea of what was happening. With the exception of the private suite, the inn was fully booked. And the suite was reserved exclusively for the owner of the White Boar or his personal guests. Before she had a chance to ask for more details, Perry was talking to her.

"Whatever your problem is, Steph, it will have to wait—unless someone is heading for Mexico with the cash and the credit card slips. In that case, call the FBI," he declared with a tired shake of his head.

"I don't have any problem," she assured him. "I'm just trying to figure out what's going on. Who's coming? The place is in a quiet uproar—if there is such a thing."

Sighing, Perry rocked back in his swivel chair. He noted her white sweater and green tartan skirt, and a faint smile touched his mouth when he looked at her face and sleek chestnut hair. The look was retro preppy—but it suited her. And the gold scarab pendant on the chain around her neck was an interesting touch.

"Guess what. Brock Canfield is making an unscheduled visit. He called half an hour ago from his cell phone to say he'd be here by two. He's driving up from Boston. Says the traffic was a nightmare on the way out." Tension etched lines in his strong face.

"Getting out of Boston is always a nightmare," Stephanie said.

"Getting in is worse. That's why we live up here, right? In the peace and quiet of the New Hampshire mountains, along with nine million other people looking to get away from it all."

"It's not that bad," Stephanie laughed.

"Not yet. Wait until summer. And we can all kiss our peace and quiet good-bye when Brock gets here."

Stephanie nodded. "Now I get why everyone is so jumpy. The big man himself is coming to inspect his property."

Perry rubbed his fingers against a spot in the

center of his forehead. "Go ahead. Joke about it. I'm the one who has to deal with the guy. Brock Canfield expects nothing less than perfection."

"I don't know what you're worrying about." Stephanie walked to the back of his chair and began to knead his tense shoulders, very gently.

"Ooh. That feels good. Ah. Right there. Yes." Perry forgot about his troubles for the moment and lolled his head back. "Scratch my ears. Throw me a bone. I wish I was a dog. Then I wouldn't have to think about anything."

"You worry too much," Stephanie scolded him gently. "Don't forget I've been keeping the books for the past three months."

"You, me, and Lotus 1-2-3. What a team."

"You know we're doing well. Brock Canfield can't possibly find anything wrong with your work and how you run the inn."

"Yeah, we've done okay," he admitted, relaxing under her hands. "If that trend continues through the ski season, we should have our best year ever."

Stephanie smiled down at him reassuringly. "That proves my point, doesn't it?"

"But if it doesn't snow—we'll have to hire topless cocoa girls or something. That'll bring the frat boys in—but they always wreck their rooms." He scowled and tensed up again.

"Perry. Calm down." She patted his shoulders, finishing the massage. "We don't let frat boys in, remember?"

"We do if their rich parents are willing to take out liability insurance." He let out a huge sigh. "Thanks. I guess Brock will judge us by what he sees on this trip. Pass or fail. Do or die. Not that I'm nervous or anything."

"He won't have any complaints." Stephanie was sure of that. The inn provided four-star service, and even the hard-to-please guests found almost nothing to grumble about. "Do you know this will be my first opportunity to meet the great and powerful Brock Canfield?" she said. "You've worked here—what? Five years? Everybody talks about him as if he were God. They practically quiver when they hear his name." She laughed. "I've heard him described as a ruthless tycoon and a gorgeous hunk of man."

Perry looked at her quizzically. "Gorgeous hunk of man? Who around here talks like that?"

"My lips are sealed," said Stephanie primly. "But I'm looking forward to meeting the real Brock Canfield."

"Well, both descriptions are pretty accurate." Her brother took hold of one of her hands and pulled her around to the side of his chair. He studied her for a long second. "Okay. You heard Connie. I have a lunch meeting that I can't miss. I'm deputizing you as my stand-in just in case I'm not back when Brock arrives."

"Me? Now wait a minute—" Stephanie began.

"Somebody has to be on hand to welcome him. Connie practically cringes every time he looks at her," Perry explained with a wry smile. "And Vic is home sleeping after twelve hours on his feet," he added, referring to the night manager. "I can't think of anyone else. Do you mind?"

"Of course not. I enjoy the company of ruthless

tycoons. What do I have to do, besides being on hand to greet him?" Despite her willingness to help, Stephanie felt a little uneasy.

"Show him to his suite, but make sure everything is in order first. No tourist brochures or junk like that cluttering up the place, and it has to be absolutely spotless. Connie is getting the flowers and Mrs. Adamson will have a bottle of unbelievably expensive champagne on ice and some pricey chocolates. Oh, and fresh fruit, just in case he's become a health nut."

Something her junk-food-munching brother definitely was not.

"What if he eats low-carb?"

"Cheese platter. Imported cashews. Beef jerky— no, that's not exactly elegant."

"Doesn't keep *you* from eating it," she said dryly.

"Pâté, then. You figure it out," he said. "But Steph—watch your step."

She was confused by the warning. "I won't say or do anything wrong—I'm not the outspoken type, you know."

"That's not what I meant." He looked her up and down. His sister was a beautiful girl and he had a brotherly duty to throw all suitors off the nearest cliff if they gave her trouble. "I was trying to say that you should stay clear of Brock Canfield. He goes through women the way a gambler goes through a deck of cards. He's rich, good-looking, powerful, and persuasive. Chicks hate that, right? I don't know why he gets them all."

Stephanie laughed. "Okay. I consider myself warned."

"I wouldn't like to see you get mixed up with

him, because I know you'd be hurt. Honestly, Steph, I'm not trying to play the heavy-handed big brother." Perry seemed to smile at himself. "It's just that I know he's going to take one look at you and get ideas. Not to be rude, but you haven't had a lot of experience with men—especially men like him."

"How do you know?" she asked, nettled.

"I just do. I'm your brother. I make it my business to know, but I don't try to boss you around or run your life."

"Oh, all right." She didn't mind that Perry was worried about her. In fact, she liked the idea that he cared enough about her to try to protect her. "Experienced or not, I think I can take care of myself."

"Of course you can—up to a point."

A smile hovered around the corners of her mouth. "Is that why you never brought him home to dinner when I suggested it during his other visits?"

"Partly," her brother admitted. "But mostly because Brock isn't your home-cooked-meal type. He's more a caviar-and-designer-vodka man."

"Very icky," Stephanie said decisively. "I hate caviar."

"Good. Then you'll have nothing to talk about."

"Wait a minute—" She wanted to ask him more, but Perry had gotten to his feet and was riffling through the papers on his desk.

"Where the hell are my notes?"

"Over here." She pointed to the low shelf next to her that concealed the ventilation system. "And if you didn't use the vent shelf for storage, you could breathe actual air. When will you be back—in case Brock asks?"

He swept up the sheaf of notes and patted her on the head in a brotherly way. "Between one-thirty and two."

"Maybe he'll be late," she said and walked to the door.

Forty-five minutes later, Perry stuck his head inside her office to let her know he was leaving for his lunch meeting. "Take care of Brock if he arrives before I get back," he reminded her.

"I already said I would. Have a great meeting. Go away."

He waved and left. A few minutes later Stephanie closed her office door to have lunch. Her appetite was all but nonexistent, so she picked at her take-out salad for twenty minutes before giving up. A few minutes before one, she got the key-card from Mary at the front desk, curious about the private suite she had never seen.

She opened the door and said an unnecessary hello. The maid had done the rooms and left. She looked around the spacious sitting room and the adjoining master bedroom and its king-sized bed. The suite was immaculate—and impressive.

Huge windows offered an unparalleled view of the White Mountains, cloaked in brilliant autumn color. Sunlight streaming through the glass made a pattern of gold on the Italian tile floor, and gave the room a welcoming warmth.

The furniture was upholstered in cream-colored leather and neutral linen, custom-built in sweeping lines that looked incredibly comfortable. A floor-to-ceiling cabinet concealed an enormous, flat-screen TV—Stephanie peeked but stopped herself from turning it on.

She checked the small, in-room bar concealed behind another cabinet whose door swung out noiselessly—it had been stocked with single malts, cognac, and good vodka. No wine coolers, no coconut-flavored rum, no sweet stuff. Brock Canfield had expensive taste in liquor and he probably drank it straight up.

She admired the flowers, which Connie had seen to: blood-red roses intermingled with bare branches in an eye-catching arrangement.

Champagne on ice—check. Cheese platter—check. It looked tempting. Pâté—check. Cashews—check. Long-stemmed strawberries—check, but minus one. She hastily arranged the others to cover the place of the berry she swiped.

She brought the juicy treat into the bedroom, nibbling on it daintily. The pale cream tones of the room's décor and its bold furniture gave it a feeling of luxurious, masculine ease.

The bathroom was a bit overwhelming, faced with marble from floor to ceiling that also surrounded a Jacuzzi. Here, too, all was in readiness, and the bath had been stocked with thick, perfectly folded towels, new bars of French soap big enough for a man's hand, and other expensive grooming products.

No doubt Brock Canfield didn't like teeny-weeny soaps and sample-size bottles. She recalled an article on decorating psychology: his style was sensual, bold, and extremely expensive. She wasn't sure if she liked it or not.

She let herself out, strawberry stem concealed

in her palm, not wanting to leave any evidence of
her presence in a wastebasket.

As she entered the lobby, she thought she preferred its traditional décor to Brock's much more
contemporary suite—it was a lot homier. The
cheery fire blazing in the massive stone fireplace
always drew visitors to the armchairs surrounding it.

The Currier & Ives lithographs changed with
the seasons, set off by the white walls and wainscoting. The brass chandelier was a nuisance to clean,
Stephanie knew, but it lent a Victorian elegance to
the airy room.

She stopped at the front desk to return the keycard. "Any sign of Mr. Canfield yet, Mary?"

The mere mention of the owner's name seemed
to unnerve the usually calm woman. "Mr. Canfield? No, not that I know of." She turned to the
bellboy. "Ben, have you seen him?"

"Nope. He hasn't arrived yet."

"I'll be in my office. Let me know as soon as he
comes."

Circling behind the registration area, she
walked down the short hallway to her office. She
left her door open. Everyone seemed to be nervous—there was electricity in the air and Stephanie wasn't immune to its volatile charge.

Before she put her bag away, she paused in front
of the small mirror on the side wall to retouch her
lipstick, then decided she looked pale. She took
out a silver compact and stroked on a little blusher.
Mascara was next. By the time she was finished,
she had completely redone her makeup.

She blew herself a kiss, just to boost her own

morale, and looked around to see if anyone was watching. Fortunately, she was alone. She wondered what Brock Canfield would think of her and then remembered Perry's warning. He usually wasn't that blunt, even if he was her brother.

"Stephanie!" Mary hissed from the doorway. "He just drove up out front. Ben's gone to help him. He's got a woman with him."

Her frantic whisper made Stephanie want to smile. Who would hear? And what would it matter? But her last comment required some thought.

"Did Perry know that Mr. Canfield was bringing a guest?" she asked the desk clerk.

Mary shook her head. "He didn't say anything to me about it."

"Um—is this a separate-room situation or what?"

"How would I know?" Mary hissed. "You ask him."

Stephanie took a deep breath, reminding herself to stay calm, cool, and collected as she started toward the lobby. What did she have to be nervous about? Brock Canfield was only a man.

CHAPTER 2

Only a man. Stephanie instantly revised the phrase the minute she saw him. Tall, dark-haired, gorgeous, just for starters. Sexy. Totally masculine. An expensive overcoat—probably Armani—hung from his broad shoulders, its dark wool contrasting with the white silk scarf around his neck.

Not for one minute did Stephanie doubt that his elegant clothes covered other than a fabulously fit, muscled body. His stride, his confidence, his healthy sexiness—everything fit Perry's description of a man who got what he wanted when he wanted it.

Stephanie felt the awesome power of his attraction before she walked up to greet him. It was even more potent when she looked into his metallic gray eyes. Their lightness was compelling, at odds with his dark brown hair.

He made a thorough appraisal of her as she crossed the lobby, but he managed to do it with class. Her pulse quickened with the inner excitement his look had generated.

So far, so good—but there was a blonde on his arm. In a baby-blue cashmere sweater, which stretched—barely—over her outsize boobs. She wore breathtakingly tight pants that made Stephanie wonder how she could breathe.

Stephanie reminded herself that Baby Blue was Mr. Canfield's guest and that was that.

"Hello, Mr. Canfield. I'm Stephanie Hall," she introduced herself, and offered her hand. "I hope you had a pleasant trip."

"It was uneventful." His handshake was firm and warm, and his gaze had narrowed with sharp curiosity. "Stephanie Hall," he repeated her name. "I wasn't aware that Perry got married. When did that happen?"

"Perry isn't married," she replied quickly, then tried to explain. "At least, not to me. I mean, he isn't married to anyone." She finally managed a more controlled, "I'm his sister."

"Right." He seemed to step back, to withdraw somehow, yet he didn't move except to release her hand. "I remember him mentioning a younger sister. Somehow I had the impression you were much younger."

Stephanie decided not to comment on that. "I'm sorry Perry isn't here to meet you himself. His meeting ran late. But he should be back within the hour."

"No problem." His nod was indifferent. The blonde arched closer to him as if to remind him of her presence. It earned her a glance from Brock, nothing more. Stephanie detected no affection in his look. "Stephanie, this is Helen Collins." The blonde managed a smile. "Stephanie's brother manages the inn for me."

And Helen is my . . . Girlfriend? Mistress? Worst nightmare? He didn't add an explanation and Stephanie wasn't going to ask for one, but she was dying of curiosity. The glint in his eye made her suspect that Brock Canfield guessed that. She didn't like the idea that he might find it—and her—amusing.

"Well—may I show you to your suite?" She hoped she didn't sound as awkward as she felt.

"Please do." His tone was faintly mocking and so was his smile.

He had a very nice mouth, she noticed. Firm lips, set in a strong, clean line. Stephanie's imagination dallied with the idea of a kiss from those lips—a sophisticated, worldly kiss—for a fraction of a second. Then she put the thought aside.

"Please follow me, Mr. Canfield." The blonde glared at her over Brock's shoulder. Forcing a smile, Stephanie turned and walked to the desk to get the key from Mary. The woman slipped two keys into her outstretched palm, and shot Stephanie a conspiratorial look. Out of the corner of her eye, Stephanie noticed Ben struggling with the luggage and knew he would be following them.

Brock and Helen had started in the general direction of the hall leading to the private suite. Stephanie would have preferred to simply give him the keys, since he obviously knew the way, but she remembered Perry's instructions—*make sure he has everything he needs.*

"Do you work here, Stephanie? Or are you just helping your brother out?" The question came from Helen, her tone on the acid side.

"I work here," she replied smoothly, and tried not to let her dislike of the other woman show.

"What do you do?" Brock asked.

"Accounting." Her answer was cool. She wasn't sure whether Brock Canfield had actually known that or merely forgotten.

"So you're the reason the monthly reports have suddenly made sense these last few months," he concluded.

The remark didn't sound entirely friendly. Stephanie was spared from replying when they reached the suite. She unlocked the door and quickly led the way inside, wanting this to be over as soon as possible.

"It's fantastic, Brock," Helen gushed. "I love it—wow!" So it was her first visit to the suite, too. Stephanie filed that fact away to tell Mary.

She released his arm when she saw the roses on the coffee table. "And roses! They're gorgeous. You knew they're my favorites." She bent to inhale the fragrance of the biggest one, and Stephanie wondered about the seam of her pants and whether the seam could stand the strain.

"There's a bottle of Moet et Chandon on ice," Stephanie murmured and gestured discreetly toward the silver container and the elegant bottle wrapped in a white damask napkin nestled inside it.

Brock Canfield's gray eyes skimmed her face, their look mocking and amused, as if he sensed her discomfort. There wasn't any need for him to comment, since Helen discovered the bottle of champagne seconds afterward.

"Ooh! Bubbly! Baby, you think of everything," she declared and plucked the bottle from the ice bucket. "Open it, Brock!"

As he shrugged out of his overcoat, Stephanie saw her cue to leave. "Well, if there's anything else, Mr. Canfield—" she began.

"Don't leave yet." His smooth order halted the backward step Stephanie had taken to begin her retreat. But he offered no explanation as to why he wanted her to stay.

She stood silently by, trying to appear as composed and calm as her jittery nerves would permit, while he tossed his coat and scarf over one armchair. A minute later his suit jacket joined them. Then he was expertly popping the cork out of the champagne bottle and filling the two glasses Helen had in her hands.

"Care to join us, Miss Hall?" he asked. "There are more glasses in the bar."

"No, thank you," she refused with stiff politeness. "I have work to do this afternoon."

"One glass of champagne won't matter." His tone was mocking, but he returned the bottle to the ice bucket.

There was a knock at the door. Since Stephanie was closest, she answered it. It was Ben, the bellboy, struggling with the luggage. She motioned him inside the suite.

"Put it in the bedroom," Helen instructed. "Where's my makeup case? Oh, good, you got it." She followed him to supervise.

"I think you'll find everything in order, Mr. Canfield." Stephanie tried again to make her exit. "I checked the suite myself before you arrived."

"I'm sure I will," he agreed.

Her opportunity was lost a second time as Ben came out of the bedroom. She was rather surprised when Brock gave him a twenty for bringing the luggage. After all, he was the owner, so it wouldn't have been necessary. Ben thanked him enthusiastically and left.

"Here are your keycards, sir." Stephanie crossed the front hall of the suite to give them to him.

He didn't immediately reach out to take them. Instead he turned to set the champagne glass on an antique side table. The soft elegance of his silk shirt complemented his supple, muscular torso without emphasizing it—but he still had an untamed look. In fact, he reminded her of a wild animal on the prowl.

Without the suit jacket, he appeared more casual, more approachable. Her unsteady pulse revealed the danger of noticing it, as she dropped the keycards in his outstretched hand.

The glint in his gray eyes seemed to mock the action that avoided physical contact.

When Helen Collins appeared in the bedroom doorway, his gaze slid from Stephanie. He didn't wait for the other woman to speak as he issued his instructions. "Unpack the suitcases, Helen, and make yourself comfortable. I'm going to be busy for the rest of the afternoon."

He was politely but firmly telling his companion to get lost, dismissing her from his presence until he had time for the toy he had brought along to play with. Stephanie watched the curvy blonde smother the flash of resentment and blow him a pouty kiss before shutting the bedroom door.

"You don't approve of the arrangement, do you?" Amusement laced his casual question.

Stephanie had to work to keep her tone equally casual—and also professional. "I wouldn't presume to pass judgment on your personal affairs, Mr. Canfield. They have nothing to do with me."

"Spoken with the true discretion of an employee to her indiscreet boss," he said. Was there an edge to his voice? She couldn't be sure.

She heard Helen squeal something about the Jacuzzi and then the jets running full blast. She was grateful the other woman wasn't listening in.

When he absently moved a step closer, Stephanie had to control the instinct to move back in an effort to keep a safe distance from him. Her nerve endings tingled with the sexual force of his attraction at such close quarters. She told her nerve endings to chill out.

"Will there be anything else, Mr. Canfield?" She made a show of glancing at her watch as if she were running late. "I really should be getting back to my office."

For a long second he held her gaze. Then his glance slid downward as he turned away and slipped his suite keycard into his pocket. "You probably should." He picked up the glass of champagne.

Taking that as permission to leave, Stephanie started toward the door. Relief was sweeping through her, the tension disintegrating with a rush. She could fully understand how curiosity killed the cat.

She was still a few feet from the door when Brock Canfield stopped her with a low-voiced question. "Did your brother warn you about me?"

Her skirt swirled around her knees as she pivoted to face him. "I beg your pardon?"

She felt cornered, trapped like a little brown mouse that almost escaped before a set of claws gently forced it back into the mouth of danger. A faintly wicked smile was deepening the corners of his firm lips.

"Perry is conscientious and thorough. That's why I made him manager." Brock let his eyes run over her slender figure. "He must have told you that I eat little girls like you for breakfast." He sipped at the champagne and gave Stephanie the impression that he was drinking the essence of her.

Her throat worked for a second before she could get an answer out. "No, he didn't say that. But he did mention that you go through women like a gambler goes through a deck of cards." She was shaking inside.

"He's right." Brock lifted his glass in a mock salute. "And I don't much care what happens to them once I'm done. Not if I'm moving on to something new." Again, he took a swallow of champagne and studied her with unnerving steadiness over the rim of the crystal glass. "After all these years of keeping you hidden away, your brother took quite a risk sending you in his place. Why did he do it? Are you supposed to distract me so I won't uncover some hidden problem?"

"There aren't any problems. Everything is running smoothly." She looked him straight in the eye.

"Perry asked me to meet you because there wasn't anyone else. The night manager is at home sleeping and Perry's assistant . . . is terrified of you. That left only me to represent the managing staff. Unless you throw out protocol—then anyone would do."

"Oh, the nervous one. Her name's Connie, isn't it?" Brock Canfield mused and wandered toward Stephanie. "She seems to be afraid of men in general. I don't think it's just me."

"She's naturally shy." Stephanie defended her brother's assistant and fought the embarrassment that was trying to color her cheeks with a stupid blush. Why should she blush when he was deliberately being obnoxious? And getting much too close for comfort.

When he reached her, Brock didn't stop but went on past her. She heard him set the glass on the table and started to turn. "Perry must have told you that if you became involved with me, I would hurt you."

His constant changing from directly personal to impersonal was keeping her off balance. Stephanie tried to adjust to this current reversal of tactics. He made a leisurely circle to stop on the opposite side of her. Her head turned slightly to bring him into focus in her side vision. He didn't seem to expect a reply from her and she didn't make one.

"It's true," he went on. "Your brother's no fool. You eat Yankee pot roast on Sunday while I have Chateaubriand. I live in hotel penthouse suites and you want a center-hall Colonial house with four dinky bedrooms. Am I right?"

His gaze fell upon the golden scarab pendant that rested upon her bosom. She was infinitely grateful that she had worn a rollneck sweater.

"Nice bug. I suppose it has some significance."

"It's just a piece of jewelry, Mr. Canfield," she said tightly. If he didn't knock off the inspection, she was going to turn and run. Her job didn't require her to put up with this.

"Oh. Sorry." He looked into her eyes and she didn't look away. "Okay—where was I? Reading your mind and foretelling your future."

And annoying the hell out of me, she thought furiously.

"Let me guess. Besides the four-bedroom house, you want children. A boy and a girl. How am I doing?"

She chose not to reply.

"I don't," he said conversationally. As if she had asked—or wanted to know. "It's time the Canfield name died."

The conversation was getting seriously weird, but she didn't dispute any of his statements. She couldn't, because there was some truth in what he had guessed about her. Her silence was ruled mostly by the knowledge that he could seduce her.

For some reason, Brock Canfield was stating all the reasons why an affair with him would never last, while at the same time he was testing her resistance to him. She couldn't raise a single objection simply because he was so near—and so devastatingly attractive. It was crazy how helpless she felt—and how much she wanted him, deep down inside.

When he moved to stand in front of her, she was

physically conscious of his maleness. Her eyes level with the breadth of his shoulders, she lifted her chin to study the strength of his masculine features, the darkness of his hair, and the burnished silver of his eyes. He threaded his hands through the sides of her hair to frame her face.

"You want a man you can snuggle up to in bed and warm your cold feet," he said. "A Mr. Commitment. Or is Mr. Safe a better name? All I want is to enjoy a woman's body, then sleep alone on my side of the bed. You and I would be like oil and water. The combination doesn't mix."

His gaze shifted to her lips. Her heartbeat faltered, then shifted into high gear, but she managed to control the downward drift of her eyelashes and kept her eyes open, offering no invitation, silent or otherwise. Brock Canfield didn't need any. Her nerves tensed as his mouth descended toward hers with excruciating slowness.

First, the fanning warmth of his breath caressed her sensitive lips. Then she was assailed by the stimulating fragrance of some masculine cologne, the scent tinged with dry champagne. The hint of intoxication swirled through her senses an instant before his mouth moved expertly onto hers.

With persuasive ease, he sampled and tasted the soft curve of her lips, not attempting to eliminate the little distance between them. Stephanie didn't relax—or resist the exploring kiss. Of their own accord, her lips clung to his for a split second as he casually ended the contact to brush his mouth against her cheek.

"You're a delectable morsel." His voice was husky and low. "Maybe I'll save you for dessert." A light kiss tantalized the sensitive skin near her ear before he lifted his head to regard her with lazy gray eyes. "If you're smart, you'll slap my face, Stephanie."

"I'm smarter than that, Mr. Canfield." She was surprised she had a voice—and that it sounded so steady. "I'm not going to fight you—and I kissed you because I wanted—"

"What did you want?" His voice was unbearably intimate.

"Because I wanted to see what it felt like."

A smile of admiration spread across his face. Stephanie's heart stopped beating for a full second, stunned by the potent charm of his smile. He withdrew his hands from her hair and stepped away to reclaim his champagne glass.

"Now you've intrigued me, Stephanie," he murmured and downed the last of the champagne.

"Believe me, I didn't mean to." She heard splashing noises from the bathroom and remembered Helen with a feeling of agitation. But the blonde hadn't seen anything—she hoped.

"Didn't you?" Brock challenged with a knowing lift of a dark eyebrow.

"No." But she couldn't hold his gaze so she looked away, lifting her chin a fraction of an inch higher.

The phone rang and Brock walked away from it, throwing an order over his shoulder. "Answer it."

Stephanie hesitated, then picked it up. "Mr. Canfield's suite."

"Stephanie?" It was her brother. He sounded surprised that she had answered. "Connie said

Brock arrived fifteen minutes ago. Why are you still there? Any problems?"

"No, I was just leaving." She was glad her voice sounded normal and not as emotionally charged as she felt. "Mr. Canfield is right here. Would you like to speak to him?"

"Sure. Put him on," Perry said thoughtfully.

She held out the receiver. "It's Perry."

Brock walked over to take the phone from her hand, without attempting to touch her. His hand covered the mouthpiece. "Just when things were getting interesting."

She refused to take the bait. "I hope you enjoy your stay with us," she offered, as if she were addressing a hotel guest and not the owner.

As she turned to walk to the door, his voice followed her. "That remains to be seen, Stephanie."

His remark held the hint of a promise that this—whatever name there was for what had happened escaped her at the moment—would be resumed at a later time. The part of her that wasn't ruled by common sense was actually looking forward to it.

Crossing the threshold into the hallway, Stephanie half-turned to close the door. Her gaze was drawn to Brock, but he had already forgotten her. His dark head bent in concentration as he listened to Perry. Very quietly she shut the door and walked swiftly down the carpeted hallway.

When she reached her office, she closed its door. It was a defense mechanism to prevent her from watching for Brock Canfield. She paused long enough at the mirror to smooth the hair his hands had rumpled, then pulled up the spreadsheet on her computer and began to correct it.

Once she heard Perry's and Brock's voices in the hall outside her office. Unconsciously she held her breath, but they didn't stop. She guessed her brother was taking Brock on a brief tour of the inner workings of the inn. It sounded logical, although Brock was probably very familiar with all that went on.

Late in the afternoon, Perry knocked on her door and walked in. "Steph, do you have those cost projections on renovating the pool house into a sauna and health club?"

Her gaze ricocheted off her brother, to be stopped cold by Brock's gray eyes. A charcoal sweater had taken the place of his tie, the collar of his shirt extending over the sweater's neckline. The casualness didn't diminish his air of male authority.

"I'll print out another copy." She dragged her gaze from Brock to click on the right icon. "No problem."

"Sorry," Perry said. "I don't know what I did with the one you gave me." He took the printout Stephanie handed him and passed it to Brock. "As you can see on page two, the costs are within range of the initial estimate. The main problem is this bearing wall." He pointed to the architect's drawing that he found in the portfolio on Stephanie's desk to show Brock what he meant.

Stephanie leaned back in her chair, unable to work while the two men discussed the problem.

The idle moment gave her too much freedom to study Brock Canfield. Sitting sideways on the edge of her desk, he listened attentively to Perry's explanations and counterproposals.

His pants were conservatively cut but his position revealed the muscles of his thighs. She liked the clean, strong lines of his profile, the run-your-fingers-through-it thickness of his dark brown hair, and his lean, well-muscled build.

What really got to her was his innate sexiness. He was handsome in a hard kind of way, but it was much more than that. She couldn't look at him without being aware that he was a man.

All the warnings didn't mean a thing, Stephanie realized—not the ones from Perry or Brock, anyway. It was like being warned against the dangers of getting too close to a fire when she was shivering. She'd take the risk for the chance to be near him.

When she looked back at Brock, he was watching her, a smile in the gray depths of his eyes as if he knew what she was thinking and the decision she had reached. It was totally impossible. But she didn't draw an easy breath until he returned his attention to the green portfolio.

"Let's do this," he said to Perry. "I'll study these blueprints and cost projections and we'll discuss it this evening. You and your sister can have dinner with me tonight." He straightened from her desk, his glance barely touching her as he rolled the blueprints. "Unless you have other plans." The remark was an afterthought, addressed to her brother, not Stephanie.

"I'm free this evening, but I can't speak for

Stephanie." There was a silent warning in the look Perry gave her that said he would back up any excuse she chose to give.

"You'll come to keep the numbers even, won't you?" The statement was issued in the guise of a question as Brock studied her with knowing certainty. "You and Helen can talk while Perry and I discuss business."

His patronizing tone irked her. In case he'd forgotten, she'd had a lot to do with how well the business was doing.

Perry picked up on her silent irritation and spoke quickly. "We could always postpone it until morning."

"Business before pleasure," Brock insisted with a glance in the general direction of her brother before his gaze returned to lock with hers. "Does eight o'clock at the restaurant work for everyone? That'll give you time to go home and change."

"Eight o'clock is fine," Stephanie agreed. She'd known she would all along, if only for Perry, but the way Brock expected everyone to be available at his convenience was beyond obnoxious.

Perry gave her an are-you-crazy look, which she ignored. Maybe she was. But she had to prove something to herself when it came to Brock Canfield, even though she was way out of her league when it came to him. Her reaction was illogical—she knew that.

But *logic* wasn't the operative word here. A much more powerful force had taken hold of her.

CHAPTER 3

"Did he put the moves on you?" Perry slipped the curly textured jacket over her shoulders, his hands lingering for a second.

"Put the moves on me? I love guy talk for inappropriate behavior. Of course he did." At his muffled curse, Stephanie laughed. "Is that a surprise? You warned me that he would."

The laughter eased the tension between them. Dining out was a luxury she experienced only rarely. Her occasional dates usually didn't want to bother, preferring to spend their money on a hockey game or a movie, neither of which required gorgeous clothes.

She had picked a rust-colored dress with simple lines, added a belt and a few delicate gold chains. She tried to consider her choice as understated elegance as opposed to being underdressed.

Luckily, Perry hadn't arrived at the house until twenty minutes earlier, so he didn't know how she had agonized over what to wear. He'd barely had time to shower and change into a suit and tie. His brown hair was still a little wet. She could feel him eyeing her with brotherly concern while she buttoned the short jacket.

"What happened, Stephanie?"

Turning to face him, she made a fuss over straightening his tie, which was perfectly straight and in no need of her attention. "I didn't swoon at his feet, if that's what's worrying you," she joked.

"Knock it off, Steph." Perry took being a big brother very seriously sometimes, Stephanie thought. "You know he doesn't take anything lightly."

"Probably not," Stephanie conceded.

"Listen, if you want to change your mind, I'll make an excuse for you. One of your friends drove up for the weekend or something," he suggested.

"Well, that's pretty rude. No." She shook her head. "What are you worried about? If he puts the moves on me again, you can beat him to death with the salt shaker or something. Besides, his girlfriend is going to be with us." The thought made her frown and she moved to the front door. "We have only ten minutes to make it to the inn."

"I forgot about her." Perry let out a sigh.

"How could you forget Mega Blonde?"

Perry followed her out of the house to the SUV he leased through the inn. "I don't know. But I'm not sure she can protect you. Brock might want to add you to his collection, you know."

"What do you take me for?" she asked indignantly.

Perry only shrugged. "He likes a challenge and

you're not easy. Are you attracted to him, Stephanie?"

"I wouldn't be human if I wasn't," she admitted. "But don't worry, Perry. I can take care of myself."

"I suppose so." But he didn't sound convinced. He helped her in, shut the door, and walked around the front bumper to the driver's side. Stephanie studied his grim profile as he turned the key in the ignition. Impulsively, she reached out to touch his arm.

"Listen, Perry," she began, "I know you'd like to fight all my battles, being my big brother, but it's my life."

"Okay, I'm being overprotective," he admitted. "But it's become a habit. I don't always remember that you're all grown up—and you get to mess up, just like everyone else."

"I know." And Stephanie did understand. She didn't resent his concern, because she knew he only wanted the best for her.

Tactfully, he switched the subject to the renovations of the pool area and pool house, which had been his idea. He was positive it would draw more customers, especially the ones who didn't want to ski. The sooner it was done, the sooner they could post photos of it on their website. So far, Brock hadn't vetoed the plan, which made tonight very important.

The inn had two restaurants, but the formal dining room was only open during the evening hours. Yet it was rarely empty. After spending the day hiking, skiing, or cycling, guests seem to welcome the chance to dress up a little and enjoy an excellent meal. Locals often booked tables as well, which made reservations almost a necessity. This Friday was no exception.

After leaving her jacket at the coat check, Stephanie let Perry lead her to the table where Brock and his blonde were waiting. He rose at their approach, his good manners and dark elegance impressing Stephanie, who tried not to show it. A ghost of a smile touched his mouth as he met her eyes. She felt oddly breathless, but her reflection in the mirrored wall didn't show it.

"Have you been waiting long?" Perry asked, more out of politeness than concern that they were late.

"No, we just got here. Perry, this is Helen Collins," Brock made the introductions. "Perry Hall is my manager. And you remember his sister, Stephanie."

Stephanie got no more than a cursory glance from the blonde, who did manage to smile at Perry. It was obvious that Helen resented their presence. She had probably looked forward to having Brock all to herself, Stephanie realized.

The little surge of gladness she felt was the result of suppressed jealousy. The discovery brought Stephanie briefly to her senses. She wasn't going to spend the entire evening lost in envy of the attention Brock paid to Helen.

"Sit here, Perry." Brock indicated the empty chair to his left—which left the chair opposite him for Stephanie.

She would have to face him through dinner, and she knew she would have to guard against staring at him. Something told her Helen Collins wouldn't be very talkative.

Her prediction proved accurate. Courtesy demanded that Stephanie make some attempt at small talk and ask where Helen was from, and all that. The other girl's replies were halfhearted at best, and she didn't seem interested in keeping the conversation going. Stephanie gave up soon enough.

She sat through most of dinner listening to the two men discuss the renovation plans, mentally adding up the costs to keep from getting bored. She was fascinated by Brock's quick mind, and his shrewd assessments of the project—and rather proud of Perry's ability to keep up with him.

But it became increasingly obvious that Helen didn't share Stephanie's appreciation of the conversation. Helen began studying the wine list, just for something to do when she wasn't staring limpidly into Brock's eyes, practically leaning on him as if to invite his embrace. Brock's reaction was a mixture of aloofness, tolerance, and amusement.

Occasionally his glance did stray to Stephanie, but he made no attempt to flirt with her. She was glad, because it would have interfered with the business discussion he was having with her brother.

After the dinner plates were removed, the waiter wheeled the dessert cart to the table. "Aren't you going to have something, Brock?" Helen protested when everyone ordered something except him.

"No." He gave her a lazy smile that remained when he glanced around the table. "I'll have my dessert later." His gaze lingered for a fraction of a second on Stephanie.

She instantly remembered his oh-so-suave remark about saving her for dessert, and fought an unsettling nervousness as she quickly dropped her gaze to the bowl of sweetened fresh fruit in front of her.

She felt constantly off balance in Brock's presence—but she'd better learn to keep both feet solidly on the ground whenever he was around. It was the only way she would survive this tumultuous interlude.

"The dining room closes at ten, you know," Stephanie said. "If you want dessert, you should order now."

"Now?" His mouth twitched with a smile as his gaze dared her to repeat that challenge. "I'd rather have it later. If I get a craving for something sweet, I'll simply raid the refrigerator."

"If you'd like, I can have a selection sent up to your suite," Perry suggested, and Stephanie nearly choked on a strawberry.

"Thanks." There was a wealth of understated meaning in Brock's bland tone. "I'll keep that in mind." The waiter was at his elbow with the silver coffeepot. "Yes, black, please."

When they finished their coffee and dessert, it was decided that Perry would contact the architect and arrange an early meeting on Saturday morning. Brock had changes he wanted made in the plans but his final approval seemed to be a sure thing. Stephanie smiled at her brother, proud of him all over again.

"Good work," Brock said, with genuine warmth. "I get the feeling your talents are being underutilized, Perry. So tell me—is this your ambition? To be in charge of a place like this?"

Perry hesitated, darting a look at Stephanie. His uncertainty was obvious. "Well, maybe not my only ambition, but I like it here, yeah. It's challenging work—and always different."

"That's a diplomatic answer. Now, what's the truth?" Brock asked.

"That is the truth," Perry laughed but insincerely.

Stephanie decided it was time to say something. "The truth is that Perry has always wanted to go to law school." She ignored the silencing look Perry sent her way.

"What stopped you?" Brock inquired. He seemed to feel entitled to say whatever he wanted, Stephanie noted with annoyance.

"My father had a skiing accident. I was needed at home," her brother explained simply.

Stephanie quickly changed the subject, since it was her fault Perry had been put on the spot like that. "Hey, guys, did you see the long-range forecast?" she chirped. "We're supposed to get a ton of snow this winter. They're predicting that New Hampshire will have its best ski season to date."

"Yeah, the reservations show it," Perry said, sounding relieved. "We're booked solid through March."

"I noticed." Brock went along with the new topic, but Helen merely continued to examine her cuticles with a bored expression.

"Excuse me," she finally said, pushing away from the table. "I'm going to the little girls' room and freshen my lipstick."

Brock caught at her hand. "We'll meet you in the lounge. Don't be long."

Helen's sullen look was immediately replaced by a bright smile. "I won't," the blonde promised and hurried away with a provocative sway of her hips.

"We should be going home," Stephanie murmured to her brother.

"Okay. It is late," he agreed, with a glance at his watch.

"Have one drink with us," Brock insisted. "We haven't toasted your new plan. Using the existing building to install a sauna is a brilliant idea, Perry—we'll save about a hundred thousand right there."

Perry nodded. "I hope so."

"So how about that drink? Will you join us?" Again there was that wide smile, all lazy charm.

After exchanging a glance with Stephanie, Perry agreed. "Just one. Sure, why not?"

Brock nodded. He was at her chair when Stephanie rose. His hand seemed to find its way to her waist to guide her to the side door leading to the lounge. His touch was impersonal, yet warm. She could feel the imprint of his fingers through the material of her dress. The sensation seemed to brand her as his somehow.

The lounge was crowded, as it generally was on the weekends. A dance band was playing—a good one that offered everything from current hits to old standards. During the off-season, the inn had live entertainment only on the weekends. In the winter, when the White Mountains were filled with skiers and snowboarders, they had a group seven nights a week.

Brock found an empty booth in a far corner of

the room. By the time they had ordered a round of drinks, Helen arrived. She ignored his invitation to join them and instead coaxed Brock onto the dance floor. Stephanie watched the blonde get up close and sexy with Brock, and knew she could never compete with such tactics.

"Want to dance? Or is that too weird?" Perry asked. "Just pretend we're eight years old and watching MTV when we were supposed to be sleeping."

Stephanie shook her head. "Oh, yeah, I remember those days. We really thought we could dance. I'm not sure I can get into it without wearing footed pajamas."

"Sure you can."

Stephanie was about to refuse again but one look at Perry's grin made her realize how dispirited she had become in the span of a few minutes. She got up and they managed without looking too embarrassingly awkward. Concentrating on dancing distracted her from the sight of Helen with Brock. And she felt comfortable with Perry, who must have been practicing some moves in the mirror, along with his air guitar routine.

When the song ended, she was breathless and laughing. "Feel better?" Perry smiled as he led her off the dance floor.

"Much better," she said, smiling up at him. "Thanks."

The lights dimmed to blue for a slow number. Her eyes didn't adjust immediately to the change of light, and she had to stop for a minute to keep from running into a table or chair in the semi-darkness.

She saw Brock and Helen on a course parallel with theirs. He bent his head to murmur something to her, but she didn't look too pleased by whatever it was he'd said. Then he left Helen to make her way back to the booth alone and crossed to intercept Stephanie.

"Mind if I have this dance with your sister, Perry?" Brock asked, although Stephanie didn't know why. He had already taken hold of her arm to bring her back to the dance floor.

She was sure Perry answered him but she didn't hear what her brother said. Almost the instant they reached the cleared area, Brock was drawing her into the circle of his arms. As usual, there were more couples on the floor to dance to the slow tunes, so it became less a matter of dancing and more a matter of avoiding others. They were soon lost amid the center of the group.

He folded her arm against his chest while his hand slid up her spine to bring her closer. Stephanie could feel her heart thudding against her ribs as they swayed together, moving their feet without really going anywhere. She was all too aware of the hard wall of his chest and the legs moving with—and sometimes between—hers in rhythm with the music.

When he released her hand to leave it against the lapel of his jacket, Brock seemed to give up pretending that they were dancing. Both of his arms were around her, his fingers spread as they roamed over her shoulders and back, slowly caressing and molding her to him.

Stephanie could barely breathe. This was what she had wanted all evening, yet she couldn't relax.

She felt like a child who had been given candy and was afraid to enjoy it too much, because she knew it was going to be taken away from her.

His chin rubbed against her temple, his breath stirring her hair. A silent whimper of suppressed delight sighed through her when he turned his mouth against her, pressing his lips gently to her temple and then to the curve of her cheekbone.

"You are so sweet, Stephanie. I'd rather have you than—"

"Just don't say *dessert*. Please." Even though she secretly wouldn't mind if he did. In the mood she was in, sappy songs and silly flirting seemed to make a lot of sense.

He found her ear and nuzzled aside the silken chestnut hair covering it, going so far as to tease her earlobe with a slight nip.

In another second she was going to melt. "That feels . . . nice." Not quite the word—*fabulous* was more like it. Her voice wasn't all that strong, her words coming out in a taut whisper.

"Is that right?" His mouth curved against the skin of her cheek.

All she had to do was lift her head and Brock would find her lips, but she lowered her chin a fraction of an inch. Her eyes were closed by the gentle brush of his mouth across her lashes.

"Any member of the opposite sex would satisfy you when you're in an amorous mood," she said softly, though she knew it was true. Brock was pursuing her simply because she was new, not because he thought she was anything special. It was just a fact.

"But you're the one in my arms. Why don't you

satisfy me?" he said, his tone both soft and challenging.

Okay, this was getting much too personal—but her heart beat faster at the thought of satisfying him and being satisfied by him. The word for Brock was *virile*. She could imagine the devastation his practiced skill could wreak if she let herself be carried away by it. Someone jostled her shoulder as the crowd moved around them and her head lifted with surprise.

In the next second, she was immobilized by the touch of his mouth against the corner of her lips. Then she was turning to seek the completeness of it, mindless of the others around them. It was a devouring kiss, hard and demanding, ending within seconds after it had begun. It hadn't seemed to help that she had both feet on the floor. Discretion had been swept aside so easily.

"Do you do this with all the women you dance with? First Helen, now me. Who's next?" She found the strength to mock him, although her voice was a little shaky.

Her head was still tipped back, enabling her to look into his eyes. The dim light in the lounge made his black pupils larger, leaving a thin silver ring around them. He was smiling at her with obvious satisfaction and supreme confidence, sure of his ability to seduce her.

Heart of glass—Stephanie suddenly remembered that old song with a feeling of chagrin. Hers was transparent, but her pride was injured that she was such an easy conquest. But was there a woman born who could deny his attraction for long?

"Nobody's next. You're the one I want. And I

think you want me, even though you seem so cool and composed," Brock said. Cool? Composed? Not her. Not now. His hand moved to caress her neck, stopping when it found her pulse point. She felt it hammering against his fingertips. "Your pulse is racing. Feel what you're doing to me."

Taking her fingers, he brought them to his neck and pressed them to the throbbing vein. She felt its wild heat, and its swift tempo, so like her own. Had she disturbed him? Or was it only desire? The vital warmth of his skin was irresistible.

"Your hand feels cool," he murmured.

That seemed impossible when she felt hot all over. When she tried to withdraw her fingers from his grasp, it tightened. He lifted her hand to his mouth and sensually kissed the center of her palm.

"I want you, Stephanie," he said as the last note of the song faded and the lights changed color again.

The sudden murmur of voices shattered the intimacy of the moment. Stephanie didn't have to find an answer to that heady comment as the exiting dancers forced them apart. He kept his hold on her hand while she let the crowd move them both off the floor.

Fixing her gaze on Perry in the far booth, she weaved her way through the tables. Before she reached it, she gave a little tug to free her hand from Brock's grip. He let it go without protest. She didn't squarely meet the look her brother gave her when she slid onto the booth seat beside him. Her glance darted across the table to Helen, whose sulky expression said it all.

"My, my. Have you fulfilled your social obligations for the evening, Brock?" Helen's irritation at being left on her own was perfectly clear.

"Stop bitching, Helen." As he sat down, he stretched his arm across the backrest behind her and picked up his drink. "You know this is a business trip." It was an unsubtle reminder, its steel edge cloaked in velvet tones.

Over the rim of his glass, his gaze locked with Stephanie's. She picked up his mood of dissatisfaction and his underlying desire, tempered with patience. She took a sip of her own drink, but the ice had melted, diluting it and leaving it flat and tasteless. She set it down and pushed it aside to glance at her brother.

"It's getting late, Perry. We should be going." Knowing he would agree, she rose and moved aside so he could slide out.

"Okay. Right. See you in the morning, Brock." He shook hands with Brock, who was also standing.

"It was a pleasure to meet you, Helen." Stephanie nodded at the blonde, not caring that it was only a polite phrase that she offered. Helen's only response was an indifferent glance.

"You're leaving on Sunday, aren't you?" Stephanie asked Brock.

"Yes, late in the afternoon," he acknowledged with a slight narrowing of his gaze.

"Well, I probably won't see you again before you leave, so have a safe trip." She placed her hand in his.

Brock held on to it when she would have withdrawn it. "Aren't you working tomorrow?"

"No." Conscious of Perry at her side, she sent her brother a sideways glance, smiling. "I have a great boss. He gives me the weekends off so I can do his laundry and clean the house."

"Hey, I do my share," Perry protested. "I wouldn't make a domestic slave out of my own sister. She'd put my socks in the garbage disposal if I did."

Brock laughed and let go of her hand. "I bet she would. Good night, all. Perry, I'll see you in the morning around eight."

Before they had taken a step away from the booth, Brock was sitting down and turning his attention to Helen, who was suddenly all smiles. Stephanie tried desperately not to remember that only moments before, he had been holding her in his arms. Now someone else was going to satisfy him. She didn't do a very good job of convincing herself that she was the lucky one, walking away relatively unscathed.

They stopped at the coat check for Stephanie's jacket and Perry's overcoat. Both were silent as they walked outside into the crisp autumn night and headed for the SUV.

Only one thing was said during the drive home, and Perry said it. "I hope you know what you're doing, Stephanie."

"So do I," she sighed.

CHAPTER 4

The dirty breakfast dishes were stacked in the sink. Stephanie paused at the counter to drink the last swallow of coffee from her cup. Her gaze automatically wandered out of the window above the sink to the foothills of the White Mountains, emblazoned with the reds and golds of autumn.

In the back of the old farmhouse, a brook rushed through the rolling acreage, complete with a romantic stone bridge. Cords of firewood were stacked near the back door of the house in readiness for the long New England winter, when a cozy fire could make all the difference in a bleak day.

Sighing, she turned away from the beauty of the clear autumn morning and set her cup with the rest of the dishes. She'd wash them later. Right now she wanted the hot water for the first load of clothes.

The back porch doubled as the washroom; a washer and a dryer were ensconced in one corner.

The floor was piled with laundry baskets and heaps of dirty clothes that Stephanie set about separating into individual loads, tossing the whites directly into the washing machine.

The day was so nice, she could hang the clothes on the line to dry. She liked the old-fashioned method—pegging out the laundry in the sun was very soothing. Besides, the clothes always smelled so much cleaner and fresher that way.

She pushed the sleeves of her old gray sweatshirt up to her elbows. It was one of Perry's, which meant it was several sizes too large for her, but it was comfortable to work in and it didn't matter if she spilled bleach on it. Her blue jeans were faded and shrunk from numerous washings, and the softened denim hugged her slender hips and thighs like a second skin.

Her hair was pulled away from her face into a ridiculously short ponytail, held with a piece of blue yarn. She hadn't bothered with makeup. By the time she washed the clothes, dusted the furniture, and swept the floors of the two-story farmhouse, there wouldn't be any trace of it left, anyway. Besides, the only one who came on Saturday mornings was Mrs. Hammermill with fresh eggs for the week.

When there was a knock at the front door, Stephanie didn't hesitate over who it might be. "Come in!" she shouted, and continued separating the clothes. At the sound of the door opening, then closing, she added, "I'm in the kitchen, Mrs. Hammermill," which was close enough to her location. "You can put the eggs on the counter. If you have an extra dozen, I'll take them. Perry wanted an angel food cake and I thought I'd make one from scratch this afternoon."

There was a movement in the doorway to the porch but Stephanie didn't glance up. She was busy examining the white shirt that Perry had somehow managed to mark up with ballpoint ink.

"Oh, no. You don't happen to know how to get out ink stains, do you?" She frowned. "Not the first time—" She looked up and saw Brock leaning a shoulder against the doorjamb, his arms crossed. She froze at the sight of him, startled. "Brock!"

"Try a stain stick. My assistant swears by hers. She says it even gets out chili sauce." There was a trace of amusement in his voice. He was dressed casually but managed to be just as devastatingly attractive as usual.

It wasn't fair, Stephanie thought crossly, especially considering what she had on. Her gaze flew past him to the cat clock on the wall, its switching tail serving as a pendulum. It was a few minutes before half-past eight.

"What are you doing here? How did you find out where we lived?" she asked in confusion, still clutching the shirt and standing amid the piles of dirty clothes. "I guess Perry told you." He nodded. "I thought you were—"

"The egg lady? Yes, I know." He finished the sentence for her and uncrossed his arms to stand up straight. "The answer to your question should be obvious. I came to see you."

"Yes, but . . . you were supposed to meet Perry this morning," Stephanie said in vague protest.

"I did, for a few minutes. Didn't take long—your brother's amazingly organized."

"Oh—well, I'll tell him you said that," Stephanie replied, feeling amazingly *dis*organized, not to mention disheveled.

"Thanks. Now, are you going to come here? Or am I going to have to wade through all those clothes to get to you?" His tone was faintly mocking.

Stephanie set the shirt over the side of the washing machine. She caught a glimpse of her reflection in the cracked mirror they kept in there, regretting her sloppy sweatshirt and faded jeans. Her face felt just plain bare, minus even lipstick.

"You should have called before coming over." Raising a hand to her ponytail, she stepped over the pile of clothes blocking her path to the doorway and Brock.

"If I had, I wouldn't have gotten a chance to see this domestic scene." Brock reached out to take the hand she was balancing with and pulled her into his arms, locking her hands behind her back while he studied her upturned face. "And you know something? You look very sexy just the way you are right now."

It wasn't exactly the compliment she wanted to hear as she turned her head away to let his kiss land on her cheek and pushed her way past him into the kitchen. The floor seemed to roll under her feet, but she knew it was only her knees quaking.

"I wasn't trying to," she declared and lifted both her hands to untie the knotted yarn around her ponytail. But she had tied it tight and the knot defied her trembling attempt to loosen it.

When she felt Brock's fingers push hers out of

the way, she tried to move past, but he put a firm hand on her shoulder to keep her in place. "Hold still," he ordered, and Stephanie stood quietly while he worked the yarn free of the knot. When it was untied, he turned her around and combed her hair into place with his fingers. "How's that?" he asked with a gleam of lazy pleasure in his gray eyes.

But he didn't wait for her to answer—he bent his head to cover her lips with his mouth, skillfully parting them as he curved her into his arms. Her fingers curled into the wool of his sweater, clinging to the only solid thing she could find in the deepening intensity of his kiss. She was exposed to a whole set of raw, new emotions that had her straining toward him in trembling need. He dragged his mouth across her cheek to her ear.

"Did you really think you wouldn't see me again before I left?" he sounded almost angry.

"I'm not sure if I believed it or not," Stephanie admitted in a soft voice. She kept her eyes blissfully closed while he nibbled his way down her neck to her shoulder.

"Where are your parents? Who else are you expecting besides the egg lady?" he demanded.

"My parents are dead," she whispered and wondered why he didn't know that. "There's only Mrs. Hammermill. She usually comes before nine."

She felt as well as heard the deep breath Brock took before he lifted his head to smile tightly at her. "In that case, why don't you fix me some breakfast? I didn't bother to eat before I came over. I thought you might do your shopping in the morning and I didn't want to miss you."

Not knowing how much she dared to read into

that statement—and a little annoyed with him for assuming she had nothing better to do than cook for him, Stephanie decided not to comment on any of it. "Uh—do you want bacon and eggs?" she asked instead. Might as well keep this unexpected encounter simple.

"What I want, I can't have at the moment." His hands slid up her back, subtly pressing her closer to him before he released her and stepped away. "Sure. Bacon and eggs will do."

"How do you like 'em?" She walked to the refrigerator, glad to have something to do. She took out the package of bacon and the last two eggs from the shelf.

"Sunny side up and crisp bacon, please."

She spied the pitcher of orange juice on the refrigerator shelf. "Juice?"

"No, thanks. Too healthy." Brock came to stand beside her while she laid the bacon strips in the skillet.

When it began to sizzle, she walked to the cupboard on the other side of him and took down a place setting. She glanced uncertainly at the kitchen table, then at him. "Would you like to eat in the dining room?" she suggested.

"No," he said with a decisive shake of his head. "I have no intention of letting you out of my sight."

His look, as well as his answer, was a little weird, but it occurred to her that he might feel as awkward as she did underneath all that macho confidence. The thought was comforting and she smiled as she arranged the plate and cutlery on the gingham cloth–covered kitchen table. She walked back to the stove to turn the bacon.

"When was the last time you had breakfast in somebody's kitchen?" she asked curiously, giving him a sidelong glance.

"Probably not since I was a kid," he admitted, as Stephanie had suspected. "Are you a good cook?"

"Bacon and eggs aren't too complicated. And no, I'm not as good a cook as Perry, but he's had a lot more practice." The bacon was beginning to brown nicely, so Stephanie kept turning it.

Brock watched her with interest. "Why was that?"

"Our mom died when I was only four. Since our dad had to work two jobs to support us, Perry had to do the cooking and look after me."

The memory of those days was poignant and it was difficult to concentrate on what she was doing. She managed to rescue the bacon before it was burned and set it aside to drain on a paper towel.

"What did your father do?"

"He considered himself a ski instructor, but mostly he earned money as a bartender and cutting firewood . . . until his accident." She cracked the eggs and cooked them in fresh butter in a different pan.

"Ah. That would be the accident that forced your brother to give up his law career," Brock guessed.

"Yes, Dad was crippled in a skiing accident." She looked over her shoulder, a curious frown knitting her forehead. "Perry's worked for you for five years. You must know all that."

He gave her a level look. "Actually, I didn't. I don't bother to inquire about my employees' personal lives unless it affects their work. Your brother's performance evaluations are always great, and the inn turns a healthy profit. He works really hard and he likes to do things right."

"That's Perry," Stephanie admitted. "But you must want to know something about their backgrounds," Stephanie insisted.

"Only their qualifications for their particular position. As long as they get results, I couldn't care less who or what they are as individuals." There was a curve to his mouth, but it wasn't a smile. "You think that's a callous attitude, don't you?"

She focused on the eggs in the pan, the bright yellow yolks staring back at her. "Yes, I do."

Brock shrugged. "White Boar Inn represents one-half of one percent of Canfield Enterprises' annual gross earnings. Maybe that will give you an idea of how many Perry Halls I have working for me," he suggested. "I couldn't possibly become involved or know much about their personal lives without losing perspective on my overall responsibility. By rights, I should sell the inn."

His indifference nettled her. "Why don't you?" She could see the logic in his argument, but she mentally recoiled from his lack of feeling. A lot of people worked at the White Boar, not just her and Perry, and there weren't enough good jobs to go around in a small New Hampshire town.

The eggs were done, so she moved away to fetch his plate from the table and slid them onto it with the aid of a spatula.

"For personal reasons," Brock answered. Stephanie didn't think he intended to explain what they were, but she was wrong. "My parents spent their honeymoon at the White Boar when they eloped. He bought it for her on their sixth anniversary. He was the one who decreed that the honeymoon suite would be reserved only for Canfields."

"Oh, okay. I could see why you'd be reluctant to sell it." Her smile was soft and radiant when she gazed at him, touched by this unexpected display of sentiment.

"Six months after they bought it, they went through a tough divorce that lasted two years. My mother remarried—several times. My father collects girlfriends." Brock watched her smile fade almost with satisfaction.

"I see. Is he . . . is he living?" Averting her gaze, Stephanie walked past him, carrying the plate of bacon and eggs to the table.

"Yes. He's retired to the south of France. I believe his current lady is a twenty-eight-year-old model. In other words, on the old side for a model, but too young for him. Of course, he refers to her as his protégée."

How disgusting is that? She didn't say it, but she wanted to. "How, um, nice. Coffee?" When she set his plate down, she searched her mind for an excuse to find something else to do.

"Black with no sugar, thanks."

Stephanie moved away from the table as he sat down to eat. "You must not have had a very happy childhood," she guessed.

"That depends on your definition of *happy*. My grandfather raised me even before my parents were divorced. They were always away on vacation in some far-off corner of the world."

"So you didn't see too much of them." She knew

she was stating the obvious, but she couldn't just stand there and watch him eat in silence.

"No. The divorce didn't seem like such a big deal. Most of the time I was away at school or else with my grandfather. From the day I was born it was expected that I would take over the company, and when my grandfather died a few years ago, that's exactly what I did."

Stephanie poured two cups and carried them to the table. "And the last time you ate in somebody's kitchen, that was with your grandfather?"

"Hardly." Brock's laugh was curt. "He had all his meals at his desk unless it was a business dinner. No, I spent a week with a friend from school." He started eating like someone was going to take the food away any minute.

"So why don't you sell the inn?" Stephanie watched him, half afraid to hear his answer. "Obviously you have no sentimental attachment to it."

Brock was slow to reply, but it wasn't due to any hesitancy. "It serves as a useful reminder of a fundamental fact."

"Which is?"

"Intimate relationships don't necessarily last forever no matter how strong the attachment may appear on the surface."

Stephanie thought that over for a few seconds. "You come up here about four times a year. But I've never heard of you bringing the same woman twice. Is that why?" The question only prompted another. "And why did you come to see me when you've got Mega Blonde back at the suite?"

Brock grinned. "Is that what you call her? It fits."

Stephanie blushed. "That kind of slipped out. Sorry."

"No need to be. Anyway, I didn't want to be with her. I wanted to be with you." He actually chuckled. "You're having a hard time trying to understand me, aren't you? Helen isn't the only one—I have a pretty healthy sex drive."

Stephanie held up a hand. "TMI—too much information. You can stop bragging now."

"I'm not bragging. And I don't pretend that a hookup like that is anything other than physical, meaning sexual. Helen got the ground rules from the beginning—no emotional claims on me or my time. In return, I treat her well, per her terms. Does that shock you? It shouldn't. Happens all the time."

Stephanie just couldn't comprehend how any feeling, intelligent person could set such cold-blooded conditions for a relationship. "I'm sure you can rationalize any behavior," she replied stiffly.

Leaning forward in his chair, Brock reached for her hand and gripped it firmly in his. The intensity of his gaze was unsettling. "What I'm not making clear to you, Stephanie, is how difficult it is for me to have the kind of relationship you would call normal—with any woman. I just don't have the time."

He let go of her hand as a tense muscle flexed in his jaw. "Tomorrow I'm driving to New York. Flying is quicker and I could have the company jet pick me up at the airport near here, but I need some downtime. When I get to Manhattan, I might hear about a West Coast merger or acquisition that would take me out there—for a month, maybe two. Or just for a day, if the details can be wrapped up online instead of in time-consuming meetings. I never know what's going to happen next."

"Okay, okay. I get the idea. You're a very important man. Well, some of us peasants have laundry to do, so you'd better finish up those eggs, even if you are the king of the world."

He grinned again. "No one talks to me that way, you know."

"Well, somebody should," Stephanie said tartly. Brock gave her a look that she couldn't interpret—not that she wanted to.

"Anyway, I have hotel suites in a dozen countries and I own a couple of houses that I'm never in. Might be six months before I see you again. So if relationships are really important to you, I'm not the right guy."

"Thanks for the warning. I mean, I didn't think you were Mr. Commitment—I'm not that naïve." She stopped, her voice choked, the futility of her feelings swamping her. "So it's hopeless, huh?"

He paused a second before continuing with his breakfast. "Sometimes I forget that it is, but the inn reminds me . . . every month when I see the name on the report."

"Oh—so that's why you said you didn't want an heir—that it was time the Canfield name died," she said, suddenly understanding.

"No one should have this much responsibility unless he wants it," Brock stated flatly.

"Well, getting back to what we were just talking about—you could sell," Stephanie suggested hesitantly.

"I'm good at what I do, unfortunately. It's not

like I could just quit and grow organic pumpkins
or something." His mouth slanted in a half-smile.
"I doubt if I could make you understand that. I
wouldn't change my life or my business, even if I
had the choice." He wiped his mouth with a napkin. "Great breakfast. Thanks. Is there more coffee?"

"Yes, of course." A little numbly, Stephanie took
his cup. After all those explanations, she was still
trying to figure out where she might fit into his
life. She scolded herself silently for even considering the possibility.

Brock must have read the bewilderment in her
eyes, because he reached out to stop her when she
started to pass his chair, his hand resting lightly on
her forearm. "When I find something I want, I
reach out and grab it, Stephanie, because it might
not be there the next time I come back. I live hard
and fast—and I love the same way. If I forget to say
you're beautiful or that your eyes are the color of
the morning sky, it isn't because I don't think of it.
I just don't waste time."

"Yes, I—" Her reply was interrupted by a knock
at the front door. It startled her until she realized
who it was. "It's Mrs. Hammermill."

"The egg lady." Brock nodded and dropped his
hands to leave Stephanie free to answer the door.

Setting his cup down, she walked toward the living room. "Hi! Come in!" The front door opened
to admit a short, stout woman in a knit hat. Two
dozen eggs were balanced under one arm on a
carrying crate.

"Sorry I'm late but hubby's been sick with the
flu. I've been doin' his chores as well as my own."

"I hope he's feeling better soon," Stephanie murmured and led the way into the kitchen. Mrs. Hammermill stopped short at the sight of a strange man and eyed him suspiciously. Stephanie quickly made the introductions.

Mrs. Hammermill was instantly all smiles. "Maybe you can talk to Perry about letting me supply the eggs for the restaurant. I would have to buy some more layers, but—"

"I'll talk to him about it," Brock assured her. Taking the egg money out of the jar on the counter, Stephanie paid the woman and tactfully hurried her on her way. She almost regretted identifying Brock, but the gossip about a strange man would have been worse.

After she had shown the woman out, Stephanie returned to the kitchen. "Sorry about that," she said with a wry smile. "What she really wants to do is latch onto someone who'll finance her egg business. She would have to buy more laying hens, which means she'd need to build a new coop—a big one—as well as the initial cost of more grain. She's a nice lady but I don't think you want to go into partnership in the egg business." At the table she stopped to stack the dishes and add them to those in the sink waiting to be washed.

"You're right. I'm not interested in chickens, eggs—or the dishes. In fact—" Brock took hold of her hand and pulled her to his chair and onto his lap. "I have only one thing on my mind—you."

Thrown off balance by his move, Stephanie was dependent on the supporting steel of his arms. Her pulse fluttered wildly as he made a sound under his breath, almost like a groan. Her arms encircled his neck, her hands seeking the irresistible thickness of his dark hair.

Their kiss was sensual and exploring, their mouths meeting in delighted discovery, the slow, heady joy of it insulating Stephanie from all thought. In the hard cradle of his lap, she felt the powerful muscles of his thighs beneath her own, the flatness of his stomach and breadth of his chest and shoulders.

As he kissed her, Brock didn't miss any sensitive spot, touching on her lips and cheek, the line of her jaw and the hollow under her ear, setting afire an urgent yearning within her. Arousing as his kisses were, she was stimulated by the chance to let her lips wander intimately over his smooth cheek and jaw, fragrant with a subtle aftershave. It was a wildly novel experience to have this freedom for sensual exploration.

His caressing hands became impatient with the thick, loose folds of her large sweatshirt. When he lifted the hem to expose her bare midriff, Stephanie drew in a breath of startled surprise that was never quite completed. Her flesh tensed under the initial touch of his hand, then melted at its firm caress.

He seemed intent on personally exploring every naked inch of her ribs and shoulders. She was quivering, her breasts straining against the lacy material of the confining bra. When he covered one with his palm, there was a rushing release of tension that was wildly gratifying.

Yet as his fingers sought the back clasp of her bra, sanity returned. She had let herself be carried away without knowing for certain that this was something she wanted. She drew away from him, pressing her hands against his chest for breathing space while she tried to clear her head of this heart-pounding passion.

"Stephanie." His voice both coaxed and commanded as he planted a kiss on her exposed shoulder.

"No." She gulped in the negative and swung off his lap, taking a couple of quick steps away from his chair while she pulled her sweatshirt down over her hips. "The first time I saw you, I knew I had to keep both feet on the ground or you'd knock me right off them. Literally." Stephanie laughed, shakily, trying to make a joke out of it even though she knew it was the absolute truth.

"I want you, Stephanie. I told you that last night," Brock reminded her. And Stephanie walked to the kitchen counter, keeping her back to him, in a weak attempt to escape the heady seduction of his voice. "If anything, it's more true right now."

The scrape of the chair leg told her he had gotten up, and she grabbed hold of the edge of the counter, needing to hang on to something. "It's all happening too fast for me," she tried to explain without sounding as desperate as she felt. "You don't understand, Brock. I can't be as casual about sex as you are."

"How much do you know about sex, Stephanie?" When he spoke, she realized he was directly behind her, his tone steady with patience and confidence.

Her knuckles were white from gripping the counter edge in an effort to keep from turning around. If she did, she knew she would be lost. To counter his sureness, she became sharp and defensive. "Not as much as you, I'm sure."

"What's that supposed to mean?" His voice was dangerously low. His fingers gripped her shoulders and forced her to turn around. She was rigid in his hold but she didn't resist him. Under the narrowed gaze of his gray eyes, her head was thrown warily back. He scowled down at her.

"Sex is just a physical act to you. I don't take it that lightly," she said, defending her hesitation and uncertainty.

He studied her face for such a long time that she felt herself growing hot.

"Are you a virgin, Stephanie?" He seemed to doubt the accuracy of his conclusion.

"Should I apologize if I am?" The challenge was a little angry, a little hurt, and a little defiant.

"How old are you?" His hands stroked her shoulders.

"Twenty-two," she answered stiffly.

"Okay. But—where did you grow up? In a convent?" Brock's tone was incredulous. "I didn't know there were any twenty-two-year-old virgins."

His remark ignited her temper. "Well, I had other things on my mind. My father's skiing accident left him almost completely paralyzed. I had to feed him, bathe him, dress him, read to him, do everything for him, for five years. Daddy never complained for himself, but he used to cry because I didn't go out and have fun. Perry took care of him, too, whenever he was home, but he never knew when an emergency would come up and he'd have to go to the inn. I dated now and then, yeah." She was angry and didn't attempt to conceal it. "But who wants to get serious about someone with a sick father? We couldn't afford to hire anyone to take care of him full-time. I'm not complaining about those five years. I don't regret a single minute of that time, because it brought me closer to my father than I'd ever been. So you can make fun of me if you want—"

He covered her mouth with two fingers to check the indignant tirade. His chiseled features were etched in sober lines. "I'm not making fun of you." He traced the outline of her mouth and became absorbed with the shape of it.

Her anger vanished as if it had never existed.

"It's just rare to meet someone with your passionate nature who hasn't, um, been around. It doesn't change anything." His gaze lifted to catch her look and hold it. The dark silver glitter of his eyes dazzled her. "I'm going to keep trying to get you into bed. Knowing I would be the first just makes me that much more determined."

Very slightly, his fingers lifted her chin. Then his mouth closed onto hers in consummation of his promise. A deep surge of desire rose within her, like a slow-burning flame fanned to burn hotter.

Brock gathered her into his arms, unhurriedly, arching her backward, his hips pinning her to the counter. The wayward caress of his hands was keenly pleasurable. He shifted his attention to the pulse quivering so wildly in her throat.

"Whose sweatshirt is this?" he muttered when his hand became tangled in the loose folds.

"Perry's." It was a shy admission, shattered by her vivid awareness of his stark masculinity.

"This has got to go." He pulled at it, saying the words against her neck, punctuating them with kisses. "From now on, if you wear a man's clothes, they're going to be mine."

"Whatever you say," she whispered with a throbbing ache in her voice. She was boneless and pliant in his arms, her forehead resting weakly against his shoulder while he rained sweet pleasure on the sensitive skin of her neck and throat.

"You know what I say." Brock seized on her submissive response, his tone fiercely low and urgent. "I've been saying it every time I looked at you or touched you. I want to make love to you—here and now. You have both feet on the floor. What do *you* want?"

But it wasn't that simple. Not for Stephanie. Not even with the twisting, fearful rawness knotting her insides. The awful confusion kept her from answering him, but he must have felt her stillness and chose not to press the point. Instead he loosened his arms, letting his hands move in a series of restless caresses over her body.

"I've postponed everything until after lunch so we could spend the morning together," he informed her in a slightly thick voice. "But there isn't any way I'm going to be able to stay in this house with you and not . . ." He took a deep breath and released her entirely. "We'd better go for a drive somewhere. At least with my hands on the steering wheel, I'll be able to keep them off you. Go and change, fix yourself up—whatever you want to do. I'll wait for you down here."

Stephanie looked at him, reluctant to agree to his suggestion, but his gray eyes warned her not to protest unless she was willing to accept the alternative. That was something that still confused her.

"I'll only be a few minutes," she promised.

CHAPTER 5

The roads were crowded with the cars of tourists, eager to see the spectacle of the autumn foliage and catch a glimpse of the scenery that defined Yankee New England—wooden covered bridges, church steeples, antique shops, and village squares. The route Brock took became less a planned drive and more a matter of choosing a path with the least resistance.

Stephanie relaxed in the contours of velour-covered seats, enveloped in the luxury of the blue Mercedes. The radio was turned low, its four speakers surrounding her with vibrant sound. A riot of color exploded outside the window: reds and yellows against the backdrop of the White Mountains and a crisp blue sky.

Traffic thinned in the lane ahead of them as Brock made the turn that would take them on the road south through Franconia Notch. An outcropping of granite loomed into view, and Stephanie looked at it a little sadly.

"That's where my friend used to be," she said quietly, breaking the companionable silence.

"What?" Brock looked around but mostly kept his eyes on the road.

"The Great Stone Face. It was a landmark rock formation shaped like a man's profile—it's not there anymore. It crumbled after a hard winter—it had been a symbol of New Hampshire since the year one." She gazed at the jagged edge that was left. "I used to make up stories about him when I was a kid—the way some kids do about the man in the moon, I suppose. Some people want to restore the side of the mountain to the way it used to be. But the Great Stone Face is gone forever."

"Good. I don't need any competition." Brock sent her a sidelong glance that was warm and desiring beneath its teasing.

"At least your heart isn't made of stone like his was." They had passed the spot where the famous profile used to be, immortalized so long ago by Nathaniel Hawthorne in his classic *The Great Stone Face*.

Stephanie settled back into her seat again, letting her gaze turn to Brock's profile, which was very much there and very alive. Just to look at him made her feel warm. "When I was little, I was sure there was a way to make him come to life, some magic I could perform, like a fairy godmother with an enchanted wand. I wanted him to tell me all the secrets of the world." She laughed softly at her own whimsy.

"Now?" Brock sounded curious, speculative.

Stephanie shrugged. "I grew up, I guess."

"No. All you have to do is touch me and I come to life." His low voice had a sexy undertone, echoed by the sensual gleam in his eye. "I can prove it whenever you want."

Swallowing, Stephanie glanced away, feeling a pleasant rise of heat in her body. She looked restlessly out the window at the passing scenery, seeking escape without wanting to find it. The interior of the luxurious car seemed suddenly very small and intimate. The click of the turn signal startled her, pulling her gaze to Brock.

"I think we could both use some air," he offered by way of explanation.

Before they reached the end of the mountain pass, he turned off and parked at the visitor's lot to the flume. When he turned off the engine, Stephanie opened the passenger door, wanting the invigorating briskness of the autumn air to clear her head. Her senses seemed freed to notice other things around her, and she took a deep breath.

As she waited for Brock to join her, she zipped the front of her cropped jacket. The legs of her jeans came down over her boots, and the short jacket added to her long-limbed looks. The air was cool enough to turn her breath into a frosty vapor.

When Brock reached for her bare hand, she automatically placed it in his, the warmth and firmness of his grip filling her with a pleasant sensation of belonging. His mouth crooked in a faint smile before they set off to join the band of tourists lined up to get on the bus that would take them to the flume.

The endless chatter of the other people negated

the need for them to talk. Stephanie didn't mind. It left her free to savor the sensation of being squeezed close to Brock on the bus seat so a third passenger would have a place to sit.

His arm was around her, her shoulder resting against the unbuttoned front of his parka, the muscled length of his thigh and hip imprinted on her own. There was safety in the knowledge that she was surrounded by people, allowing her to simply enjoy the closeness, now that the temptation to take it to a more intimate degree had been removed.

As the bus slowed in approach of their destination, Brock murmured in her ear, "If you tease me too much, I'm going to wring your beautiful neck—after I take a bite of it."

Her head turned sharply in alarm. She looked up, relieved to see that he was smiling. The remark had been meant to let her know he was deriving his own kind of pleasure from having her body crushed to his side. He lightly brushed his lips against the wing of her eyebrow in a fleeting kiss.

An older woman behind them whispered to her companion, something about them being a wonderful pair of lovers. Which deepened the corners of Brock's mouth without curving them. Stephanie glanced to the front, feeling a little self-conscious.

When the bus stopped to let them out, neither of them rushed to join the mass exodus. They let the other tourists hurry on ahead while they followed more slowly. Stephanie wasn't as comfortable with the silence between them as she had been. When Brock removed his hand from the

back of her waist to button his parka, she paused
with him. Ahead was the railed sidewalk winding
through the cool shadows of the gorge.

"It's really better to come in the summer when
it's hot," she said to fill the silence. "Then you can
appreciate the coolness and the shade."

"If you want to get warm, just let me know. I can
help with that." When she smiled at him, he
reached out to pull her toward him, lightly strok-
ing her cheek. He smiled gently. "You don't know
what to do next, do you?"

"Um—no. I assume you're talking about—" she
stopped, embarrassed.

"Sex. Sorry. I'm just saying what's on my mind,"
Brock stated, gazing deep into her blue eyes. "On
my mind every time I'm near you." The vibrancy
of his low voice made her breath catch. "Does that
bother you?"

"Yes. But in a good way. I think—I'm pretty confused. I guess you noticed," she said ruefully.

"Don't worry." He spoke gently, his mouth
swooping down to feel the coolness of her lips
against his own. Straightening, Brock wrapped an
arm around her shoulders to turn her toward the
boardwalk.

They entered the deep ravine in silence, walking side by side until the boardwalk narrowed and
Stephanie moved ahead. On both sides, sheer rock
walls towered upward nearly seventy feet. Moss
grew thickly on the moist rock, hugging the stri-
ated crevices. In the spring and summer, delicate
and rare mountain flowers blossomed in the shadowy darkness of the gorge.

A laughing stream tumbled over the rock bed

running alongside and below the boardwalk. The long chasm had been carved by the elemental forces of nature and the swift waters of the Pemigewasset River, centuries before the glaciers had moved across the land.

The cool temperature and the high humidity combined to pierce the bones with a chilling dampness. Stephanie shoved her hands deep into the pockets of her jacket to protect them from the numbing cold. They strolled along the boardwalk that twisted and curved with the ravine. Red and gold leaves swirled downward from the trees high overhead to float in the little stream like colorful toy boats.

Stephanie paused at the end of the flume where the boardwalk made a right-angle turn with the gorge. Leaning against the railing, she gazed down at the stream. A sodden clump of leaves had formed a miniature dam, but the rushing water had found a spillway at one end and was fast eroding the fragile blockage.

"It's peaceful here, isn't it?" She glanced at Brock, standing beside her, leaning a hand on the railing, but it was she who had his undivided attention.

"Have dinner with me tonight, Stephanie," he said suddenly. "Just the two of us. In my suite—with wine, candlelight, and soft music. I'll hire a car and driver, and send Helen wherever the hell she wants to go—Boston, New York, Miami. We'll have the whole night and top it off with breakfast in bed in the morning."

Helen. Definitely someone she didn't want to think about. She must be totally, completely out of her mind to even think about getting involved with a man who could kick a woman out of his bed so easily. Okay, Helen wasn't particularly pleasant, but she was still a human being. Brock didn't really seem to care about anybody but himself.

Yet she could not find the will to fight her incredibly powerful attraction to him. Stephanie moved away, full of doubts that she knew she couldn't ignore, but Brock blocked the attempt, shifting his position to trap her on the rail, one strong hand on either side of her.

"Hey—I met you less than twenty-four hours ago," she said weakly. "You have another woman with you. I can't just pretend you didn't show up with her."

"Helen came along for whatever she can get, Stephanie—as usual. I know it sounds crass and cold, but she doesn't really want me any more than I want her."

"So why is she with you?" Stephanie asked.

"Because I invited her," he said bluntly. "I didn't know you existed. We started fighting the second you walked out the door of the suite."

"Yeah, well—maybe that was because of me."

Brock shook his head. "Helen didn't hear a thing."

Stephanie wasn't convinced. "You brought a woman you don't even like with you, and now you're kicking her out because I happened to catch your eye. That's just crazy."

"Yeah. It is." He began brushing kisses over her neck and cheek, and Stephanie didn't resist this persuasive technique of a master in the art of love. She was conscious of the warmth of his breath and the coolness of his mouth against her skin, making her tingle with awareness.

"Pretend that when we met yesterday afternoon, it was two weeks ago. Dinner was a week ago and this morning was yesterday. Time is something I don't have. We have to make the most of it," Brock said softly.

"Two weeks ago isn't exactly an eternity," she pointed out. "And I'd rather not pretend anything. I hardly know you."

"Just trust me."

She shook her head, beset by doubt.

"Stay with me, Stephanie. We'll have all night to get to know each other—in every way there is."

She shuddered with exquisite longing and drew back, tossing her head with a wary kind of defiance. "You don't understand, Brock. I want to be something more to you than just someone you slept with in New Hampshire." A dry leaf fluttered down in a lazy spiral and she caught it and crumpled it in her hand. "You won't remember me any more than you'll remember this leaf."

His look became stony as he straightened from the railing. "All right," he said grimly. "Forget about tonight. I can understand why you would want to wait—and trying to rush you into it was a mistake." His balled fists sought the pockets of his parka and he put a little distance between them. "Look, I have to leave right after lunch tomorrow—by noon at the latest. What are you doing in the morning?"

The question caught Stephanie off guard. "I . . . I usually go to church. Me and the other local virgins. We sit in a special section. No guys."

"Right." He had to smile but there was a bleakness in his gray eyes that chilled her. "Okay. I suppose you're going to ask me to come with you. But I'd still be thinking about you. I don't want to add total hypocrisy to my long list of sins."

Her mouth opened but she couldn't think of anything to say. His hand came out to take her elbow and guide her along the boardwalk. The serene and quiet setting only intensified her mixed feelings.

Not a word was exchanged until the others came back and the bus made its return journey. It seemed to take forever. They walked to the car and Brock started it up. "Will I see you before you leave?" Stephanie risked a glance at him as she asked the question in a subdued voice.

"Not tonight. I haven't got that much self-control. Not where you're concerned."

He didn't even look at her as he reversed out of the parking space. Before he turned onto the road, he let the car idle and looked at her. There was a softening in the hardness of his expression—and a surfacing patience.

"We'll get together in the morning . . . before church. In the meantime"—he pushed back the sleeve of his parka to see his watch—"it's time I was back at the inn. Perry and I are meeting the architect at one."

At the farmhouse, Brock didn't bother to get out of the car. When he looked at her, not moving, Stephanie leaned across the seat to kiss him. His hands didn't touch her and his response to the contact of her lips was minimal, barely warm.

Vaguely dejected, Stephanie walked to the

house and paused at the door to watch Brock drive away. She didn't really blame him for his attitude, but she wasn't going to change her mind just to suit him.

On Sunday morning, Stephanie awakened earlier than usual. Since Brock hadn't given her any indication when he might call or come, she didn't take the chance of being caught unaware. She was dressed, complete with light makeup, when she went downstairs to make coffee and collect the Sunday paper from the doorstep.

She had read most of it without remembering a word and finished her second cup of coffee when she realized how nervous she was. Waiting for the phone to ring or for the sound of a car driving up the lane was an exercise in futility. But knowing that Brock was leaving soon and that she had no idea when he would be coming back weighed heavily on her mind.

A noise in the living room sent her rushing out of the kitchen, sure she had missed hearing Brock's car, but it was a bleary-eyed Perry she encountered.

"Brr, it's cold in here! Why haven't you started the fire?" he grumbled, shivering in his Polarfleece robe. His hair was tousled from his night's sleep, and a pair of old slippers covered his large feet as he moved toward the wood-burning stove. "You're up and dressed early this morning. How come?" He waved aside her hesitant attempt at an answer, kneeling to stuff tinder and small logs inside the cast-iron door of the stove. "I remember.

You told me at supper that Brock was supposed to come over in the morning."

"Yes, he is." While her brother got the fire going, Stephanie walked to the front window to look out. "You got in late last night."

"I know." He didn't offer any explanation. "Coffee on? Is that the Sunday paper?"

"Yes to both questions. I'll bring you a cup."

It wasn't long before the fire was crackling merrily and chasing out the chill in the room. When she returned, he was stretched out in his favorite armchair, his feet on the footstool, his eyes closed. She set his coffee on the lampstand beside him and dropped the sports section in his lap. Perry stirred, slowly opening one eye and yawning.

"Why didn't you sleep later?" Stephanie chided. "You never get up this early." Theoretically, Sundays were his days off, except in winter, but he usually stopped by the inn in the afternoons.

"I'm really bushed," he admitted. "But I woke up and couldn't go back to sleep."

While he sipped at the steaming hot coffee, Stephanie wandered to the hooked rug covering the wide floorboards in front of the fireplace. The living room was large and open, with exposed beams and hand-planed wainscoting. The sliding glass doors, a more recent addition, were decorated with October frost, partially concealing the view of the hills rising behind the house.

"I always think I'm doing well until I come away from a meeting with Brock. That's where I was last night."

Stephanie nodded sympathetically. She knew the feeling.

"He picks my brains until there's nothing left. And he asks so many questions," he sighed.

"About what?" Stephanie turned to study her brother, wondering if Brock had asked about her.

Perry started to answer, then caught her eye. "No, he didn't ask about you. But he did bring up the subject of me giving up going to law school after Dad's accident."

"Why? What did he say?"

"A lot of stuff. Mostly about going back part-time and in summer." His mouth tightened. "Which would take me forever, plus there's the problem of commuting and keeping the inn running smoothly. No, it just isn't possible."

"What else did you talk about?" Stephanie wasn't going to argue about a subject she and Perry had discussed many times. She was too eager for any snippet of information about Brock.

"Everything from how to hire and keep good staff to the renovations to turning it into the most famous ski lodge in New England." Her brother paused. "You know, Stephanie, most of the time I feel like I'm an experienced guy, but last night he was in his suite getting calls from half the world and e-mailing the other half from his laptop. My whole life is centered around the inn, but I doubt that its annual earnings would even pay his travel expenses for a year. We're pretty small potatoes in his business empire. The place could burn down and he'd never miss it."

"Why are you thinking like that?" His defeated attitude wasn't like Perry.

"I don't know. Hell, maybe I'm jealous." He laughed shortly. "There I am, sitting in his suite trying desperately to concentrate on a business discussion, and that blonde keeps waltzing in and out of the bedroom in a robe. I spent more time imagining—"

Stephanie turned pale and he shut up the second he noticed it.

"Sorry, Steph. But don't make a fool of yourself over him."

"Please," she protested softly. "There isn't anything you can say that I haven't told myself already." She turned, needing a few minutes by herself. "Excuse me. I'm going to get more coffee."

When she returned to the living room, Perry was buried in the sports section and hockey updates. Stephanie sat on the sofa to drink her coffee in silence. The minute it was gone she was up, walking to the window to look out. Back and forth she went, too nervous to stay seated, while the grandfather clock ticked away the minutes.

"What's up? Besides you, I mean," Perry remarked on her tenth trip to the window.

"Nothing." She crossed to the fireplace to add another log to the fire.

"It's getting late," he observed. "I'd better get dressed for church. Are you coming?"

She rose and glanced toward the window. "I . . ." Then Stephanie saw the blue Mercedes coming up the drive. "He's here!"

She dashed to the door and was outside by the time Brock stepped from the car. Her smile froze in place when she spied Helen sitting in the passenger seat. Her gaze swung in hurt confusion back to Brock as he approached, his face grim.

"I have to leave. With luck, I'll make it to New

York in time to catch an afternoon flight from JFK to Geneva," he said.

Stephanie couldn't speak but only stared at him with rounded blue eyes. The frosty chill of the October morning wasn't nearly as cold as she felt. He was leaving, and they wouldn't even have the morning together.

"I came to say good-bye," Brock continued. "I should have called, but . . ." His jaw hardened. "I knew this would happen." He grabbed her by the shoulders as if he was going to shake her.

His brusqueness was almost welcome. In the next second, he was yanking her into his arms and giving her a kiss that left no doubt to anyone watching that there was something going on between them. His passion engulfed her, leaving her weak and breathless when he broke the contact.

He turned away to walk to the car, hiding his emotions as he said good-bye.

She couldn't even get the word out—couldn't even say his name. He started the car and was turning it around. Helen had flipped down the visor and was looking into the makeup mirror, pretending not to see Stephanie.

But she didn't move from where she was standing at the door. There was no last glance from Brock. No wave. Nothing. Tears misted her eyes, blurring her vision. She didn't see his car disappear from view down the long lane.

Entering the house, she sensed Perry's concern and spoke quickly. "He had to leave . . . for Geneva." Her voice was choked and very small. Her brother looked at her for a long minute but didn't say anything as he turned to climb the stairs.

Stephanie walked blindly into the kitchen where she cried slow, silent tears.

The north winds came to strip the trees, exposing the dark trunks and branches, and leaving heaps of brown leaves to carpet the ground. The first snow flurry of the season came the last weekend in October. It was even colder when November arrived.

Stephanie had written Brock two letters, avoiding the easy connection of e-mail and sticking to news of the inn, minus any personal messages. The only address she had was the one the monthly reports were sent to. She couldn't be sure if they would reach him. Last week, she had sent only a postcard.

No reply came, and she convinced herself that he had forgotten her. But she couldn't shake the feeling that she had been on the brink of discovering something wonderful, only to lose it.

Her office phone rang and she allowed herself the luxury of a nice, long, lugubrious sigh before she answered it. "Stephanie Hall, White Boar Inn. May I help you?"

"How are you?" a familiar male voice inquired.

Stephanie tightened her grip on the receiver. "Brock?" She could feel her voice choking. "Where are you?" Wherever he was, she could hear a hum of voices in the background.

"Can you believe it? In the middle of a board meeting." His short laugh was quiet. "I don't know who the hell they think I'm talking to, but I had to call you."

"I'm glad." Her answer was hardly above a whisper.

"The snail mail caught up with me this morning. Thanks for writing. E-mail is quicker, you know. "

"I . . . I wasn't sure you wanted me to contact you at all," she whispered.

A voice intruded, speaking clearly enough for her to hear. "Mr. Canfield, here are the cost breakdowns you wanted."

"Thanks." Brock's response was muffled, then he came back to her. "You still there?"

"Yes," Stephanie assured him, her voice regaining its strength.

Brock started to say something, then changed his mind. "This is frustrating." His tone was low and charged with irritation. "I can't see you or touch you."

"I know." Just the sound of his voice was getting her hot and bothered.

"Mr. Canfield?" The same person interrupted Brock again.

"Dammit, can't you see I'm on the phone?" he demanded. He sighed with exasperation and then spoke to her. "I'm sorry, it's no good, I can't really talk now. But I'm trying to schedule a trip to New Hampshire in December or January."

That long? Stephanie thought but she didn't say it. Instead she kept her tone light. "The height of the skiing season. Maybe you'll have enough time to hit the slopes. We already have four feet of good powder."

"I don't give a damn about the snow." He controlled the impatience in his voice to add a promising, "I'll see you . . . soon, I hope."

"Good-bye, Brock."

The line went dead before Stephanie hung up the phone. She stared at it until a slight movement caught her attention and she looked up to see Perry in the doorway.

"Was that Brock?" He studied her quietly.

"Yes." She was unwilling to discuss it.

A sadness came over her brother's face. "Don't let him break your heart, Steph." His hand slapped at the doorjamb in a helpless gesture as he turned to walk down the hallway to his office.

CHAPTER 6

There weren't any more calls from Brock. Stephanie continued to write to him but only occasionally, and she still avoided e-mail. Other than to say she looked forward to his next trip to New Hampshire, she didn't make any possessive references to him. She knew that the next time she saw him, things might be very different, and she didn't want to risk any potential embarrassment later on.

The forecast for Thanksgiving called for snow. It was falling steadily in fat flakes, accumulating on ground that was white from previous snowfalls. It was a workday as usual, the Thanksgiving weekend being one of their biggest of the holiday season.

When Stephanie entered the kitchen that morning, her brother was at the back door, bundled up in boots, muffler, and gloves. "Let's forget about breakfast. The roads are a mess and they're only going to get worse. We can eat when we get to the inn."

She glanced out the frosty window at the falling snow. The gray-white hills nearly disappeared behind it.

"We're in for a big storm," Perry prophesied. "It wouldn't hurt if you grabbed some clean clothes and toiletries and stuff. If this keeps up, we'll just sleep at the inn tonight. The lane is always the last to get plowed out." He grimaced and ducked out the back door amid a whirl of snowflakes and frigid air.

She gathered up their things in a practiced hurry and joined him outside. He was scraping snow from the windows and had just finished. The drive from the farmhouse to the inn usually took ten minutes but the limited visibility and the slippery roads increased it to twenty-five. The radio forecast said it was going to get worse.

Before breakfast was over, the area slopes were closed to skiers. The inn suddenly seemed more crowded than usual because all the guests were virtually confined to the inn. They congregated in the lobby around the fireplace, the games room, the lounge, and the restaurants. There was even a line to use the recently completed sauna and exercise room, and the computer alcove had several people waiting to check e-mail and doodle around online. Almost every flat surface had been commandeered for card games and laptops, and chess and checkers tournaments were under way.

Shortly after twelve noon there was a mild panic when it was discovered that two cross-country skiers hadn't reported in from an overnight trip. Perry and Stephanie had just sat down to the restaurant's turkey dinner. The adventurers were finally located at another lodge, but their dinners were cold when they returned.

Then the influx of stranded drivers began. Although they were full, Stephanie temporarily doubled up rooms where she could, shifting all the members of one family into a single room and so forth. She helped housekeeping figure out how many spare blankets, sheets, cots, and pillows were on hand and how many new arrivals they could handle before letting people bunk down wherever they could for the night.

"Don't forget to save *us* a place to sleep," Perry reminded her at one point when she was working out the capacity of the sofas in the lobby.

"There's always the floor," she said with a laugh.

It was almost a relief when the storm knocked the telephone lines out late in the afternoon and the switchboard finally stopped beeping. The dinner hours didn't bring a letup in the frantic pace. With so many extra people, both Perry and Stephanie lent a hand in the restaurant kitchen, doing everything from helping to fix the food to running loads through the industrial dishwasher.

At nine-thirty Perry laid a hand on her shoulder. "You've done enough, Steph. Time to call it a night."

"Okay," she agreed wearily. "What about you?"

"I'm going to the lounge. Freddy needs some help behind the bar. And,"—he breathed in tiredly—"I'd better stick around in case someone gets rowdy when we run out of beer."

Stephanie was tempted to insist that he let someone else serve as a bouncer, but Perry took his responsibility as manager too seriously to hand it over to anyone else. "Then I'll see you in the morning."

"Wait a minute!" He called her back when she started to turn away. "Where do I sleep tonight?"

"On the couch in your office . . . unless it's already occupied," she joked. "In that event, you're on your own."

"Thanks a lot, sis," he retorted in a mock growl.

Stopping at her office, Stephanie picked up the small overnight bag she had packed and started down the hallway. She didn't know which sounded more fabulous—a shower or sleep. With luck, she would be able to have both.

Before she knocked at the door of the suite, she heard childish giggles coming from inside. Her knocks produced some shrieks and more giggles. The door was opened by a young woman, not much older than Stephanie. She looked tired, harassed, and exasperated, her smile growing thin.

"Of course. Come in." But the woman was distracted by an impish five-year-old girl who appeared in the connecting doorway to the bedroom. "Amy Sue, you get back in bed this instant!" she threatened, and the little nightgowned figure fled in laughter. "I'm sorry. I've been trying to get the girls asleep for the last hour. They think this is some kind of party."

"It's all new and exciting. And confusing—by the way, I forgot your name. I'm Stephanie Hall."

"I'm Meg Foster. And these are my naughty daughters, Amy, five, and Hayley, four."

Amy quickly scurried under the covers. The

king-size bed seemed to swallow up the two small, dark-haired girls. The pair studied Stephanie, peeping curiously over the blanket's satin edge.

"Hello, Amy and Hayley." Stephanie smiled. The two looked anything but sleepy with their bright brown eyes.

"Hello. Who are you?" the youngest asked, obviously not shy with strangers.

"My name is Stephanie," she repeated.

"My friend in day care has that same name," Amy piped.

"Will you read us a story?" Hayley dived for the storybook on the nightstand beside the bed. "Read mine."

"No, mine!"

"Girls!" Meg Foster attempted to put a note of authority into her tired-sounding voice.

"I don't mind," Stephanie said. "I'll read to them while you relax in the tub." When the woman hesitated, obviously tempted, Stephanie assured her again that she didn't mind—in fact, she would enjoy it.

"Thanks. I really appreciate it," the woman said. "All day long, trying to drive in that storm—I'm exhausted, let me tell you. The girls have been bouncing off the walls, not that they mind being stranded here. I won't be long, I promise."

"Take your time," said Stephanie with a laugh. "I'm not going anywhere."

"Read my story, please?" Amy begged.

"I'll read them both," Stephanie promised. "But we'll start with Hayley's first."

She set her overnight bag on the floor by the

bed and walked over to sit on the edge where the bedside lamp was lit. Hayley immediately pressed her book into Stephanie's hands.

They grumbled when she insisted that they had to crawl under the covers and lie down before she would read to them. They didn't give in until she'd agreed to show them the pictures on each page.

Her ploy worked. By the time she had read the first story for the third time, both girls had fallen asleep. When the bathroom door opened, Stephanie held a silencing finger to her lips. Meg Foster smiled and shook her head in disbelief.

"You must have one of those magic voices, like my husband Ted. I can read until I'm hoarse, but they go right to sleep for him," she whispered. "I don't think my head is even going to have a chance to touch the pillow before I'm asleep. The bathroom is all yours and it's like heaven."

"Good." Stephanie flexed her shoulders as the fatigue began to set in. She picked up her bag and started toward the marble bathroom.

"Oh, Stephanie . . . do you mind if I leave on the light on my side of the bed? The girls don't like to sleep in the dark and they're in a strange place. If it doesn't bother you . . ."

"No, not at all. I'm like you," Stephanie explained. "I can sleep through just about anything."

"The girls don't toss and turn very much, so they won't bother you."

"It's okay. I'm sorry we couldn't provide you with a room of your own," Stephanie apologized.

"Listen, I'm grateful for a bed to sleep in. And

heaven knows this one is big enough to hold two more," Meg smiled. "Go and take your bath. And good night."

"Thanks. Good night."

The hot bath made Stephanie realize how physically and mentally exhausted she was. It was an effort just to dry off and put on a nightgown. All three of her unexpected guests were asleep when she reentered the bedroom. She moved quietly to her side of the bed and got in. She, too, drifted into sleep within minutes.

A coolness roused her, a vague suggestion of a draft. Stephanie tried to pull the covers tighter around her neck, but something held them down. She started to turn onto her side, only to become conscious of something heavy on the edge of the mattress.

Her eyes opened just a little, then widened as she realized there was a familiar-looking person— a man—sitting on the bed beside her. It was a few seconds before she realized who it was.

"Brock?" Was she dreaming? She said his name softly in case she scared his image away.

But his hand touched her face in a light, cool caress, and she knew it wasn't a dream. "Hello."

"What are you doing here?" she breathed, keeping her voice low.

He looked tired and drawn—she could see that in the half-light from the lamp. But the glint in his gray eyes was anything but weary.

"Here you are, finally in my bed, and there isn't room for me." His gaze moved to the sleeping children in the center of the bed, their angelic faces illuminated by the soft glow of the bedside lamp.

"The storm—" Stephanie started to explain in a whisper.

"Yes, I know. I stepped over sleeping bodies in the lobby." Without warning, Brock folded back the covers and slid his arms beneath her, picking her up in one smooth motion.

Stephanie clutched at his neck, too stunned and sleepy to struggle, and too conscious of the possibility of waking the children or their mother. "What are you doing?" The question was asked with confused excitement, her pulse accelerating at the contact with his leanly muscled frame.

"I'm taking you into the other room with me," he said softly, and carried her through the connecting door to the sitting room. "We have an hour of Thanksgiving left and I intend to spend it with you."

Brock didn't put her down until they were inside the other room and the door was shut. A single light burned in the far corner. Outside the window the snow was still falling, but slower and not as thickly as it had been earlier.

Not quite able to believe he was really there in the flesh, Stephanie gazed at his handsome face, the darkness of his hair, and the melting grayness of his eyes. His hands encircled her waist, gliding over the silken material of her nightgown to bring her slowly closer as if he enjoyed the feel of her.

When his mouth began a downward movement toward her, Stephanie went on tiptoes to meet it. He took possession of the yielding softness of her lips with a gentle sensuality. It was so different from any other kiss that she could hardly understand what was happening to her.

His hands were at the small of her back, caressing but firm against her skin and holding her close to the hard muscles of his thighs. Her blood ran with fire as he practiced the subtle art of seduction with effortless ease. Stephanie was lost to his skill and she didn't care. When at last he released her lips to seek the bareness of her shoulder—the nightgown had slipped down over one—she sighed in enchanted contentment. It gradually dawned on her that the coolness she was feeling against her scantily clad body wasn't from a draft in the room. It was Brock who was chilled.

"You're cold," she murmured in concern.

"So?" His mouth was against her ear, his tongue circling its sensitive hollows. "Warm me up."

Taking him at his word, Stephanie pressed closer to him. "How did you get through the snow, anyway?" she asked, her mouth brushing against his shirt at the shoulder. "I still can't believe you're really here." She sighed at the miracle of being in his arms. It felt utterly safe—and right.

"Neither can I." His arms tightened fiercely for an instant. "There were times when I wondered whether I would make it," he admitted in a tired and rueful voice.

"Why did you come?" Stephanie lifted her head, shuddering at the thought of him out in the blizzard. Her hand glided along the smoothness of his jaw and he rubbed his cheek into her palm without answering.

"Why did you take such a risk?" Her voice was tender.

"I wanted to be with you." He gazed deep into

her eyes, letting his look add a heady force to his statement. "I didn't want to spend the holiday without you."

"You should have called—let me know that you were coming," Stephanie admonished, but she knew she would have been worried sick about him.

"I wanted to surprise you." His mouth twisted in a wry line. "It was an eighteen-hour obstacle course—closed airports, canceled flights, trains not running, highways closed. When I finally accepted the fact that I might not make it, the telephone lines were down and the cell networks were overloaded. I couldn't get through to tell you I wanted to be here."

"Brock . . ." His determination—and foolishness—touched her.

"Never mind. I made it, didn't I?" The circle of his arms tightened as he pressed a kiss to her temple.

"But how?"

"I rented a four-wheel-drive monster and bribed a road crew to let me follow their snowplow," he explained.

"And how did you guess I'd be at the inn?"

"I didn't. I went to your home first," Brock told her.

"But the lane—" Stephanie's eyes widened in alarmed protest.

"Was blocked," he finished the sentence for her. "I had to leave the car on the road and walk back to the house. Good thing you and Perry left the back door unlocked. I yelled a few times, but I figured you'd both gone to the inn when no one answered. Of course, I never expected to find you sleeping in my bed." He let out a bearlike growl and she giggled.

"Did the desk clerk tell you where I was?"

He nodded. "I didn't want to go around knocking on doors in the middle of the night trying to find you. Perry would have had some irate guests to deal with in the morning."

She was impressed all over again by his single-minded determination to find her. It had to mean something. He wouldn't bribe his way past a hard-working road crew and risk the wrath of a protective big brother for no good reason. Just thinking about it made her feel slightly euphoric.

"Come." Brock took hold of her hand and led her to the side of the room. "I took the big cushions off the sofa and the spare pillows and blankets from the closet to make us a bed in here."

Stephanie stared at the blanket-covered cushions on the floor and the two pillows lying side by side on top. Brock was studying her, waiting for her reaction. But there was none—at least, not a negative one.

"I'll turn out the light." Releasing her hand, Brock moved to the opposite side of the room.

Stephanie watched him. There wasn't any conscious decision on her part. She was only aware of how much he had gone through to get to her, despite the paralyzing storm. All arguments for and against going to bed with him paled in comparison to that unshakable fact. It was truly the only thought in her mind.

When the click of a light switch darkened the room, she sank onto the firm cushions. A sublime calmness settled through her as she folded back the blanket to slide beneath it.

She loved Brock. The quiet knowledge wasn't a rationale for her decision, but it was the simple truth. Implausible as it seemed, as short a time as she had known him, she loved him. The unshakable strength of emotion made her feel mellow and warm, ripe with the fullness of it.

Brock was a dark shadow as he approached the makeshift bed. Not until he had joined her under the covers did he take form and substance. Lying on his side, he reached for her to draw her into his embrace.

Her hands encountered the muscled bareness of his chest, its crisp hair sensually rough beneath her palms, his legs shifting to tangle with hers. The sweet intimacy sparked a hot desire within her as his mouth sought and found hers.

He demanded a response that she had no wish to hold back. He mastered her with a fiery hunger, possessing her heart and soul, which she was only too willing to give into his keeping. With a surrendering sigh, she slid her arms around his brawny shoulders to bring more of his weight onto her.

The blanket slipped to a position over their hips as Brock pushed the silken strap of her nightgown off a shoulder. His mouth explored the rosy nipple that he could just see—the muted exterior lights of the inn reflected from the deep snow outside. He caressed both her breasts and suckled one. The sensation made her toes curl. Then his mouth returned to her lips while the hair on his chest brushed across the sensitive skin of her bare breasts.

A moaning sound came from his throat, his warm breath filling her mouth. The thin material of her nightgown was no barrier to his ardor—but he stopped.

Reluctantly, Brock drew away from her to roll onto his back, his arm flung above his head on the pillow. Stephanie was confused by his withdrawal, and left aching. Turning onto her side, she rose onto an elbow to gaze at him.

The gleam in his eyes seemed to have faded, although it was difficult to make out his expression. He reached out to slide the strap of her gown back up on her shoulder, his hand remaining to silently caress her. A half-smile was lifting one corner of his mouth. Even that seemed to require a lot of effort.

"What's wrong, Brock?" Stephanie whispered uncertainly, wanting to curl herself into his arms, but not doing it because of the lack of an invitation.

"Oh—I've been working long hours the last few days. Taking care of business so I could come up here and see you. And that trip through the snow did me in, I guess." His hand moved to caress her silken hair, running through it gently. "I've had six hours of sleep in the last three days. That's what's wrong."

She heard the weariness in his voice but in the dimness she could only guess at the fatigue etched in his features. When he chuckled softly, she frowned.

"Don't you see the irony of this, Stephanie?" Brock murmured. "After all this time, you're finally beside me, just the way I imagined it. And now I'm too damn tired to do anything about it," he sighed.

Her personal dissatisfaction was forgotten in a rush of loving concern for him. Leaning forward, she kissed his lips with infinite tenderness. A loving smile curved her mouth when she straightened.

"You'd better get some sleep before you collapse," she advised, and turned to sweep back the covers to return to her own bed.

"No." Brock stopped her with an outstretched hand. "Stay with me tonight."

Her hesitation lasted only a fraction of a second. She lay down once more beside him. Brock turned her over onto her side with her back to his belly and spooned her against his length. His arm was around her waist, his hand possessively cupping a breast.

Stephanie was warmed by the memory of Brock saying once that he preferred to sleep alone. So he shared her need to be close—a need that transcended every thought and feeling that might have been true in the past. What they had was unique. Stephanie knew it instinctively. And she suspected Brock did, too.

Hugged close to him, she heard his breathing grow deep and heavy as his utter exhaustion overcame him. She closed her eyes, not sure that she could drift off so easily, but blissful contentment soon whisked her away. They slept enfolded in an embrace of passive desire.

Morning light streamed into the room through the large windows and Stephanie opened her eyes.

She became conscious of a sleeping body next to hers—a very male body—radiating a delicious heat. She snuggled closer.

She was facing a broad chest and even broader shoulders, and Brock's muscular, heavy arm was thrown across her. His hand cupped her hip in firm possession, while one of his legs entwined with hers. Looking through her lashes, she studied the unrelenting strength of his face in sleep and the sexy stubble that outlined his jaw. Sensual and powerful, he stirred all her senses.

She felt a very strong impulse to kiss him awake but the brilliant sunlight and the muffled voices of others in the outer hall warned Stephanie of the lateness of the hour.

Reluctantly she slid out of his hold and rose from the makeshift bed on the floor. Her bare feet made no sound as she entered the bedroom where Meg Foster and her little daughters were still sleeping. With her overnight bag in hand, she slipped into the bathroom to wash and dress.

There wasn't a sound from anyone when she came out. She hesitated in the sitting room, but Brock was still totally out. He had left the keycard to the suite lying on an end table. She left it where it was in case he or the Fosters needed to get in and out—she could always get another one from the front desk—and quietly exited the room through the hall door.

She went directly to the restaurant kitchen. The inn was already astir with early morning breakfasters digging into tall stacks of pancakes dripping with locally made maple syrup. The smell was heavenly.

Outside, the sky was clear—almost too blue against the pure white snow that had formed enormous drifts. She set china cups and a pot of coffee on a tray to take to the suite.

As she was passing through the lobby to pick up another keycard, her brother appeared. "Stephanie!" he called out to stop her. "Brock's here," he said when he reached her side. "He arrived last night."

"Yes, I know," she nodded. "I'm taking him some coffee now. He's still sleeping. He made a bed on the floor of the sitting room." She didn't mention that she had shared it with him. It wasn't an attempt to conceal anything from Perry, but she preferred to choose her own time to tell him.

Perry glanced at the tray, then at her, studying her closely. "Why is he here? Did he say?" he questioned.

"He wanted to have Thanksgiving here." She hesitated over making the explanation longer, but she didn't have to.

Her brother filled in the important part. "With you, right? He wouldn't make that trip for a plate of turkey."

"Yes," Stephanie nodded, unable to keep the radiance from shining in her eyes.

Perry shook his head in amazement. "In that blizzard? Wow. I'm impressed What a hero." He bit his lip. "Maybe I was wrong about him," he said thoughtfully. Whatever else he was about to add, he changed his mind and flashed her a wry smile instead. "Better take that coffee to him before it gets cold."

"I'll be right back," she promised.

"No rush," Perry insisted. "After all the hours you put in yesterday, you can take your time this morning."

Her smile was full of affection for her brother. "Thanks, boss."

At the door to the suite, Stephanie had to set the tray on the floor to have her hands free. The cups rattled on their saucers as she entered the sitting room, but the delicate noise didn't waken Brock, who was still sleeping soundly on the floor. Only silence came from the bedroom where the young mother and her two little girls were.

Stephanie carried the tray to the low table and set it down. Knowing how little rest Brock had had in the last few days, she didn't pour him any coffee yet, only a cup for herself. The thermal pot would keep the coffee hot for a long time. She walked to a chair, unconsciously choosing one that would permit her to watch Brock in sleep.

The blanket was down around his hips since the heat in the inn had been kicked up to high. His lean, tanned torso rose and fell with his deep breaths, his flat navel barely visible in his hard abs. He was lying on his side, facing her.

Stephanie let her gaze wander upward to his strongly defined mouth and the thick, dark lashes resting against his cheekbones. His brows were thick as well but nicely arched. His rumpled dark hair fell across his forehead. Even in sleep, Brock exuded an incredible virility. She wanted to touch him so much—but she didn't.

When he stirred, she held her breath. His hand moved across the empty cushion beside him, as if instinctively seeking something. Was he looking

for her in his dream? What a wonderful thought—
then she saw his hand freeze for a full second. He
awoke instantly, turning onto his back, alarm in
his expression.

"Stephanie?" He called out for her in an impatient voice before he saw her seated in the chair.
His expression changed immediately to one of satisfaction.

"Good morning." Her voice was husky with the
knowledge that he had missed having her sleeping
beside him.

"Not so good," Brock said a little woozily. "I
mean, you weren't here." He patted the pillow beside him. "Why didn't you wake me up when you
got up?"

"Would you like some coffee?" Stephanie rose,
conscious of the way he took in her fully dressed
appearance, detail by detail. Without waiting for
him to say yes, she walked to the table and poured
a cup for him.

"Why did you get dressed right away?" he asked.
He blinked at the sunlight that flooded the room.
"What time is it?"

"Almost nine o'clock. Don't forget there are
people in the next room." She carried the cup to
him.

The blanket slipped a little farther downward,
giving her a tantalizing glimpse of the elastic waist-
band of his white briefs. It was crazy the way her
body reacted to the sight, yet she had folded about
nine million pairs of identical male underwear for
her brother and it hadn't done a thing for her.

"I suppose you have to work this morning." He
pulled up the blanket and looked up at her as she

stood by the crude bed. He was still supported by his elbows and half-reclining.

"No. Perry said it was okay if I was late," she assured him, and knelt down to give him his coffee.

But Brock didn't reach for it. "In that case, come back to bed." He looked at her lips and then into her eyes.

Stephanie couldn't find her voice. She recovered it after he'd sat up and circled one arm around her waist while his hand curved itself to the back of her neck, pulling her toward him.

"I'm going to spill the coffee," she warned a breath before his mouth covered her lips to hungrily remind her of what he had wanted to do last night.

Her hand gripped his hard shoulder for balance while the cup of coffee jiggled in its saucer in the opposite hand, the steaming liquid sloshing over the rim. But she offered no resistance to his kiss, melting under his heady domination.

"Get rid of that coffee and those clothes, and come back to bed with me," Brock ordered against her mouth, and proceeded to outline her lips with his tongue.

He kissed her thoroughly and sensually before drawing away. Stephanie felt deliciously stupid, barely capable of thought when she met the gray darkness of his eyes. A sound intruded, but just barely registered until she noticed something moving out of the corner of her eye.

Five-year-old Amy was standing in the doorway wearing her flannel nightgown, one bare foot on top of the other, eyeing them curiously. Stephanie was brought sharply back to reality, grateful that Brock was decently swaddled in the blanket.

Brock turned to look behind him and barely stifled a curse of frustration rather than anger. His eyes held a glint of amusement when he looked back at Stephanie.

"Who's that man?" Amy wanted to know. "Is he your husband?"

Brock rescued the cup of coffee from her shaking hand and arched a mocking eyebrow in her direction.

"Uh—no. He's a friend," Stephanie explained a little self-consciously.

The little girl padded quickly across the room as if invited. "Why are you sleeping on the floor?" she asked Brock, and bounced over the cushions to sit on a pillow with her legs under her.

"Because there wasn't any other place for me to sleep," he replied, regarding Amy with a patience that surprised Stephanie a little.

"There was lots of room in our bed," Amy insisted. "Why didn't you get next to Stephanie?"

"Ah—your bed was for girls only. This one is for guys." He rolled his eyes for Stephanie's benefit. Talk about questions no one wanted to answer— kids know how to ask them.

A drowsy Hayley entered the room, rubbing her sleep-filled eyes and hugging her storybook in front of her. She pattered quickly to her older sister's side and perched on the edge of the pillow, sitting cross-legged and yawning.

Brock took a sip of his coffee and murmured to Stephanie. "Two's company. Four's a crowd."

"Can we watch cartoons?" Hayley asked. "Who are you?"

"Ah—is your mother awake?" Stephanie asked. "They're serving pancakes downstairs, girls. But she has to go with you. You can't go alone."

"Not yet." Not even pancakes could distract the children from their fascination with Brock. "Do you have any children?" Amy asked him.

"Um—no."

"Wouldn't you like to have a little girl of your own?" Amy seemed puzzled. "Daddy says it's wonderful, especially when you have two. But he doesn't like spending so much money on Barbie clothes."

"Adds up," said Brock solemnly. "I bet he's saving for college for you two already."

"How did you know that?" The little girls looked at him with renewed interest.

"That's what dads are supposed to do," he replied.

"You should have daughters. You could have sons, too, but boys aren't as nice. Joey Barnes stepped on my doll and broke its head on purpose."

"But Daddy fixed it," Amy reminded her, before turning back to Brock. "Which do you think you'd rather have?"

"I don't know. What do you think, Stephanie? Boys or girls? Or one of each?"

"I—" She was spared from answering that astonishing question by the sound of Meg Foster's voice coming from the bedroom.

"Amy? Hayley? Where are you?"

"We're in here, Mommy," Amy answered immediately.

"What are you . . ." The question was never finished as the young mother appeared in the doorway.

The sight of Brock sitting on the floor with Stephanie and her daughters made her suddenly conscious of the very short nightie she was wearing. She stepped behind the door in embarrassment.

"You girls come here right now," she ordered. "You haven't brushed your teeth yet," she added, as if that was the reason.

The pair hopped blithely to their feet and dashed into the bedroom. Meg sent Stephanie an apologetic look before closing the door.

"Now." Brock caught at Stephanie's hand to pull her off balance and into his arms. "Where were we before we were so rudely interrupted?" His mouth had barely touched her lips when there was a knock at the hall door. Releasing her, he muttered, "This place is turning into Grand Central Station. You'd better toss me my pants—there's likely to be a parade through here next."

Before she answered the door, Stephanie handed him his pants, which had been draped over a nearby chair. She opened it to see one of the housekeepers, doing a routine room check. When Stephanie turned around, Brock was on his feet, zipping up the dark pants but still bare-chested. The sight made her knees go weak.

"More coffee?" she suggested innocently. Anything to keep him around where she could look at him.

"Since circumstances don't allow anything else, why not?" he said with a wry smile.

She had just started to fill up his cup when the telephone rang. Brock motioned her to stay where she was. "I'll get it." He answered it, then hesitated, glancing at Stephanie as he listened to the caller. "Just a minute." He covered the mouthpiece and pointed to the bedroom. "Is her name Meg Foster?"

Stephanie nodded.

"Her husband's on the phone. Guess the line's working again. There's an extension by the bed she can use."

"I'll tell her." She handed Brock his cup before she walked over to knock on the connecting door. "Meg, your husband's on the phone."

The delighted shrieks of the two little girls came first from the bedroom, then echoed into the sitting room through the phone in Brock's hand. He set the receiver back in its cradle and looked at Stephanie.

"How do you suppose she's going to explain that a man answered?" he mocked.

"Well, with the storm and all, I'm sure he'll understand." She retrieved her coffee cup from the side table to refill it.

As he was pouring the coffee from the thermal pot, Brock came up behind her, sliding an arm around her waist and bending to kiss the side of her neck. "Believe me, if I called you and a man answered—other than your brother—you'd have a lot of explaining to do."

"Really? Have we gotten that far?" A delicious tingle danced over her skin at his nibbling kisses. "I'll answer the phone myself," she giggled.

His arm tightened. "I'm not kidding, Stephanie. Just thinking of someone else touching you—"

Someone rapped very softly on the hall door. Brock cursed under his breath as he broke away from her and crossed the room with long, impatient strides to jerk the door open.

Perry stood outside, looking startled. "Uh—I wasn't sure if you were up yet."

Brock's laugh was harsh. "I'm awake, all right. Thanks to two little girls, their mother, and a telephone call from their father—not to mention a visit from the housekeeper. Come on in. Everyone else has." His irritation negated his attempt to be funny. "I suppose you're looking for Stephanie."

"Yeah. Indirectly." Perry's expression was apologetic. "Steph, I need the revised rate schedule we came up with yesterday afternoon. I looked on your desk but I couldn't find it."

"Folder in the top right-hand drawer of my desk," she said automatically. "And it's on my computer."

"I don't know the password."

"So, what are the roads like? Can I get out of here?" Brock demanded unexpectedly. She stared at him, not willing to believe the implications of that question. Brock didn't even glance her way.

"The airport is still closed, but the highways are open. The snow is drifting in places, but otherwise it's in good shape, according to the highway patrol report we got this morning," her brother replied.

"You aren't leaving?" Stephanie almost accused.

"I have to." Then he flashed her an angry look, noting the obvious hurt in her expression. "Dammit! I don't like it any more than you do!"

Very quietly, Perry slipped out of the room, leaving them alone. Stephanie turned away from Brock, trying to hide her bitter disappointment. She heard him set his cup down and walk up behind her. His hands settled hesitantly on her shoulders.

"Twenty-four hours was all I could spare, Stephanie," he explained grimly. "I've already used more than that, most of it trying to get here."

"I understand that." She turned and was confronted by the naked wall of his chest. Lifting her gaze she looked into his face. "Honestly, I'm glad you came . . . for however long or short it has to be."

His gray eyes no longer smoldered with resentful anger, but burned with a sultry fire as they lingered for a moment on her parted lips. There was no longer any hesitation in the touch of his hands as he drew her up to meet his descending mouth.

His kiss seared her with the rawness of his sexual hunger, arousing her to full awareness of his need. Her arms wound around his neck as she was crushed willingly against his chest. Before the embrace got out of control, Brock set her from him with a groan.

"You'd better go now," he said tightly. "We aren't going to have any more time alone. And I'd rather say good-bye now."

"Brock!" she protested.

"Believe me, it's better this way," he insisted. "I'll see you when I can—you know that, don't you?"

"Yes." She tried not to think about how long that might be.

He walked her to the hall door, brushing her lips with a kiss before she left the room. Her throat was raw and her eyes burned, but she didn't cry. An inner voice warned her that these farewells were something she had better accept, if she planned to have any relationship with Brock Canfield.

Perry didn't say anything when she walked into her office to find him going over the schedule he'd been looking for. There was gentle sympathy in his look, and a suppressed concern.

For nearly two hours she waited, clinging to the hope that Brock would stop by to see her one last time before he left. But he went without seeing her again. Squaring her shoulders, she began concentrating on her work.

Keeping busy was the one sure way to make the time pass faster until she saw him again. The feeling that he cared deeply about her, as she did for him, made it seem easier somehow. There was strength to be drawn from that.

CHAPTER 7

"Mistletoe?" Perry held up the sprig by its red bow and cocked an eyebrow at Stephanie, kneeling in front of the fireplace to arrange the nativity scene on its snowy blanket. "What on earth do we need mistletoe for in this house?"

"That's a good question." She sent him a teasing glance over her shoulder. "Maybe for the new elementary-school teacher—Joyce Henderson. I understand she came into the restaurant for dinner again last night. I also understand that you happened to take your break at the same time."

"The restaurant was crowded," he defended himself, a redness spreading upward from his neck. "It seemed logical to ask her to sit at my table."

"But twice in half a week?" she inquired archly. "I didn't realize schoolteachers around here made enough money to afford the entrées at the White Boar. Or did she pay for her own meal both times?"

"Pattie really has a big mouth," Perry sighed.

Stephanie only laughed at his reference to the cashier, her source of information, who had betrayed the fact that Perry had bought the pretty young teacher dinner the night before. "She's worried about your single status."

"It's none of her business."

"Maybe not," she conceded. "But in case you decide to invite Joyce over for a glass of holiday cheer, why don't you hang the mistletoe from that center beam? It looks like a strategic location to me."

"Who said I was going to invite her over?" Perry bristled.

"Not me," Stephanie countered with wide-eyed innocence. "But if you do, let me know. I can always spend the night at the inn."

"Hang up your own mistletoe." Perry set it aside and reached into the box of decorations to take out the Christmas wreath for the door.

"Get me the ladder and I will," she agreed, realizing that the subject of the new schoolteacher was a touchy one.

A sigh slipped from her lips as Perry stalked out of the room to get the ladder. She regretted ribbing him. It must be more than a casual flirtation for Perry to be so sensitive about it.

She certainly wasn't in any position to make light of someone else's relationship. She hadn't heard from Brock since Thanksgiving, which was two weeks ago. And two weeks could seem like an eternity, if she let herself obsess over it.

Perry returned with the ladder, not saying a word as he set it up beneath the beam where Stephanie had suggested that the mistletoe be hung. Leaving behind the smaller hammer, he took the heavier one and a couple of thin nails, as well as the Christmas wreath of evergreen garlands, pinecones, and red bows, and flipped on the outside light. He stepped outside and closed the door to keep the cold night air from chilling the living room.

Finished with the nativity scene, Stephanie took the sprig of mistletoe, the hammer and a tack, and climbed the ladder. One step short of the top, she stopped and stretched to reach the hardwood beam.

They traditionally hung their decorations after the tenth of December, but didn't put up the tree until the week before Christmas. Stephanie realized, a little ruefully, that neither of them was exactly filled with the holiday spirit this year.

The phone started ringing before she had the mistletoe tacked into place. Stephanie hesitated, then continued to tap with the hammer, ignoring the commanding ring of the phone. The front door opened and Perry glared at her.

"Can't you hear the phone?" he snapped.

"That's only the third ring," she retorted just as impatiently.

"Fourth," he corrected, and walked briskly over to pick up the receiver and silence the annoying sound. "Hello. Deck the halls," he answered in a not particularly friendly tone. Stephanie winced at his awful pun. "Just a minute." He set the receiver on the table with a thump. "It's for you."

The tack bent on the last strike of her hammer, which meant she had to start all over again and find a new tack. "Find out who it is and tell them I'll call them back."

"I already know who it is—Brock." Just for a moment his expression softened. "Do you really want me to tell him you're too busy to talk right now?"

That got her scrambling down the ladder, nearly knocking it over in her haste to get to the telephone. When she grabbed for the receiver, it slipped out of her fingers and crashed to the floor. Thinking she had broken it, Stephanie clutched it to her ear.

"Brock? Are you there?" Her voice was a thin thread of panic. "I dropped the receiver. I was on the ladder hanging the mistletoe when Perry answered the phone." She hurried her explanation. "I didn't realize it was you calling until he told me. Then I was . . ." It was too embarrassing to admit how excited she had been, so she changed her sentence. "Anyway, I dropped it. I'm such a butterfingers."

"Glad I called, huh?" He seemed to see right through her attempt to cover up her feelings. His voice grew warmer.

"You know I am," Stephanie said softly, and noticed her brother slipping out of the room so she could have some privacy. "It's been so long since I heard your voice. I . . ." She stopped, unable to actually admit the rest.

"You what, Stephanie? What were you going to say?" Brock wasn't going to let her slide. "Did you miss me?" He guessed right again.

"Yes, I've missed you." Her voice vibrated with the intensity of her emotion.

"Why didn't you tell me that in your letters?" he demanded. "I couldn't stand it any longer, not knowing whether you've been as miserable as I have. The way you write, I get the feeling that everything is white and wonderful back there."

"Have you really missed me, too?" She hardly dared to believe it was true.

"I've been out of my mind." An urgency entered his tone. "Stephanie, I have to see you. I can't wait any longer."

"I want to see you, too." Her hand tightened on the receiver, trying to hold on to this moment. "C-can you come here?"

"No." He dismissed it as out of the question. "I'm in Palm Springs. I don't have a chance of getting away, not until closer to the holidays—maybe." He stressed the last word. "I want you to come here, honey. I'll make all the arrangements. You can leave tomorrow morning and be here by noon. I'll only be able to spare a few hours in the afternoons to be with you over the weekend, but we'll have the nights. All of the nights."

"Brock." She was overwhelmed by the invitation and his determination to see her, whatever the cost.

"Don't worry about packing much or digging out your summer clothes. We'll go on a pre-Christmas shopping spree. Just you and me."

"You don't need to buy me anything," she said swiftly.

"I want to," he replied. "I wake up nights, thinking you're going to be lying beside me. I can't describe the hell I go through when you aren't there. Stephanie, will you come?"

Yes was on the tip of her tongue when she realized why she couldn't say it. "Brock, I can't." Disappointment throbbed in her tone, acute and painful.

"Why? What do you want me to do—beg?" He was angry and seemed not to believe she was refusing. "Why can't you come?"

"I have the payroll to finish and the Christmas bonuses. Tomorrow is the last day everyone's going to be there."

"Oh, come on. I want you here with me. Can't someone else do it?" Brock argued.

"No one else is qualified."

"Your brother can do it. And don't tell me he doesn't know how," he retorted.

"He's overworked as it is, with the inn booked solid and temporary winter help. I couldn't stick him with it." What Brock was asking was unreasonable and Stephanie tried to make him understand—not easy, considering that he didn't want to listen.

Okay, so he had an international staff to handle things like that every time he snapped his fingers—she didn't. "It isn't that I don't want to. The payroll is my responsibility and that's that. I can't come."

"You can if you want to badly enough." He stubbornly refused to see her point of view. "Tell everyone they'll have to wait until next week for the paychecks. I don't care. Stephanie, I've got to see you. I want you to fly here."

"It's impossible. I can't do what you're asking. If you'd think about it, you would understand why." Her voice was growing tight with a mixture of anger and hurt confusion. "You aren't being fair."

"Fair? The way I'm feeling isn't fair," Brock argued. "I need you."

"Please don't do this." She was close to tears. "I can't come."

There was a long silence before he came back on the line, sounding grim. "All right, if that's the way you feel about it."

"That isn't the way I feel. It's just the way it is," she choked.

"Have it your way." Brock sounded disinterested and very distant. "Good-bye."

Stephanie sobbed in a breath as the line went dead. She stared numbly at the telephone for a long time before she finally wiped the tears from her cheeks. She was sniffling when Perry came into the room a short time later. He handed her his handkerchief, but didn't ask what was wrong.

He didn't say a word when she stuffed the mistletoe in the bottom of the box of Christmas decorations and carried the ladder out to the back porch. Perry didn't have any desire to hang it and Stephanie thought it was highly unlikely that she would have a need for it.

It was almost a week before she summoned up the courage to write Brock a short letter, saying only that she was sorry he hadn't understood her reason for turning down his invitation.

And she doubted that he had the patience to even start something as time-consuming as a real letter, and that was why she still avoided e-mailing him. She could just imagine the resulting flurry of hasty exchanges, which, unfortunately, could be read and reread and misinterpreted on both sides. Silence in this case was definitely golden.

But she made it clear that she still believed she had made the right decision. After that, she didn't write to him again. If he could be that selfish when she put her responsibility to the staff first—she knew that many of them lived from paycheck to paycheck—then he could just figure out for himself how wrong he was and grow the hell up.

Perry was great—good old Perry, who never said I-told-you-so. Instead, he did his damnedest to cheer her up whenever she sank into the depths of despair, which was often.

They had weathered many depressing situations together. His support gave Stephanie the hope that she could do it again.

The week before Christmas their church had a caroling party. A minor managerial crisis at the inn—the head bartender had joined AA and quit his job on principle—forced Perry to cancel at the last minute, but he encouraged Stephanie to go without him. Regarding it more as a religious celebration than a social event, she agreed.

He dropped her off at the church with instructions to call him when she was ready to go home and he would pick her up. It wasn't necessary, however, because she met Chris Berglund, whose parents owned the farm a mile from theirs. They had just about grown up together, first as playmates and then schoolmates. Some people even thought they were related, which they weren't.

Stephanie hadn't seen much of him since their

high school graduation. Chris had gone on to college, coming back only for term breaks, which was why he was here now.

When he heard she was without a lift home, he immediately volunteered to take her since it was right on the way to his parents' place. They chatted, exchanged personal news, and recalled funny incidents from their childhood days.

As they turned into the lane leading to the farmhouse, Stephanie leaned back in her seat and sighed. She couldn't remember when she had laughed like this and felt so lighthearted. She glanced at Chris, with his curly brown hair and dark-rimmed glasses, a bulky parka adding size to his lanky body.

"I still can't believe you're going to be a doctor," she remarked. "I can remember when you used to squirm at the sight of blood."

"Okay, I outgrew that," he laughed.

"Dr. Chris Berglund," Stephanie tried it out. "It has a very professinal ring to it."

"Sure does, doesn't it?" he agreed. "But I still have two years of med school, plus an internship to get through, before I'm a real doctor. There's more to it than 'open your mouth and say *ah.*' "

Stephanie laughed, as she was meant to do. "I'll bet your bedside manner will be impeccable."

"You know it." Chris slowed the car as he approached the farmhouse. "Hey, looks like Perry's waiting up for you. Front light is on. He takes that big-brother stuff seriously."

"Oh, Perry really cares. I wouldn't trade him for anything," she replied, and meant it.

"He's a good guy," Chris agreed, and stopped

the car beside the shoveled sidewalk to her front door.

Stephanie got out, joined by Chris as he walked around to see her to the door. "Want to come in for a cup of cocoa? Perry would love to see you."

"I'd better not." Chris turned down the invitation reluctantly. "I just got home this afternoon. With Mom being in charge of the caroling party and all, I haven't had much of a chance to visit with them. The minister and his wife and a couple of Mom and Dad's friends are coming by the house tonight. I think they want to show me off."

"Naturally." Stephanie understood. Stopping at the door and turning to him, she said, "I'm glad you're home, Chris. It isn't the same when you aren't around."

"Next time I come, I'll bring a couple of guys from my fraternity. I'll introduce you to one of them." He winked. "Can't have my favorite girl turning into an old maid." He locked his hands behind her waist and pulled her closer. "You're much too pretty."

"You're right," she laughed, but there was an ache in her heart all the same.

His kiss was a warm, friendly one, innocent and meaningless. It didn't occur to Stephanie to object—any more than it would have if a member of her family had kissed her. It was the same with Chris. Neither of them was hiding any secret passion for the other.

He was smiling when he moved away to leave. "Tell Perry I'll stop by the inn tomorrow. Maybe we can all have coffee together."

"Okay," she agreed, and added with a quick

wave as he disappeared down the sidewalk, "Thanks for the ride!"

His answer was a wave. Stephanie turned to enter the house as the car door slammed. Hurrying inside out of the cold, she paused to shut the front door and stomp the snow from her boots on the heavy mat inside.

"Hey, Perry!" she called to her brother as she turned and began unwinding the wool scarf from around her neck. "Guess who's home for Christmas?"

She had barely taken two steps into the living room when she saw a dark-coated figure standing beside the fireplace. She faltered in surprise before a thrilling joy ran through her.

"Brock!" she cried happily, and started forward with lighter steps.

"Surprise, surprise." The sarcasm in his voice was unmistakable.

His left hand was thrust in the side pocket of his overcoat. In his right, he held a glass of whiskey. It had to be whiskey since that was the only drink they kept in the house. He stood with his legs slightly apart in a challenging stance that stopped her from rushing to him. But it was the look of anger in his eyes that froze Stephanie. His masculine features might have been carved out of stone.

"When did you get here?" she managed finally. "Why didn't you let me know?"

"Fifteen minutes ago. What's the matter?" Brock asked coolly. "Are you wishing I'd come fifteen minutes from now so I wouldn't have witnessed that tender little scene out front?" His mouth thinned as he took a swig of whiskey. "I bet you would've liked to know I was coming. You would have done a better job of juggling the men in your life so they wouldn't meet each other coming and going."

"Brock, that's not how it is," she protested in a pained voice.

"You mean that's not an example of how you wait for me?" he challenged her. "I saw you kiss him."

Stephanie half turned to glance at the glass pane on the top half of the front door, the outside light illuminating the entrance. If Chris had kissed her in the living room, they wouldn't have been more visible. Out of the corner of her eye, she saw her brother appear in the kitchen opening, drawn by Brock's angry voice.

"It was Chris." She unconsciously appealed to her brother to make Brock understand how innocent the kiss had been.

"He's a neighbor—" Perry began, trying to come to her rescue.

"That's convenient," Brock snapped.

"You don't understand," Stephanie insisted helplessly.

"I understand, all right." His voice was low and controlled. "I understand that I was a fool."

He set the glass down and stalked out, so quickly that she didn't notice Brock was moving until he swept past her. By the time she turned, the front door was slamming. She wrenched at the doorknob, the lock momentarily jamming from her haste.

She managed to jerk it open in time to see

Brock striding around their vehicle to where his Mercedes was parked. The boxy SUV had hidden it from her view when she came in with Chris.

Had he driven up all the way from New York again? He must be exhausted—but that was no reason he couldn't listen. She was going to make him listen, whether he liked it or not.

As she ran down the sidewalk after him, she heard the car door slam and the motor roar to life. Before she reached the driveway he had reversed onto the lane. Stephanie had a brief glimpse of his profile and the forbidding grimness of his expression before the car accelerated down the long drive.

"Stephanie?" Her brother was calling to her from the open front door.

She paused long enough to ask. "Are the keys in the SUV?"

"Yes. Where are you going?" he asked, already guessing.

"I've got to explain to him. I can't leave it like this." The answer was tossed over her shoulder as she ran.

She lost sight of the Mercedes taillights when she turned onto the main road. Judging by the direction Brock had gone, she took a chance that he was going to the inn.

His car was parked in the section reserved for employees, steam rising from its hood when she arrived. An image of him, steaming in the same way just because he wouldn't listen, came to mind. She smiled a little, parked the SUV beside his car, and hurried inside.

Slowing her steps to a fast walk through the lobby, she ignored the questioning look she received from the desk clerk, and didn't stop to explain what she was doing there at that hour of the night.

Her heart was pounding when she reached the door to Brock's suite. Before she lost her nerve, she knocked rapidly three times and felt a tense kind of relief when she heard hard strides approaching from the other side of the door.

It was jerked open by an impatient hand. Brock's eyes narrowed on her in icy anger.

"I deserve the chance to explain what you saw," Stephanie rushed out the words before he could order her to leave. Minus his overcoat and suit jacket, he had on a white shirt, his tie askew from an attempt to loosen the knot. His hand returned to finish the job as he pivoted away from the door, not closing it.

Stephanie moved hesitantly into the room, shutting the door behind her and watching the suppressed fury in the way he stripped the tie from around his neck and tossed it onto a seat cushion.

Without a word, he walked to the minibar and poured out a shot of single malt. He took a quick swallow and moved away—not speaking, not looking at her.

"I . . ." It was difficult to know how to begin when she was being so frigidly ignored. "Chris Berglund and I grew up together."

"You must have had a very joyous reunion," Brock remarked caustically.

"It was wonderful to see him again." Stephanie

refused to deny that. "Chris and I are old friends. That's all we've ever been. We're more like brother and sister. I know how it might have looked—"

"Do you?" Brock spun around, his voice icy. "Do you have any idea what it's like to break appointments, to tell insanely busy CEOs you're trying to get on your side to go take a running jump into a lake because there's a woman you can't get out of your head—and if you don't see her, you're likely to go crazy? So you take off, drop everything. Then you're there, in her home, waiting for her to come back from church. How sweet." He tossed her a disbelieving look. "You hear a car drive up and voices. You're so anxious to see her that you nearly go flying out the door. But there she is— kissing someone else."

"But it didn't mean anything. Perry can vouch for me." Her voice was hoarse, scraped by the rawness of the emotions he had displayed, his feeling of betrayal.

"Perry is your brother. Of course he would cover for you."

"Then ask someone else."

"I don't have to."

She was silent for only a moment as her own anger rose. "Well, I don't have to put up with crap like this from anyone."

"Why didn't you write me after we argued on the phone?"

"I did once. But you just sounded so angry—I didn't want to get near you. You had no right to lose your temper like that. It was incredibly immature. And it's not like I can make you grow up."

"I know that!"

At least he was angry at the right person, Stephanie thought: himself. But she had no idea how this would play out.

"Look, when those letters stopped, I thought I'd lost you. I came all this way to apologize for being a selfish, arrogant bastard."

"Good."

He crossed the room to stand in front of her, his hands on her shoulders. "Can you blame me for being a little crazy?" He groaned. "For wondering . . ." There was a wild look in his eyes. "How many men would fly halfway around the world to be with you?"

"Brock, there's only you," Stephanie whispered, lifting a trembling hand to let her fingertips trace the iron line of his jaw.

"That's what you say." A rueful look flashed across his face. "But I don't know what you do when I'm not here."

That was it. She'd had enough. She slapped him—hard.

"Get out of my life. If you feel entitled to say things like that to me—if you don't trust me— then go back to that blonde bitch. I have had it with you." Her voice was chillingly calm and he actually backed away a few feet. "Just because you own this place doesn't mean you own me or the people in it."

"Is that all you have to say?"

"Brock, I love you—but I shouldn't."

He shook his head and looked ashamed.

For what it was worth, Stephanie thought furi-

ously. "By the way, I shouldn't have to prove anything to you. Do I ask you how many women you've
slept with since you've met me?"

He raked a hand through his hair, looking like
he wanted to howl. Well, she had the floor and he
was going to get an earful. "Brock, you travel with
a two-legged entertainment system, for God's sake.
What kind of things do you think I imagine when
you're gone?"

"I don't know," he said wearily. "And Helen is
history. But where do you and I go from here?"

"Right now? Absolutely nowhere."

And she meant it.

CHAPTER 8

She waited a few days before she got up the nerve to call him. They exchanged meaningless small talk—and wonder of wonders, he asked her up to his suite. She agreed to come by at the time he said was convenient, after a moment of proud hesitation.

"Good. I'll see you then," he replied, clipped and to the point. "Good-bye."

Yes . . . good-bye," Stephanie said. Then there was a click and then no sound on the line. She wondered if she had made the right decision by contacting him first. Brock couldn't have sounded more indifferent.

Stephanie spent the afternoon lolling in a bubble bath, washing and blow-drying her hair, and trying on a half a dozen outfits before finally deciding on the rust-colored dress she'd worn to dinner the first day she'd met him.

Without transportation, since Perry had the

SUV, she had to call a cab—not that the local taxi service was ever on time. But somehow at exactly five o'clock she was standing in front of the door to Brock's suite. She mentally rehearsed the short speech she planned to make, then knocked on the door.

Brock opened it within seconds. There was a moment of silence as their eyes met. Stephanie thought she saw a flicker of emotion in the gray depths of his, but it was quickly veiled. Her senses reacted to the dark gray silk shirt he was wearing, unbuttoned just enough to give her a tantalizing glimpse of sun-browned skin and dark chest hair.

"You're right on time. Come in." A smile curved his mouth but it lacked warmth.

"Thanks," she murmured as he stepped to one side to let her in. She nervously fingered the metal clasp of her purse, ill at ease with him and not understanding why.

His sharp gaze noticed the way she was fiddling with her purse. "Would you like a drink?" he suggested.

"Please." She needed some kind of fortification. At the questioning lift of his eyebrow, Stephanie added, "Um—vodka and whatever. Juice, I guess."

He crossed the room to the minibar. "Cranberry juice okay? I don't have Cointreau."

She nodded.

"Two semi-Cosmopolitans coming up."

He mixed the drinks while she looked around the room, which was immaculate. Except for his attaché case sitting on the floor near the phone, there wasn't any evidence that the sitting room had been used. The door to the bedroom was shut, but Stephanie suspected the same would be true in there.

Yet the atmosphere in the living room seemed to be alive with dangerous undercurrents that made her edgy. Her gaze moved back to Brock, aloof and yet totally compelling. He held the two drinks carefully and walked over to hand her one—but he didn't add an invitation to sit down.

Stephanie accepted the brimming glass and sipped a little of the tart drink. She was rapidly beginning to regret her boldness.

"You said you wanted to see me," he reminded her.

"Yes," Stephanie lifted her gaze. "Okay—I was totally offended by some of the things you said," she began and searched his expression, hoping for at least a hint of remorse.

But his face was an impassive mask. She realized he had no intention of making this easier for her. The speech she had so carefully rehearsed was suddenly and completely forgotten.

Everything was thrown out as she made one last attempt to reach him. "If you want me, I'll stay with you tonight. I do love you, Brock. I keep coming back to that. Maybe we can work it out if we really try."

Her words didn't seem to make any impression on him. "Love, huh? You'll get over it," was his cool response.

Stephanie couldn't believe that he could shrug it aside with that much disinterest. She stared at him, too stunned to hear the connecting door to the bedroom open. It was only when a voluptuous blonde in a practically see-through robe waltzed into her vision that she realized she and Brock weren't alone.

"You two know each other," he said casually.

Stephanie felt like throwing up. "Uh, yeah. Hello, Helen. What's going on? If somebody wouldn't mind telling me."

Helen linked her arms around Brock's and pouted, not seeming to care that she wasn't even dressed, strictly speaking. "Honeybunch," she cooed, "you promised we'd be alone for the rest of the evening."

"This could get interesting," Brock drawled. Stephanie turned pale, transfixed by his mockingly cold smile. "Just my luck, huh? She was able to join me for the weekend—otherwise I might have had to endure a night of amateur entertainment."

His taunting words shattered her. She dropped her drink, not hearing it crash to the floor, turning to rush from the room, nearly blinded by tears. Shame and humiliation consumed her. Conscious only of the desperate need to escape, she wasn't aware of the stares or turning heads as she ran through the lobby and out the front door.

Not even the zero temperature cooled her scalding tears. Sobbing, she realized she had no place to run, except home. The SUV was parked to one side in front of the entrance. Hurrying to it, she glanced inside and had to wipe the tears away before she could see the keys dangling out of the ignition.

Climbing behind the wheel, she started the engine and reversed out of the parking space. The tears refused to stop falling, now that the deluge had begun. As she turned onto the main road, she nearly sideswiped an incoming car, swinging the wheel to avoid it just in time.

Shrugging free of Helen's hold, Brock walked over and shut the door Stephanie had left open. His shoes crunched on the broken glass around the cranberry juice stain on the floor. He gulped his own drink, trying to wash down the bad taste. His gaze flicked uninterestedly to Helen's display of flesh.

"The show is over. Cover up, Helen," he ordered in a flat voice.

She shot him a disapproving look and disappeared into the bedroom with a swirl of polyester sateen. He finished the rest of his drink and waited for its deadening effect to begin—he had given Stephanie a lot less vodka. It didn't work with its usual swiftness and he walked to the bar for a refill.

He brought the vodka bottle back with him to an armchair. He stretched out and put his long legs up on a matching ottoman, staring broodingly out the window at the snow-covered mountains.

He barely glanced up when Helen returned, covered from neck to ankle in a black robe trimmed with white fake mink. Her hair, bleached to platinum, looked just about as fake.

Without waiting for him to suggest it, she walked to the bar and made herself a gin and tonic.

"Want me to call a maid to clean up this mess?" she asked, gesturing to the broken glass and the spreading pool of liquid.

"No." Brock shut his eyes. His lungs felt as if they were about to burst.

"Did you have to be so rough on her?" Helen complained. "Couldn't you have dumped her in a nicer way?"

"It was the best way I knew—I had to be sure she got the message." He heard the weariness in his voice, the utter fatigue.

"Sometimes I'm not sure you have a heart, Brock Canfield," she retorted.

"Got to be cruel to be kind." He lifted his glass in a morose salute, the lines in his face showing deeper in the waning light of the winter afternoon. "Isn't that how the song goes?"

A wall of tears blurred Stephanie's vision. She knew that she was putting herself in danger by not pulling over, but she didn't care. There was no one else on the road ahead or behind her. When the SUV began to skid—so much for four-wheel drive, she thought blackly—she stopped trying to control it and let it go wherever it wanted. It spun out and bumped something, coming to an abrupt halt. The suddenness of it catapulted her forward against the steering wheel, but her seat belt worked well enough.

The airbags didn't inflate and it didn't occur to her that she'd had an accident. She simply took advantage of the steering wheel's support, folding her arms to rest her forehead against them and cry her heart out.

*   *   *

"Planning to get drunk, Brock?" Helen asked from her reclining position on the sofa. "Or are you holding on to that vodka bottle for security?"

Brock glanced at the frosted bottle and the empty glass beside it. The glass hadn't been re-filled. "I'm considering it."

But it didn't seem worth the effort. The stupor would eventually wear off and he'd be back to square one. A knock at the door made him lift his head—and a hand to cover his eyes.

"Answer that," he told Helen. "Send whoever it is away. I don't want to see anyone."

With a soft rustle of material, she swung her legs off the sofa to rise and saunter to the door in high-heeled slippers. Brock looked wearily at her movie-star affectations and watched her open the door with a dramatic flourish. "I'm sorry, but Mr. Canfield can't see anyone right now," she murmured coyly.

"He'll see me." Perry Hall pushed his way into the suite.

"Brock, it's the brother," Helen said with mock dismay.

Brock let his hand drop to the armrest. He could do without a confrontation with Stephanie's brother, but he had been expecting it. "What do you want, Perry?" he sighed.

"I want to know where Stephanie's gone." He stopped in front of Brock's chair, square-jawed and stern.

"How should I know?" Brock's gaze narrowed faintly. "She isn't here."

"But she was here. And I'm betting that *she*—"

Perry gestured toward Helen "is the reason Stephanie ran out of here crying."

"Well, you'll have to ask Stephanie." Brock unscrewed the top from the vodka bottle and refilled his glass. To hell with the cranberry juice.

"When I find her," Perry replied. "She drove off in my SUV."

Brock shrugged. "Then she probably went home."

"She didn't. I called and called, but there wasn't any answer. Her cell goes straight to voice mail. I got hold of the neighbors and they went over to the house, but she wasn't there."

The announcement rolled Brock to his feet. "Are you saying that she's missing?" The demand came out as a smooth question.

"Yes. I don't know what happened here or what was said, but I do know the kind of state Stephanie was in when she ran out of the lobby," Perry retorted. "And she wasn't in any kind of condition to be driving. Since you were responsible, you can just loan me your car so I can go and look for her."

"I'll get the keys." Brock walked into the bedroom and came out wearing his parka. "I'm coming with you."

"Forget it," Perry said. "I don't need you along."

"I'm not asking your permission." Brock moved toward the door. "Since, as you say, whatever's the matter with her is my fault, I'm going along to make sure she's all right."

"You should've thought about that before."

"Maybe," Brock countered. "But what happened today will ultimately turn out for Stephanie's own good. You and I both know that, Perry."

"I warned her that you would hurt her but she wouldn't listen," Perry sighed.

"I didn't hurt her as much as I could have."

Perry stiffened. "Hey, that's my sister you're talking about. I oughta punch you out right here, right now—"

"Let's go," Brock said wearily.

Stephanie felt drained and empty, without the strength to even lift her head. Her throat was dry and aching, scraped raw by the last sobs. Her eyes burned and there wasn't even any relief when she closed them. She hurt all over—she hadn't realized it was possible to hurt so badly.

She heard a noise, then sensed an influx of cold, fresh air, but she didn't welcome its revivifying effect. A voice called her name. It sounded so much like Brock's that Stephanie was convinced she was dreaming. She moaned in protest when she was gently pulled away from the support of the steering wheel and forced to rest against the back of the seat.

"Are you hurt, Stephanie?" It still sounded like Brock. "Can you hear me?"

"Yes," she rasped thinly, but didn't bother to open her eyes. None of this was real, anyway.

The familiar and caressing gentleness of Brock's hands was exploring her face, smoothing the hair away from her forehead. The sensation was sweet torment.

"I can't find any sign of a cut or a bruise." Brock's voice again, low and concerned.

"Stephanie, do you remember what happened?"

The second voice made her frown. It belonged to her brother. "Perry?" Mustering her strength, she opened her eyes.

Again there was a sensation of being deep in a dream. Brock was half-sitting on the driver's seat and facing her. A deep furrow ran across his forehead and his eyebrows were drawn together. She felt weepy again but there weren't any tears left.

Something made her glance sideways. There was Perry, bending low and trying to crowd into the car.

"I'm here, Stephanie," her brother assured her. "Do you remember what happened? How long have you been here?"

"I don't . . . know." The last question she could answer but the first meant pain. Stephanie looked at Brock. None of it was a dream. She knew exactly where she was and why. She pushed his hand away from her face. "Why are you here? You should be back at the suite being entertained by the blonde bombshell," she said, her voice breaking. "Go away and leave me alone!"

But he ignored her. "Did you hit your head when the car spun into this snowdrift? We'd better call 911, Perry." His hand went back to her head, feeling for bumps.

"No, no, I wasn't hurt at all," she insisted huskily, and pushed his hand away again. "I lost control on a patch of ice, I guess. Is that what stopped me—a snowbank?"

"You're lucky it wasn't a telephone pole," Brock muttered and reached for her arm. "Come on, let's get you out of the car."

"No!" Stephanie eluded his hand and turned to

her brother. "I want to go home, Perry," she said tightly, edging along the seat to the passenger side.

She caught a glimpse of her reflection in the rearview mirror. Her face was pale and colorless, her eyes swollen and red from the tears, and her cheeks stained with their traces. She looked like a wrung-out mop. It wasn't fair that Brock had seen her this way.

She hadn't wanted to give him the satisfaction of knowing that he'd crushed her. That was why she had run. She stared at her hands, twisting them white, as Brock stepped away from the driver's side to let her brother slide behind the wheel.

He started it again, and put it into reverse. The tires spun, then found some traction, and they were bouncing backward out of the hardpacked snow. Brock stood by the roadside, his hands in his pockets, watching them. For a moment he was outlined there, alone, his gaze lingering on her. Then the SUV was moving forward.

"Why did you have to bring him along with you?" Stephanie choked painfully on the question, her eyes misting with tears again.

"It was his car. He insisted." His gaze left the road, swinging to her. "Are you okay?"

"No, I don't think so." She stared out of the window at the bleak landscape of snow and barren trees. "All those lines always sounded so melodramatic before—but Perry, I wish I could die."

When they reached the house, Stephanie went directly to her room. Without changing clothes or turning on a light, she lay down on her bed, huddling in a tight ball atop the covers. It was nearly nine when Perry knocked on her door and entered the room carrying a tray with a bowl of hot soup and crackers.

"Go away, please," she requested in a flat voice.

Setting the tray on the bedside table, he switched on the lamp. "You have to eat, Stephanie."

"No." She rolled away into the shadows on the opposite side of the bed.

"Just a little," he insisted in that patient voice of his. She rolled back and he smiled gently. "Sit up." He fixed the pillows to prop her up and set the tray on her lap. For his sake, she ate a few spoonfuls, but it had no taste to her. When she handed it back to him, Perry didn't attempt to coax her into eating more.

It was nearly midnight before she roused herself enough to change into her nightgown and crawl beneath the covers. She didn't sleep, at least not the kind of sleep she normally knew.

With dull eyes, she watched the dawn creep into her bedroom through the east window. She heard the church bells ring their call to early service, but didn't leave her bed to respond to them. Perry came in with orange juice, coffee, and toast. She sampled a little of each of them . . . for him.

All morning she stayed in her room. When Perry came to tell her he was going to the inn for an hour or so, Stephanie merely nodded. She heard him come home in the middle of the afternoon, but she didn't leave her bedroom.

Perry came in around seven o'clock. "The food's on the table."

"I'm not hungry." She sat in the center of her bed, hugging her pillow.

"Stephanie, you can't stay in this room forever," he said with a sigh. "It was rough. It hurt like hell, I know. But it's over. You've got to pick up the pieces and start again." She stared at him, hearing this truth that was so difficult to put into practice. "Come on." He offered his hand. "The longer you stay here, the harder it will be to leave."

Hesitantly, she placed her hand in his and let him help her off the bed. Together they went downstairs to the kitchen. She sat down at the table with its platter of Yankee pot roast, potatoes, onions, and carrots. The irony of it was painful— she remembered Brock had said she was all about pot roast while he was all about Chateaubriand.

"Has . . . has Brock left?" she faltered on the question.

The carving knife was poised above the meat as Perry shot a quick glance at her. "Yes."

A violent shudder quaked through her but she made no sound.

The next morning she was up before Perry, having decided that routine was something solid to cling to in her shattered world. She made coffee, fixed their breakfast, dressed, and drove to the inn with Perry. There was one difference. She closed her office door when she went to work—she was no longer interested in the comings and goings of the inn's guests.

There were well-meaning questions from her fellow workers but she turned them aside. She knew they were making their own guesses about

what might have happened, but she didn't offer
them any information that would fuel more gossip.

All around her were festive Christmas decorations, cheerful voices calling holiday greetings, and
the merry songs of the season drifting through the
halls. This time, no spirit of glad tidings lightened
her heart.

Chris Berglund came over several times while
he was home for the holidays—at her brother's request, Stephanie suspected. But mostly he talked
to Perry while she made certain there was plenty
of cocoa, coffee, or beer for the two of them to
drink. She was grateful that Perry was trying to fill
her empty hours. In a way his methods worked.

The coming of the new year brought changes.
Stephanie's appetite was almost nonexistent. She
ate meals because they were necessary, but she lost
weight. She rarely slept the whole night through.
In consequence, there was a haunted look to her
blue eyes, mysterious and sad. She rarely smiled
and laughed even less frequently. Her chestnut
hair was worn up, away from her face, in a neat
French twist, which only added to her touch-me-
not look.

Unless Perry took her, Stephanie skipped most
social functions. Even longtime friends saw little of
her. Except to shop or go to the inn to work, she
rarely left the farmhouse.

A few old ladies, New Hampshire natives,
clucked softly when she walked down the streets,
saying that she would end up—oh, dreaded fate—
an old maid. Nowadays it was called being single
and free, Stephanie thought wistfully. She knew

that some wondered what she would do if her brother got married, now that Perry was going out with his schoolteacher practically every night.

But Stephanie couldn't look ahead any further than the next day. It was the way she had gotten through January, February, and March. It hadn't been easy. She wondered if it ever would be. But the worst was over . . . definitely over.

CHAPTER 9

Precariously balanced on a metal folding chair, Stephanie reached as far as she could, but she still couldn't get the dust on the rear top of the filing cabinet. Sighing, she straightened to stand on the unsteady chair.

The door to her office opened and Perry entered. "Hi."

Affection warmed her gaze, though her smile was barely there. "Hi, yourself. Your timing is perfect." She carefully stepped down from the chair. "I need your long arm to dust the back of the cabinet."

"What's this? Spring-cleaning time?" Then good-naturedly, he took the duster she handed him and stepped onto the chair, waving it around like a symphony conductor before dealing with the dust.

"It's the right time of year," Stephanie pointed out. The calendar on the wall was open to April and she had changed the screen saver on her computer to hopping pink bunnies. They looked happy in their flowery meadow—maybe too happy, she thought glumly. "Besides, I didn't have anything else to do this afternoon."

"Mud season is always the slow time of year," he joked. "Want me to dust the top of the other filing cabinet?"

"As long as you're here, be my guest." Taking a spare duster, she started toward the shelves where the extra stationery and forms were kept. The back of the shelves looked like someone had been fingerpainting in the dust.

Perry wielded his duster with abandon, raising a cloud that made him cough. "Wow, I can see why women love doing this," he said.

"Yeah, right," said Stephanie. They worked on for a few more minutes in companionable silence, and then Perry spoke. "By the way—"

She looked up with alarm. His tone was far too nonchalant. "What?"

"Brock's coming."

She had lived in dread of those words. They hit her, spinning her around toward Perry. Accidentally she knocked the wooden cylinder filled with pens and pencils from her desk, scattering them on the floor.

"Damn!" She choked out the word and bent hurriedly to pick them up, grateful for a reason to hide the tears that sprang into her eyes.

She had forced them back by the time she had gathered all the pencils. Her hands were shaking when she returned the cylinder to the desk. Perry was pretending to be interested in the sharpness of her letter opener, giving her a chance to recover.

"When . . . ?" She had to swallow the lump in her throat and try again. "When is he coming?"

"This weekend. On Friday," he added.

"Oh." The duster was twisted into a tight ball in her hands.

"Are you going to run and hide?" His question was really a challenge.

It made her feel like a first-class coward, because it was exactly what she wanted to do. "No." But it was a very small sound.

"Good girl," her brother praised. She lifted her head, letting him see the anguish in her eyes. "Come on," he cajoled, "let's see that New England backbone."

"Sure." She took a deep breath and turned away.

He clamped a hand on her shoulder in a firm display of affection. "There isn't much happening around here today. We'll leave early this afternoon, around four, okay?"

"Do you have a date tonight with Joyce?" she asked, trying to follow his change of subject.

"No, not tonight. See you later." He moved toward the door.

Stephanie walked back to her desk and sat down. Brock was coming. It twisted her inside until she wanted to cry out, but she didn't. She had been bracing herself for this moment. Now it had come—her first true test. After nearly four months, surely she would survive it.

* * *

Friday. Friday. Friday. Each beat of her pulse seemed to hammer out the word. When she arrived at the inn that morning she was a nervous wreck, despite her well-disciplined outward show of calm.

It took her twice as long as usual to get the payroll checks ready for Perry's signature. Especially the last few, because that was when Perry stuck his head in the door to tell her Brock had just driven up. After that, she mentally jumped at nearly every sound, expecting him to walk in.

She skipped lunch to finish the payroll, finally getting it done at two o'clock. Gathering the checks and papers into a folder, she walked down the hall to Perry's office. The door was standing open but he wasn't there.

Probably with Brock, Stephanie thought unhappily, and walked in to leave the folder on his desk. Out of habit, she paused to straighten the leather desk set that had belonged to their father.

"Excuse me." Brock's voice ran through her like a lightning bolt. "Could you tell me where I could find Perry Hall?"

It dawned on her that the question was being addressed to her. She turned slowly to see him framed by the doorway. Tall, dressed in a gray suit, he was just as compelling as she remembered him, if not more so. She watched disbelief, then recognition, flash across his face.

"Stephanie," he murmured her name and took a step into the office. "You've changed. I didn't recognize you."

His gray eyes seemed to examine every detail from her willowy figure to the new, sophisticated way she wore her hair. His inspection left the sensation that he had physically touched her. Inside, she was quaking.

"Yes, I've changed," she admitted. *But not where you're concerned, Brock.* The love she felt was just as strong, if not tempered by the separation. She turned away, pretending to straighten some papers to keep from giving in to the impulse to throw herself into his arms. "I'm afraid I don't know where my brother is. Maybe you should check at the desk."

"How are you?" Brock asked, his voice coming from only a few feet behind her.

"I'm fine." That was a lie. She was dying inside. But she turned to face him and lend strength to her words.

Close up, she could see that he, too, had changed. Still ultramasculine, he looked leaner in the face. The hollows of his cheeks were almost gaunt. More lines were carved into his skin or else previous ones had grown deeper, especially the ones around his eyes, where they fanned out. And he seemed harder.

"Got the reports. Looks like the inn did exceptionally good winter business," he remarked.

"Yes. It's pretty empty now, but spring is generally slow." Why was she letting this conversation continue? Why didn't she leave? Stephanie was angry with herself for lacking the willpower to walk out the door. With a defiant tilt of her chin, she flashed him a cold look. "But I'm sure that won't bother you, since you bring your entertainment with you." She was even angrier for stooping to that remark. "Excuse me. I have work to do."

She brushed past him, hurrying from the room before she made a complete fool of herself. She met Perry in the hall.

"Brock's looking for you. He's in your office." Her voice was brittle with the force of her control.

His concern showed in his eyes. "Are you okay?"

Her answer was a silent nod. He touched her arm as he walked by her to his office. Stephanie slipped quickly into her own and leaned against the door, shaking in reaction. It was several minutes before her legs felt strong enough to carry her to the desk. At five o'clock, Perry came to take her home. As they drove away from the inn, he said, "You don't have to worry about fixing dinner."

"I suppose you're eating out tonight." *With Brock*, she added silently.

"You're half-right," he replied cheerfully, and she realized he had been in a good mood when he picked her up. "We are eating out tonight."

"Perry, I—" Stephanie started to refuse.

"Consider it a celebration," he said and glanced at her. When he saw the desperate look in her eyes, he smiled. "Brock isn't going to be there. At least, he isn't invited."

Then he actually laughed in a big-brotherly kind of way. Good old Perry, thought Stephanie ruefully.

"No, it's just you, me, and Joyce. She's meeting us at the inn."

Celebration. Joyce. Comprehension dawned. "Are you . . . ?" She felt a rush of happiness for him. "Perry, are you and Joyce getting married? Are we celebrating your engagement?"

"Um, not exactly. No. I haven't asked her yet," he hedged. "Do you like her, Stephanie?"

"Sure. She'd make a great sister-in-law," Stephanie said. "But don't tell her I said so until you buy her a diamond, okay?"

"No problem. No sense in rushing things, right?"

"Right. Getting back to this dinner—what are we celebrating tonight if it isn't your engagement?"

"That's a surprise. I'm saving it for dinner," Perry declared complacently. "And you haven't got all night to dress. I promised Joyce we'd meet her a little after six, so you have to hustle."

One small consolation of losing weight without even trying was buying new clothes. It wasn't nearly as difficult to choose what to wear after several sessions of retail therapy. Since Perry said tonight's dinner was a celebration, she picked an aquamarine dress of flowing silk.

Joyce Henderson was waiting for them when they returned to the inn. The petite brunette was super-smart and outgoing by nature—perfect for Perry, as far as Stephanie was concerned. Her brother tended to be too serious at times.

"What's all this about, Perry?" Joyce asked. "You were so mysterious on the phone this afternoon."

"Just wait," he insisted, taking her arm and guiding her to the restaurant entrance.

"Has he told you, Stephanie?" She tried to look over Perry's shoulder at Stephanie.

"Not even a hint," she replied.

"You'll both find out soon," he promised. After they were seated at a table, he waved aside the dinner menus. "We'll order later. Bring us a bottle of champagne. Bring two."

"Champagne?" Stephanie frowned. "You really meant it when you said this was going to be a celebration! How much longer are you going to keep us in suspense?"

"Wait for the champagne." Her brother was enjoying the secrecy.

The champagne arrived. Because the waiter was serving his boss, there was a little extra pomp and ceremony attached to popping the cork and pouring a sample for his approval. Finally the three glasses were filled with the sparkling wine.

"All right, the champagne is here. Now out with it," Joyce demanded.

Perry lifted his glass and started to speak, but his gaze focused on a point to the left of Stephanie, then ran swiftly to her. It was the only warning she received before Brock spoke.

"May I join you?" he asked.

Stephanie was grateful that he was alone, but she wished that Perry would tell him no. Especially since the empty chair at their table for four was next to her.

"Of course, Brock. Sit down," her brother said with subdued enthusiasm and motioned to the waiter to bring another place setting.

Stephanie sat silently through Perry's introduction of Joyce to Brock, aware of the dark-suited shoulder and arm next to her. But she wouldn't look at him. She couldn't look at him.

It didn't seem to matter. Her senses were filled with his presence—the deliciously male smell of his cologne, the warm, rich sound of his voice, and the feeling that she had only to reach out to touch him.

Another glass of champagne was poured for Brock. "Have you told them the news?" he asked Perry.

"Not yet," he admitted.

"You know what it is?" Stephanie sent Brock a surprised look and her gaze was caught by the enigmatic grayness of his.

He held it for an enchanted instant, then his gaze slid to Perry. "I know about it."

"The suspense is killing me. Will one of you tell us?" Joyce asked with faint exasperation.

Perry hesitated, bouncing a glance at Stephanie. "Brock is selling the inn."

"That doesn't come as a surprise." Although it was possibly a cause for celebration, even if she didn't feel it at the moment. She fingered the stem of her wineglass, darting a look in Brock's direction. "The inn was really a nuisance to you, anyway. I'm sure you'll be glad to get it off your hands."

"I will, but not for your reason," Brock replied, but didn't explain what his reason was.

"Okay—is this what we're celebrating?" Joyce was confused.

Perry glanced at her and smiled. "He's selling it to me. You're sitting with the future owner of the White Boar Inn."

"What? I don't believe it!" Joyce was incredulous and ecstatic at the same time. She was laughing while tears glittered in her eyes. "Perry, that's wonderful!"

"I think so," he agreed.

"I'm glad for you," Stephanie offered. For herself, she knew how much she would miss the previous owner.

But her brother didn't seem to notice her lukewarm congratulations as glasses were raised in a toast. Stephanie barely sipped at her champagne, not needing its heady effects when Brock was sitting beside her, disrupting her composure and destroying her calm.

"Perry didn't explain the proposal I offered him," said Brock, glancing at Stephanie over the rim of his glass. "Actually I gave him two choices."

"Yes, well, I made my choice," her brother shrugged. "It's what I really want. There isn't any question in my mind."

"What was the other choice?" Stephanie glanced from her brother to Brock. She sensed there was something significant here.

"I explained to him this afternoon that I'd decided to sell the inn," Brock began. "If he wanted to buy it, I agreed to personally finance it for him or . . ." he paused "I offered to give him a full year's pay plus a bonus—more than enough to pay his tuition through law school."

"But . . ." She stared at her brother. "I don't understand."

"Neither did I, until Brock offered me the choice." He shook his head, as if a little amazed by it himself. "But when it was right in front of me, I knew that what I really wanted was to be here. All my life I thought I wanted to be a lawyer, but when it came right down to it, I couldn't give up this place."

"I know the feeling," said Brock. "The inn isn't

the only thing I'm selling. Quite a few of my other companies are up for sale. And I'm consolidating the rest of my holdings." He set his wineglass down, watching the delicate bubbles rise to the surface. "As a matter of fact, I'm looking at some four-bedroom homes. Nothing fancy—standard Colonials on an acre or two. White picket fence. Everything but the golden retriever."

Stephanie's heart stopped beating. She was afraid to breathe or move, terrified that she was reading something into that statement that Brock didn't mean. Her wide blue eyes stared at him. Slowly he lifted his gaze to look at her.

"Would you be interested in helping me pick out a house, Stephanie?" he asked huskily. "I don't want there to be any question about what I'm doing, so I'm asking you in front of your brother— will you marry me?"

"Yes." Where was her pride? Quickly Stephanie shook her head. "No." Then she wavered. "I don't know."

"You need a more private place to convince her, Brock," Perry suggested.

"Will you let me at least try?" He studied her.

"Yes," she whispered.

"Excuse me." Brock rose from his chair and waited for her to join him.

She felt like a sleepwalker lost in a marvelous dream as Brock escorted her from the restaurant, his hand lightly resting on the small of her back, but definitely possessive. She stiffened in mute resistance when she realized he was guiding her to his suite.

It was the scene of too many conflicting and

painful memories. Anywhere else and she might have melted right into his arms the minute they were alone. But when he closed the door she put distance between them.

"After all this time—why, Brock?" she asked, remembering the days of hell she'd been through.

"Because I made the same discovery Perry did. I always thought I had the life I wanted—until I met you. Even then I didn't recognize what was happening. I couldn't see the choice that was in front of me. For the last few months, I did everything, had everything my way—as usual. But I finally realized that if I lost it all tomorrow, I wouldn't care, as long as I had you."

"But—" Stephanie turned, searching his face, wanting desperately to believe him. "What happened here—with Helen—what was that all about?" It was such a painful memory that she couldn't put it into words.

"I know how much I hurt you." A muscle flexed in his jaw as he clenched it. "I wanted you from the moment I met you. I fooled myself into believing we could have an affair—a nice, long affair. Hey, later I even thought if we married, I could still do whatever I wanted. Then I acted like a jealous idiot over that neighbor of yours."

"I remember," she said wryly.

He sighed. "Then you told me how uncertain and anxious you felt when I was away—and I knew that constant separations would ultimately ruin what we had. I was being ripped apart by them already. I can only imagine what you were going through."

"Why didn't you explain that?" she asked, aware that he was moving toward her.

"Because, my gorgeous Yankee—"

She held up a hand. "Now wait a minute. That sounds like a *Playboy* feature. Gorgeous Yankees."

"You'd be the star, Stephanie."

"Oh, shut up." But she had to smile.

"Anyway," Brock continued, "after that fight, when you chewed me out but good—"

"You deserved it," she interrupted. "You *so* deserved it."

"Yes, I did. But I was too mad to think straight. And when you called asking to see me, I knew you were coming with the intention of making up. I put you off and called Helen." His hands began to move in restless caresses over her shoulders. "I wanted you so much I couldn't trust myself alone with you—I knew I couldn't talk you out of or into anything you didn't want to do."

Her eyes narrowed. Was he going to pretend that was a good reason for parading a bleached-blonde bimbo around—and breaking her heart?

Brock held up his hands. "I know what you're going to say. I never should have pulled such a stupid stunt. If you hate me for staging that scene, I understand. You're right. It was easily the most idiotic thing I ever did."

"How could you?" she whispered. "I should smack you again—but that wouldn't be enough."

"No." His eyes shone with profound regret. "But I never for a minute thought that one of the first things you would say was that you loved me. The hardest thing I've ever done was reject you and your love. I thought it might be easier for you if I made you hate me."

"It wasn't easier. But you nearly succeeded!"

"Nearly?" He cupped her chin in his hand and raised it to study her face. "You mean you don't hate me."

"No, Brock, I love you. I've never stopped loving you," Stephanie admitted.

His arm brought her slender curves to the muscular hardness of his body as he bent his head to seek her lips, parting them hungrily, needing her as desperately and completely as she needed him. Love flamed, wild and glorious, sweeping them up in its radiant heat. Breathing shakily, Brock lifted his head. "Okay. Whew. This could get out of control real fast. I mean, I want it to but not yet. We have to discuss this like adults, right? And then we can lose control—"

She put a finger on his lips. "Why did you wait so long?"

Brock sighed and thought a moment before replying. "Because nobody was there to offer me a clear-cut choice—you or the Canfield legacy. I was too damn stupid to realize it was that simple. But you can believe this." He framed her face in his hands, gazing at her as if she were the loveliest work of art in the world. "I worship the damn ground you walk on, Stephanie. And I don't care if I never have another glass of champagne, sleep in another hotel penthouse suite, or eat Chateaubriand for the rest of my life."

"Looks like you've got your priorities in order," she said impudently. "But you're going to have to promise me more than that to make up for the dumb blonde. Keep going."

Brock grinned. "Okay. Picture this. Our first Christmas. I'll be hanging the garlands on the white picket fence and you'll be baking something that smells great. I'll come inside with cold hands and warm them up on your—"

"Chocolate chip cookies," she interrupted. "Fresh from the oven. With cold milk."

"Gee, I don't know," he said doubtfully. "Sounds kinda wholesome."

"Brock, wholesome is sexy."

"Promise?"

"Wait a minute," Stephanie laughed. "You were promising me stuff. Our first Christmas, remember?"

He nodded and took her in his arms once more. "Okay. The tree is decorated, all our friends just went home, and there's a crackling fire."

"Chestnuts roasting?" she asked hopefully.

"Chestnuts. Cookies. Whatever you want. This is your fantasy, Stephanie, but I'm going to make it come true."

She nestled against his warm, muscular chest. "Mmm. I like it so far. But what do you want?"

"Just to be alone with you," he said simply. He kissed the top of her head. "You and me, on Christmas Eve. How does that sound?"

"Sounds wonderful," she whispered. "I never thought I'd be this happy again." Joy filled her heart and shone in her eyes.

"Give me a chance, Stephanie. Just remember that everything I said tonight—about selling and consolidating, I mean—might take at least a year.

In the meantime, I'll still have to travel a lot. After that it'll only be a few times a year. Then you can come with me."

"Whatever you say," Stephanie murmured. "It's going to be crazy."

"It'll be okay. We're both crazy in the same way, right?"

She laughed a little.

"Just let me love you, let me make up for all the pain I've caused you." His mouth moved onto hers, gently at first, then more sensually, for several very pleasurable minutes. He broke the kiss with a husky sigh.

"Wow. Mmm. I don't want to stop. Aren't we supposed to be talking?"

"This is better."

He stroked her hair tenderly. "How much time will your brother need to find a new bookkeeper so I can marry you?"

"You mean I have to give up my thrilling career in accounting? Damn." She looked up at him with a sly smile. "Well, I do have some influence with the boss. Maybe a week, two at the most."

"Where would you like to spend your honeymoon? The Caribbean? Maybe the Virgin Islands?"

"Ha ha."

"Well, what about Europe?" he continued. "Or maybe right here in the honeymoon suite where it all started?"

"Here." Stephanie didn't even hesitate over the choice.

"Okay. But I'm having that king-size bed replaced." His hands captured her slim waist. "I might lose you in it."

"Think so?" She brushed her lips across the corner of his mouth.

"I'm not going to take the chance," Brock murmured before he took her teasing lips in a passionate kiss.

"Oh—" She shut up and surrendered. "Mmm. Nice kiss," she breathed at last.

"That's the happily-ever-after kind." Brock grinned. "Want more?"

"Yes."

In case you missed it,
here's a peek at Janet Dailey's
CALDER PROMISE,
available now from Kensington Publishing.

"What happened, Laura? Did you forget to look where you were going?" The familiarity of Tara's affectionately chiding voice provided the right touch of normalcy.

Laura seized on it while she struggled to collect her composure. "I'm afraid I did. I was talking to Boone and—" She paused a beat to glance again at the stranger, stunned to discover how rattled she felt. It was a totally alien sensation. She couldn't remember a time when she hadn't felt in control of herself and a situation. "And I walked straight into you. I'm sorry."

"No apologies necessary," the man assured her while his gaze made a curious and vaguely puzzled study of her face. "The fault was equally mine." He cocked his head to one side, the puzzled look deepening in his expression. "I know this sounds awfully trite, but haven't we met before?"

Laura shook her head. "No. I'm certain I would

have remembered if we had." She was positive of that.

"Obviously you remind me of someone else then," he said, easily shrugging off the thought. "In any case, I hope you are none the worse for the collision, Ms.—" He paused expectantly, waiting for Laura to supply her name.

The old ploy was almost a relief. "Laura Calder. And this is my aunt, Tara Calder," she said, rather than going into a lengthy explanation of their exact relationship.

"My pleasure, ma'am," he murmured to Tara, acknowledging her with the smallest of bows.

"And perhaps you already know Max Rutledge and his son, Boone." Laura belatedly included the two men.

"I know *of* them." He nodded to Max.

When he turned to the younger man, Boone extended a hand, giving him a look of hard challenge. "And you are?"

"Sebastian Dunshill," the man replied.

"Dunshill," Tara repeated with sudden and heightened interest. "Are you any relation to the earl of Crawford, by chance?"

"I do have a nodding acquaintance with him." His mouth curved in an easy smile as he switched his attention to Tara. "Do you know him?"

"Unfortunately no," Tara admitted, then drew in a breath and sent a glittering look at Laura, barely able to contain her excitement. "Although a century ago the Calder family was well acquainted with a certain Lady Crawford."

"Really. And how's that?" With freshened curiosity, Sebastian Dunshill turned to Laura for an explanation.

An awareness of him continued to tingle through her. Only now Laura was beginning to enjoy it.

"It's a long and rather involved story," Laura warned. "After all this time, it's difficult to know how much is fact, how much is myth, and how much is embellishment of either one."

"Since we have a fairly long walk ahead of us to the dining hall, why don't you start with the facts?" Sebastian suggested and deftly tucked her hand under his arm, turning her to follow the other guests.

Laura could feel Boone's anger over the way he had been supplanted, but she didn't really care. She had too much confidence in her ability to smooth any of Boone's ruffled feathers.

"The facts." She pretended to give them some thought while her sidelong glance traveled over Sebastian Dunshill's profile, noting the faint smattering of freckles on his fair skin and the hint of copper lights in his very light brown hair.

Despite the presence of freckles, there was nothing boyish about him. He was definitely a man fully grown, thirty-something she suspected, with a very definite continental air about him. He didn't exude virility the way Boone Rutledge did; his air of masculinity had a smooth and polished edge to it.

"I suppose I should begin by explaining that back in the latter part of the 1870s, my great-great-grandfather Benteen Calder established the family ranch in Montana."

"Your family owns a cattle ranch?" He glanced her way, interest and curiosity mixing in his look.

"A very large one."

"How many acres do you have? I don't mean to sound nosy, but those of us on this side of the Atlantic harbor a secret fascination with the scope and scale of your American West."

"So I've learned. But truthfully we don't usually measure in acres. We talk about sections," Laura explained. "The Triple C has more than one hundred and fifty sections within its boundary fence."

"You'll have to educate me," he said with a touch of amusement. "How large is a section?"

"One square mile, or six hundred and forty acres."

After a quick mental calculation, Sebastian gave her a suitably impressed look. "That's nearly a million acres. And I thought all the large western ranches were in Texas, not Montana."

"Not all." She smiled. "Anyway, according to early ranch records, there are numerous business transactions listed that indicate Lady Crawford was a party to them. Many of them involved government contracts for the purchase of beef. It appears that my great-great-grandfather paid her a finder's fee, I suppose you would call it—an arrangement that was clearly lucrative for both of them."

"The earl of Crawford wasn't named as a party in any of this, then," Sebastian surmised.

"No. In fact, the family stories that were passed down always said she was widowed."

"Interesting. As I recall," he began with a faint frown of concentration, "the seventh earl of Crawford was married to an American. They had no children, which meant the title passed to the son of his younger brother." He stopped abruptly and swung toward Laura, running a fast look over her face. "That's it! I know why you looked so familiar. You bear a striking resemblance to the portrait of Lady Elaine that hangs in the manor's upper hall."

"Did you hear that, Tara?" Laura turned in amazement to the older woman.

"I certainly did." With a look of triumph in her midnight dark eyes, Tara momentarily clutched at Laura's arm, an exuberant smile curving her red lips. "I knew it. I knew it all along."

BOOK YOUR PLACE ON OUR WEBSITE
AND MAKE THE
READING CONNECTION!

We've created a customized website just for our very special readers, where you can get the inside scoop on everything that's going on with Zebra, Pinnacle and Kensington books.

When you come online, you'll have the exciting opportunity to:

- View covers of upcoming books
- Read sample chapters
- Learn about our future publishing schedule (listed by publication month *and author*)
- Find out when your favorite authors will be visiting a city near you
- Search for and order backlist books from our online catalog
- Check out author bios and background information
- Send e-mail to your favorite authors
- Meet the Kensington staff online
- Join us in weekly chats with authors, readers and other guests
- Get writing guidelines
- AND MUCH MORE!

**Visit our website at
http://www.kensingtonbooks.com**